BLOOD IN
THE STREETS

THE BLOOD TRILOGY

Book 2

BY

PAUL DAVIDS

Dedicated to all my children and step children.

Sapphire, Saffron, Shaw, Saxon, Ryan and Callum.

CONTENTS

CHAPTER 1

A Struggle

The moonlight glinted off the knife as it sliced through Del's skin; he was conscious and felt every passing swipe. The huge man wielding the weapon was silent. Del instinctively knew it was a man but didn't know how as it was just a pure white silhouette. The shape was faceless, just a light figure slashing at his body. Del was not tied up or restrained in any way but found it impossible to move. He was helpless as chunk after chunk of his flesh flew off in front of his eyes. His struggle was immense, straining every sinew in his body, to no avail. The pressure to move and escape was overwhelming, more overwhelming than the pain. He was trying to shout, trying to scream but all that would come out of his mouth was an unfathomable senseless moan. The skinning stopped abruptly and the faceless figure stood motionless for a second and then slowly turned the knife towards itself. Del's panic increased tenfold and his attempt to scream became violent... Del shot upright in his bed and screamed at the top of his voice, "Nooooooo!"

His hair was a mess, his eyes were red and watering and he was so covered in sweat that he looked as if he had just come out of the shower. His breathing was fast and his heart was beating at an extreme rate. His wife Janice was in bed next to him and woke as Del screamed 'no'. She sat up and put her hand on his sweat-soaked shoulder.

"Another one, babe?" she said softly. Del slumped back down on the bed with a sigh and just said one word.

"Fuck!"

"Was it the same as usual, babe?" Janice was sat up, looking down at her husband with a worried look on her face. She stroked his forehead, it was hot and running with panicked sweat. The dreams had been going on for a while now. She felt completely helpless; she wanted to make it better but there was nothing she could do.

"Yes, same one," panted Del. His breathing was still fast and his heart was continuing to race. He had been having the same nightmare for a few months now; he didn't know why they had started but knew exactly what they were about. Del was a detective inspector and had been for over a year now. He had taken over from the previous inspector who had turned out to be a serial killer. Not just any serial killer, he was the Butcher and Del had been caught and nearly murdered himself. He sat up and pulled his legs off the end of the bed. He sighed as the harrowing experience ran through his mind's eye once again. Del had thought he had put it all behind him, until recently. The figure in his dreams was faceless but Del knew instinctively that it was Bos, his old boss. He knew it but didn't understand why he was being haunted by it now. He had struggled to come to terms with the entire warped situation but it was all over a year ago and he had moved on.

"Do you want a drink of water darling?" Del stood up on shaky legs.

"Yes but don't worry babe, I'll get it, I could do with a little walk." It was always the same after one of those damn dreams, he would not be able to get back to sleep for a while. He padded barefoot down to the kitchen. They had just moved there. They didn't need a big place as it was just Del and Janice. Janice was not able to have children; he was sympathetic obviously but it came as a bit of a relief to him as he never really wanted kids. It wasn't necessarily the kids that were the problem, it was being a parent he didn't want. One of his favourite lines was to say, "Most children would grow up happy and stable if it wasn't for their bloody parents." So a two-bedroom house was perfectly okay for them; they could definitely afford more now he was earning a full-time substantive detective inspector's wage but why do that? In his view life was for living, not saving up to leave it to someone else once you die. He poured a glass of water from the cold dispenser in the fridge and stood staring out of the kitchen window in his boxer shorts. It was not an awful sight he was a well-proportioned man in his late thirties, not that anyone would be watching. The kitchen clock said 02:46 and it was mostly dark outside.

The street lamp about eight metres away lit up a portion of the road. As he watched he saw a cat run across on its nightly adventures. His mind flashed back to the night when Bos had restrained him, it was a similar time and he was watching another person being butchered in front of him. It was difficult for him to recall his feelings exactly now, but he must have known that he was going to be next. He couldn't remember being too concerned with that at the time. At that particular moment he was still unaware that Bos was the killer. Every memory looking back now was tainted with the knowledge that it was his colleague they were after.

"Bizarre!" he said and drank some of the drink. Janice walked in behind him at that point.

"Have you calmed down a bit now, love? Your heart was going ten to the dozen for a while then." She had thrown one of Del's old night shirts over herself and had only done a couple of buttons up, so ample flesh could be seen through the gaps.

"Yes babe, I'm a little better." He put his glass down on the side and walked towards his wife.

"It's still all a bit of a mindfuck to be honest. I tell you what though, that shirt looks better on you than it does on me." He put his arms forward, slid them in between the gaps in the shirt and leant his head down towards her, and kissed her. He pulled her closer and the few buttons that were fastened popped open. They kissed for a few seconds and then wordlessly stopped and walked back to the bedroom.

CHAPTER 2

The Beginning

It was 06:45 and Del's alarm clock was bleeping away.

"Bugger!" He turned over, sneered at the illuminated numbers and then smashed his arm down on the snooze button on the top of the clock. "That can't be the time, no way was that a full night."

Janice moved next to him and smiled without facing him.

"Well a full night's sleep it wasn't. If you wanted a full night of sleep, actually going to sleep would have been a good idea, babe." She playfully slapped his behind under the covers. Del clicked the alarm off and dragged himself out of bed and off to the bathroom. This time there were no boxer shorts to hide his assets from full view. Janice whistled; Del smiled and continued on his way to the toilet, his bare feet slapping on the tiles. Del finished his ablutions and then made two lots of toast and coffee. He took Janice her breakfast.

"Here you go babe, enjoy. What are you up to today then?"

Janice sat up and thanked him for the toast and drink. "I'm having lunch with Sue but I have nothing else on so may catch up on some sleep I missed." She smiled at him and bit into her toast.

Del kissed her on the forehead and said, "Well lucky you. I will see you tonight, say hello to Sue for me."

Janice had known Sue for a while now, about nine or so months he guessed. They had met each other at a yoga class, hit it off and had been friends since. Del had met her a few times at the house. She was an extremely attractive fifty-ish-year-old woman who was always well turned out and seemed quite intelligent. Del had mentioned this once and then regretted it as Janice liked to tease him about it now. Del went to the kitchen and finished his breakfast. After half an hour he was ready to go out of the door. He gave Janice a kiss and left her to continue to sleep.

*

He drove to the station in good spirits considering the nightmare he had last night. He entered the police station via the front entrance.

"Morning Del," said Sergeant Smith on the front desk. She had known Del for quite a while and they got on well. She was one of the people you could rely on for speaking their mind.

"Morning Mags, how are you?"

"Not as good as you obviously. Got lucky, did you?" Maggie chuckled and continued to file her nails.

Del continued whistling through the station to his desk. His colleague was already sat there waiting patiently for him. He was Sergeant Harry Gorham, a well-dressed, dark-haired, clean shaven man in a sharp blue pinstripe suit. Since the last inspector had been going around murdering people it was thought that working with partners was a good idea. It was after the newspapers obviously hammered them for the Butcher killings that the new procedures were put in place. Some of the newspaper headings were awful and affected staff quite a lot, others were more amusing and he could remember a couple being put on his desk. 'Bungling Bobbies in Butcher Balls-up' was one that stuck out. A more damming and hurtful one was headed: 'Who Polices the Police?' and went on to hint that most police couldn't be trusted, and to do so was tantamount to taking your life in your own hands. This particular one was not humorous at all and was the source of many tears, not to mention some staff quitting. Del and Harry had not hit it off immediately, like Del and Bos, but that was to be expected. Del was under a bit of a cloud for a while with people doubting him. Some thought that if they were working with a serial killer they would have known earlier, however those people were not the majority and it did pass. Most staff in the station knew Bos and knew him to be an exceptionally clever man.

"Hi Del, you alright?" Del sat down.

"Actually I'm in quite a good mood considering I had another nightmare last night." Harry had made a drink ready and pushed it across the table to him.

"Same one as normal!"

Del picked up the mug and blew the billowing

steam from the top of it. "Thanks, yes it was exactly the same, scary as hell." Harry was just about to ask something else but he was stopped as Del's phone rang.

"Hello, Inspector Martin, how can I help?" It was silent for a moment and then he said, "Right." Another small break and then, "What do you mean?" It was quickly after that when he put the phone down, and he turned to his colleague. "Come on, we have a body."

Sergeant Gorham asked what they had.

"Don't know yet, a body at the docks." Both men stood up and abandoned their drinks.

*

On the drive towards the docks Harry asked what he had been told. Del had passed the info on.

"Well as you know I wasn't on the phone for long, Control just said Uniform on scene already, requesting senior officers as we have an odd one."

"What do they mean 'odd'?"

Del looked over to Harry and told him that he didn't have a clue, they wouldn't add to that. So it was with interest and a little trepidation that they pulled in towards the docks. The word 'docks' conjures up images of passport control, large ships with containers and a busy, smoke-filled, noisy workplace. The fact is, that picture could not be further from the truth. It was an abandoned quay front that at the height of its use had around two ships at any one time. Where it had picked up the grand title of 'the docks' had been lost in the mists of time but that was what everyone called the deserted, run-down hole now. Del drove towards the area and saw a marked unit in the distance so headed directly for it. He pulled his car up just before the marked unit and climbed out. There was, on closer inspection, a further two marked cars a little closer to the waterfront. Del and Harry looked at each other and shrugged. They started walking towards the first car they had seen and there was a PC rummaging around in the boot. Del looked across to Harry and put his finger up to his lips and winked. He crept towards the PC, hoping that he would not find what he was looking for quite yet. He was in luck because the officer was not only looking intently but also mumbling to himself. Del could hear sporadic words like, "Useless fucks, should have checked," and, "Stupid dicks."

A pace before he reached the vehicle Del shouted, "Lost something?"

The reaction really was quite something to behold. It is rare to see a person jump, spin, scream and swear in one cohesive movement but the man managed it. The jump landed him a clunk on the head and he spun around at the same time and screamed like a girl, which automatically turned into, "Aaaahhh, you fucking wanker, piece of…" If that wasn't perfect enough – to see the realisation on his face, mid-flow, that he had just called a senior officer a wanker, was a picture that Del would have loved to have framed and placed on his desk. Harry smiled.

"Excuse me, do you think that is any way to speak to a senior officer!" The PC stuttered and stammered in apologies and Del and Harry smiled.

"Don't worry about it, it was a shitty thing to do. What's going on and what are you looking for?"

The PC explained that he was looking for some police barrier tape. "Teach me to check the bloody car before I take it over."

Del nodded.

"Yep that would be a simple lesson learnt. What have we got as a scene then?" The boot was shut with no trace of any tape being found.

"It's a bit of an odd one really." He pointed in the direction of the other units and said they should head that way. The two inspectors walked towards the other cars; they were parked next to some buildings on the quay front. They reached around five metres away when they saw another PC; this one noticed them and started walking towards them.

"Hello sir." Del knew the officer as PC Roach, a dependable and rather serious character.

"Morning. What do we have?"

The PC explained that he had started a scene log and would place their details in when he got back to the car. He then said, "CSI are not here yet but follow me and I'll show you." PC Roach turned round and walked to the door of the concrete building. He didn't say another word, he just pointed.

"Fuck me!" were the words that came from Del.

Harry said, "No, you're fine, but what the hell is this freaky shit?"

The concrete building had an electric garage door. It had a handle in the centre where someone had tied a rope. Hanging from the rope was the body of a male.

The male was naked and there was a large puddle of blood on the floor below him as his throat had been slit. This was nasty but they were used to nasty. What was disconcerting was the graffiti on the body. From where they were, about 4-5 metres away, it looked like he had lines drawn all over him. As they walked closer the lines came into focus more. His body had been separated into sections and each section had writing on it. 'Chunk', 'ribs', 'loin', 'sirloin' and 'round' were some of the words scrawled on the body.

Harry looked at Del. "I don't want to say it but what does that look like to you?" His look was not returned but his query was answered.

"I know, it looks like a butcher's shop window."

Del put his hands up to his temples. "Shit, and the day started so well." He walked to the body but couldn't get too close due to the quantity of blood. He walked into the unit and had a quick scan; there was nothing particularly untoward noticeable. He turned to leave and noticed something. The man who was hanging had something in his mouth. He bent down and got as close as possible without standing in the blood. It looked like paper.

"I have a bad feeling about this," he said, standing up and making his way out of the unit.

"What's up?"

Del shook his head at Harry's question.

"I think there is something wedged in his mouth. I have a dodgy feeling about this one."

CHAPTER 3

The Killer Speaks

Del had combed the surrounding streets for any available CCTV coverage and had spent the next day with Harry sifting through it. The day after started in a similar vein. The public had been asked via all media if they had any information, to call the hotline provided. Uniform had visited house to house extensively too and the result of all the work so far was on their desks. It was a lot but it usually was first thing; most info gathered would be discarded quite quickly. Through all the footage so far there was not a thing out of place that would suggest the crime that was about to take place at the docks.

"This is a joke, we don't know what we're looking for!" Del threw the remote for the TV onto the desk in frustration. It hammered across the table, bouncing between mugs like a pinball machine.

"I have looked through the paperwork the units have sent and none are marked as urgent. The area it was in was bound to give us a slow start."

*

Harry was a pacer, he had been pacing up and down for a while. There was a knock at the door and a messenger handed Harry an envelope. It held the CSI initial report – 'the docks'. He looked at the cover and handed it directly to Del. "Here you go, perhaps this will give us something to bite on."

Del stood up, grabbed it and opened the envelope with vigour. He pulled out pictures of the scene and put the envelope on the desk. He could see quite clearly that the body had been marked into joints of meat. In one photo there was a close-up of the victim's mouth – it had a ruler next to it that measured the distance the piece of paper was peeking out. He ran through the pictures, stopped at one and froze. It seemed to Harry to last for quite some time, until all of a sudden Del slumped into the chair he was sitting in before. He closed his eyes and sighed. "Fuck."

Harry was used to Del and had never seen him react like this. Del was close to the edge with his emotions but this sigh was from the pit of despair.

"What the hell is in that report?" Del opened his eyes and raised his hand with the photo so as to pass it to Harry.

"I'm not ready for this fucking shit, not at the moment." He shook his head and shut his eyes again. The paper was taken with intrigue and more than a little concern and Harry looked at the picture. The picture was that of a piece of paper; it was on a flat surface with a ruler measuring the size. It was 15cm by 15cm. He read out what was written on the page.

So you think you stopped 'The Butcher' do you! You haven't seen anything yet. You thought Butcher Bos was sick, watch and learn.

Harry now sat down too.

"So we have a copycat Butcher."

Del opened his eyes.

"No, no we do not. If we had a copycat killer we would have a mutilated body in a tree. This is a determined note to let us know we have more to come."

Del leant forward and picked up the envelope and pulled out the papers. He scanned the detail, looking for a specific reference.

"Another key difference, our body is still an unknown, so we know our new Butcher does not feel the need to string up criminals. We need to find out who this man was. A good detective told me once that if you find the patterns you will be closer to finding the killer." Del then went quiet and read some more. He looked up a second later.

"Okay, it was the fucking killer we were looking for that told me it, but still good advice!" He smiled at Harry and then put the page down to his side. "Right, let's get this out of the way from the start. Harry, are you hanging people up and killing them? I don't think I could handle a second colleague doing that."

Harry laughed. "Yes, I could see that would be an irritant. No, I haven't, but let's face it, you could have asked him that and he would have said no too."

"Okay but as long as you know, if it is you I won't be very happy about it." Del winked and then said,

"Come on, let's catch this bastard!"

They both then had a look at the report. It said that the time of death was between 23:00-03:00 of the morning they found him. He was hung while alive and his throat cut. He had contusion marks on his wrists that suggested he was bound but the marks suggested handcuffs.

"Shit, let's try and stop that being public knowledge, shall we? We don't want people thinking another copper is going around mutilating people." The report also said that blood alcohol content levels were at .25%. This was high and meant he was intoxicated when he was killed. Del stood up and waved to Harry to follow him. They walked through the corridors until they entered through a large wooden door that was labelled 'Conference Room Three'.

"Right, I know this is going to sound weird but this is the room we used during the hunt for The Butcher. Don't ask me why but I think I want to use it now!" Del went over to the phone that was near a computer terminal at the side and dialled a couple of numbers.

"Hello Jim, it's Del, Inspector Martin. Can you do me a favour please?" This hung in the air for a little while. "Can you scrape together six of those large portable white boards and get them up to conference room three for me?" He waited and laughed. "Well I don't know but you are a resourceful fellow, I'm sure you can find them somewhere, that's why I called you." Another gap while the other person spoke. "Now I'm sure if you had that written on your head you would not be working as maintenance, with that type of title you would be top brass for sure. Oh, a pack of Blu Tac, some string and some dry-wipe pens would be handy too." He waited again and ended with, "Yes, I have been told that before, Jim, thanks."

Harry waited for the call to end. "Well?"

"Jim is going to pull together as many white boards as he can find and we're going to set up this room and map out our info on them."

Harry was a little bit perturbed by this sudden change in the way they worked. "Why? We don't usually do this for a murder."

Del nodded and then scratched his head with his left hand and with his right he waved the CSI report. "No, but this is not going to end with one body. My arse twanged as soon as we turned up at the docks, this is going to pick up speed like a train and if we don't put the brakes on it early... well let's just say I have a feeling we'll be under the wheels before we know it." Harry nodded.

"Okay, you're the boss, but promise me one thing?"

"What's that?"

"We don't always have to do what your arse wants!"

*

The two men collected the paperwork that had been piling on their desks and swapped all the CCTV footage discs to the conference room so everything was in one place. On the last trip back just before they reached the room Jim came along the hall pushing one of the white boards.

"Ahh Jim, you're a star!" shouted Del from behind a cardboard box in his arms.

"Don't give me that shit, I'm an arsehole for putting up with your shit." He threw a pack of pens and some Blu Tac in Del's box of discs.

Del winked at him and said, "Okay, a chocolate star, but a star nonetheless."

With that one Jim broke into a smile and continued into the room with the board. He wheeled it into place and left, saying that he had another two for definite and would continue to hunt for the others. Del thanked him and moved the board up against the longest wall but right in the middle of it. He undid the pack of pens and took a red and a blue out, then walked back to the board.

"Right, this one is the centre board, any new ones will be added to the sides." He took the blue pen and wrote 'The Butcher' at the top. At the bottom he wrote 'copycat' in red. He then wrote a question mark next to both.

"Why the question marks?" Harry asked.

"Well it's odd but it is the question I have been asking myself for a while now and it is more relevant now than ever, and it fits for the copycat too… Why?"

Harry was sitting in a chair on the other side of the conference room watching what Del was doing. "I take it you're wanting more than 'they are fucking mad'!"

Del expelled air in a half laugh, half sigh type of action.

"A little more precise would be nice, but that is the thing I have struggled with." He stuck the pen in his mouth and rattled it in his teeth for a small while. "Bos was not 'fucking mad', as you put it, he was a bloody good copper. I know he was asleep at the time but you still need a reason, mad or not, so will this bastard."

Harry said that in his view the new one would be easier to categorise. "I find it hugely unlikely that this killer will be asleep, so I think it's probably one of a couple of reasons."

"Enlighten me. What are the reasons?" Del sat on the edge of the large wooden table and waited for Harry to expand on his statement.

"Well as far as my logic goes, this killer has mentioned the first Butcher so it must be linked in some way. It will either be revenge for something that happened during that case—"

Del butted in at that point. "Revenge for what?"

Harry thought for a little while and said, "Well it could be revenge against the police in general, it could be revenge against Bos because this one somehow thinks they are the Real Butcher, or revenge against you for stopping him. The other option is that it is a complete wacko that was fixated with the Butcher killings and wants to add their name to the story."

Del turned and faced the board and stared for a couple of minutes; he then wrote 'revenge' in brackets underneath 'copycat'. His pen hovered next to the Butcher tag but he didn't write anything. The pen went back and forth to the board but nothing else.

"Okay, we need to find out about Bos. I know he was asleep but it still makes no sense the way it stands."

Del turned to face Harry who was still sat in the chair at the other end of the room.

"Harry, can you concentrate your efforts on finding out everything you can regarding Bos's past? I think this is key for understanding this."

Harry sat forward with his hands together. "I will, as long as you're sure you don't need my help with the new one."

He was told that he should still work out of conference room three so they could swap info between each other.

Jim came in with another two boards this time. "Here you go Del, another two." Del went over to help move them.

"Thanks for these, it is appreciated and will be a great help, but can you find seven now because I need a separate one for Harry!"

Jim tutted and jerked his head up. "You really do take the fucking piss, don't you? But yes, I have found seven that I can 'borrow' for you." Del slapped him on the back.

"Perfect. What would I do without you?"

"Piss off someone else, I should imagine." Jim smiled and walked out. They continued to build up a spider diagram across the boards. Del placed some Blu Tack near 'The Butcher' and then tacked string running in a separate direction for each murder from the original case. By the end of the shift they had string attached to each murder with other info, like victim's name, address and victim location. It spread across the six boards. On the end of the six boards was a gap and then a blank board – this was going to be for Harry to add bullet points about Bos's past. They stood back and admired their work.

"I like that," said Harry.

"Yes, hasn't got us a huge leap forward but gets us ready for the shit storm I'm expecting!"

CHAPTER 4

Dinner

Del entered the house after his shift and wiped his feet on the welcome mat. He heard light, easy listening music coming from the dining room. He walked into the room and found the lights turned down a little lower than normal and the table set for three with all the nice silverware and crystal.

"Babe!" he shouted.

Janice answered from the kitchen, "I'm in here, go get washed and changed and dinner will be close to being done."

Del turned and walked upstairs. Who was he to argue with that? He washed the grime from his day away and came down. It was minutes later and he had showered and changed. This time he walked into the dining room there were plates too, with food. Janice was in one seat smiling at him, and her friend Sue was sitting elegantly in another.

"We thought we would all have a meal together." Janice picked up her glass of wine and raised it towards Del. Sue was wearing a satin, figure-hugging red dress. It was cut low to show her cleavage but not so low as to leave nothing to the imagination. She had long, straight, dark hair. Her makeup was sparing apart from the striking red lipstick that covered her full lips. She was a stunning lady. Sue picked up her glass also.

"Cheers to the Great Inspector." She smiled, showing a set of beautiful pearly white teeth. Del wasn't the shy, hiding in the corner type of man, but he did feel a little odd, maybe a little naked standing in front of Sue's stare.

"Why thank you, the Great Inspector title will have to be on hold for a while depending on how my new case goes." Del sat down and noted as he did so that Sue moved her chair just a little bit nearer to him. If inner feelings and emotions were visible both Janice and Sue would have seen a large question mark and exclamation mark rise out of Del's head at that point. He was conscious about keeping his eyes well and truly for his wife and not lingering too long on some of the obvious assets on show to his left.

Janice took a sip of her wine. "What new case is this then?"

Del picked up his glass and took a sip. "I have just picked up a murder case that I think is going to turn into a bit of a problem; I think it may be linked with the Butcher."

Janice put her glass hastily down on the table. "What! What do you mean? Why?" The concern was very apparent in her voice.

Sue looked over to Janice. "What's the matter,

hun? You look worried. Who is your butcher?"

Janice did not take her eyes off Del. "What do you mean, linked?"

Del was treading thin ice with Janice when talking about the Butcher as he knew she got very uneasy due to the recent dreams he was having.

"I'm not really sure yet, just a similarity, could just be a coincidence." He smiled at his wife, put his hand on hers and added, "Don't worry."

Sue leant forward. "Del, who is your butcher and why is Janice so uptight about him?"

Del turned to his left and was around six inches from Sue's face because they were both leaning forward. She smiled a very sensual smile and Del's stomach lurched oddly and his tongue dried up immediately. *Bloody hell, she is gorgeous,* he thought, and was compelled to sit back. He started to speak but his voice went very shaky, so he cleared his throat and started again.

"It's not a real butcher, it's a name we called a serial killer over a year ago."

"Oh no, do you think he is back again?"

Del shook his head. "He better not be – we buried him."

Janice took an intake of breath in shock. "Del!"

Sue frowned, put her head to one side and looked at Janice. "But if he is dead why are you so worried, hun?"

Janice took a larger sip of her drink. "It was not a nice time and Del suffered after that case, and still is!"

Del put his hands on the table. "Look, I shouldn't have mentioned it, it's probably nothing anyway. I shouldn't have worried you, babe."

This time Sue put her hand on his. "Don't you worry, talking is one of the things friends do." She furtively winked at him and never removed her hand from his. Del was not used to this type of behaviour particularly from someone as good looking as she was. He was in a bit of a panic. It seemed like an eternity he sat with her hand grasping his, not knowing how to react. He got to his feet and grabbed the bottle of wine with his right hand, slipped his left away from Sue's and grabbed his glass. He poured himself more wine, even though he had hardly touched its original contents.

"Refill anyone?" he said.

"You do seem very nervous, babe. Let's just eat, shall we?" Del was thankful to concentrate on something other than Sue. He delved into his food and tried not to look up. "We're going to check out a new gym tomorrow Del, then we're going shopping." Del just nodded.

"Yes. I want to go into Silk and Satins, it's a new luxury lingerie establishment in the high street. I know I'm single but you never know, do you?"

Del choked on a piece of food at that precise moment. To try and cover up his timing he looked at her. "So Sue, what do you do for a living?"

Sue told him that she was a lady of leisure. She was from a very rich bloodline and lived off the wealth that they accumulated.

"I know it sounds a little lazy but why knock

yourself out working when you really do not need to?"

Del said he thought he would get bored.

"Oh, honey there are plenty of things in life to keep me occupied. Janice is helping me with some of that."

"Only happy to oblige my wealthy friend."

*

It seemed a long night for Del; he felt like he was under a spotlight the entire evening. The spotlight was the gaze of an attractive woman right in front of his lovely wife. The conversation eventually came back to work and Sue asked Del who he worked with.

"I work with a Sergeant called Harry now, he is a good man."

Sue had finished her meal at that point and was dabbing her mouth with a napkin. "Now? Have you changed staff then?" It was an uncomfortable subject but it did often raise its head.

"The last partner I had tried to kill me."

Before he could say any more of the sentence Sue laughed. "Well you must be one hell of a person to work with then." Del did smile.

"Yes, does sound a bit odd, doesn't it? But the Butcher case I mentioned earlier, it happened to be my partner that was doing it so it didn't end well." Sue sat static with her mouth open. *She really does look fantastic,* he thought.

"I don't know what to say to that. Congratulations Del, I'm only usually speechless if I have something in my mouth and you have managed it without putting something in it." She winked at him. Del's face went very warm and Janice burst out laughing.

"You are so bad, Sue, you could make a pimp blush."

Del actually laughed with them and it was pure relief that his wife heard and understood the sexual connotations to the sentence from Sue. It somehow made him feel at ease that his wife was comfortable with her actions and from her reaction it sounded like it was her regular behaviour.

*

Eventually the evening was over and a cab arrived to take Sue home.

"We must do this again; next time I will host." Sue went towards Del and grabbed him. She kissed him on the lips. "Thank you, see you soon."

He did not know what to say but she then went to Janice and kissed her full on the lips too.

"Thanks hun, see you tomorrow." Janice closed the front door and Del let out a sigh.

"Jesus, babe, she's a bit strong."

Janice walked towards him. "It's just her way, she doesn't mean anything by it. Come on, let's go to bed."

CHAPTER 5

Initial Search

Harry sat at his normal desk thinking. It was a bit of a daunting task; he had to look into the background of someone. That was not out of the ordinary, what was making this one a bit of a mind melt was that the person in question was a well-known and once well-respected inspector. Not only that but he was also now a well-known serial killer. Quite an unusual combination. The first thing he tried to do was to look for any information that was kept on their systems, however, anything and everything that was connected to Jeff Boston was security blocked. He could gain no information whatsoever from their files without going through a top brass release request and he didn't want to go through all that hassle and time. He knew he had to look into Bos but that did not mean he was comfortable with it. He stood up and decided to go about it in a different way. Harry knew where Bos had lived when he was an inspector, and that his house was empty as it was still going through the legal red tape. He had discovered this information through his conversations with Del. He knew Del was struggling with trying to come to terms with what had happened, even over a year later.

Harry drove to the house that was once home to 'The Butcher'. It was still a lovely area but the house had become a bit of a blot on the landscape. It had become rather overgrown and unfortunately had a little graffiti around its outside walls. He walked through the front garden which was once well kept but now had weeds overgrowing and hanging over the pavement, and litter strewn around the place. He tried the front door but predictably enough it was locked. Harry walked around the building reading the spray paint, trying to find some way in. The word 'butcher' was prominent on the walls along with numerous expletives. All of a sudden he stopped; he could see a small window left slightly ajar. Due to the frosting on the window he presumed it was to a bathroom. The window was just to the left of the balcony terrace on the top floor. Harry inspected the wall below but could not find any leverage or foot holes to lift him up to that level.

"Who'd be a burglar, hay!" he said out loud to himself. He continued around the side of the property. In the undergrowth of the shrub bed he could see an old green wheelie bin. He fought his way to it and tried to drag it out. It took a while and some considerable effort to release it from the clutches of the overgrown shrubs and bind weed. It didn't look in the best of conditions either, with moss growing up the side, but it may do the job. He pulled it juddering in protest towards the balcony area. It was difficult to pull as it only had one wheel left attached and that was buckled beyond repair. It was placed against the wall and shaken to see if it was secure. Harry lifted his right leg and started to try and climb onto it. The buckled wheel gave way even more and the bin lurched to the side just as Harry put his weight on it.

"Fucking hell, Jesus," he said, falling off, but he managed to land on his feet. He pushed and pulled the bin again, trying to find a better level, and failed miserably. The bin was then put on its side and Harry booted the one dodgy wheel – it was more than a little stubborn. It took a few well directed kicks from his size tens before it handed in the towel and flew off to lick its wounds in the sanctuary of the shrubbery. Harry tried again and this time it seemed a lot more static than before. He climbed up and gingerly edged himself towards the balcony; it did take quite an effort on his part but he did then manage to haul himself over the balcony wall. Harry dusted himself down and walked towards the patio doors that lead to the bedroom.

"Bollocks." These were locked too. *Why are people so security conscious when you don't bloody want them to be?* he thought. He was going to have to try and get in via the small window. Unfortunately it was a little away from the balcony so more climbing was to be necessary. The only saving grace Harry could see was that there was a bit of a lip sticking out where the plaster ended and the brickwork started. He would have to try and shuffle along that. He pulled himself over the edge and started edging past the end of the balcony.

"What the fucking hell am I doing!" He reached his left hand out and grabbed hold of the side of the window frame. He was still not close enough but inch by inch it was getting nearer. Harry had his right hand clinging to the side of the building now and his left was finding its way under the open window. With a big lurch he moved his right arm to join his left. He was now fully standing on a plaster lip holding on to the open window. The window was just a little above head height so this was going to be a strain, and he knew it. He stayed standing in one place for a while building up his will.

"Right, now or never you mad twat." He lifted his body with the strength in his arms and his head slipped through the window well enough but that was it. Panic started then as he thought, *Shit, if I fall now I'm likely to be decapitated or impale myself on the bloody window latch.* His legs scrambled up the wall for any leverage possible; they looked like he was on a vertical treadmill. They pumped like mad but were getting absolutely nowhere. His arms were starting to burn now and sweat was running down his face and down his back, not just due to exertion, but panic too. All of a sudden some plaster crunched off the wall and his right foot was able to get some purchase. This was all the help that he needed and he clambered up and through the window. He landed in a heap in a lovely oval bath and lay there panting for a little while.

"Fucking hell." He shook his arms with relief, they were burning with effort. A minute or so passed and he finally thought he had recovered enough to move. Still a little shaky in the legs, he climbed out of the large bath and went to the door.

It was a lovely place – a little dusty but lovely. He started in the bedroom and searched through the wardrobe, cupboard and drawers but nothing of any interest as far as Inspector Boston's past went. Harry then decided to go for the living room and hunted through the desks and drawers. He did find a photo album, it was flicked through and along with the lady he presumed to be his wife that was killed, were a couple of pictures of Bos when younger. He was with a male and female.

"Yes, what do we have here? Mummy and Daddy I believe." Harry took the photo out and put it in his pocket. There was a lot of paperwork to go through and most of it was irrelevant crap as far as Harry was concerned, until he flicked over a postcard. It was a normal beach scene however on the back it had:

Son, thank you for the lovely present, it was a lovely holiday, wish you would have come too. This is the beach we were next to.

Love Mum and Dad

To Harry's joy it had a sender's address on it and it was from about thirty miles away.

"Yes." Harry grinned from ear to ear and put the postcard in his pocket along with the photo. He headed for the front door and left for his car. After his dodgy entry he was very happy with the result and even more happy to be able to use the door.

The car started and he headed off to Farnham to have a chat with Mummy and Daddy Butcher. The house in Farnham was a normal two-up, two-down terraced home, the garden was immaculate with shrubs and flowers and a very lush green covering of grass. Harry knocked on the door and a minute later an elderly gentleman answered, peeking around the corner of a security chain.

"What?" Not exactly a greeting, more a demand.

"Hello, are you the father of Jeffrey Boston?" The answer was nearly as short as his first remark, but a whole lot blunter.

"Fuck off." And the door was shut. Harry was stunned for a moment then laughed a little. He knocked again and could hear voices behind the door, it sounded like a bit of an argument. The door opened and this time it was a female, she too opened it with the security catch on.

"Yes?" she said. Harry could hear the male in the background.

"Tell him to fuck off, fucking bastards." The voice then mumbled incoherently.

"Shut up, you silly old sod." She looked back through the crack in the door. "Mind you, if you don't give me a decent answer it is exactly what I will be saying. Who are you and what do you want?" Harry was smiling; he liked old people, especially ones that still had a bit of a kick in them. Before he could answer, "Come on, hurry up. I'm getting on, you know, don't really wanna die on a doorstep waiting for you to find your tongue!" Harry took out his warrant card and handed it to her through the gap in the door.

"I'm Sergeant Harry Gorham and I'm investigating a murder, could I come in and speak to you and your husband please?" The lady hummed for a little while and then shut the door. Harry waited for a moment but nothing happened, then the door opened and this time without the safety chain.

"Come in then. Sorry about that but we have had some right shit at our door over the last year." Harry nodded his head and could quite understand what she meant, this old couple were parents to a notorious serial killer. The elderly lady led the way into the old-style living room and sat down in a single floral-designed seat. Her husband was sat opposite her.

"Sit down then. How can we help?" Harry was wondering how to approach this after the reception he had received at the start.

"I'm sorry but it is about your son Jeff."

The male in his seat huffed loudly. "See? Told ya, told ya you should of told him to fuck off. Always the bloody same, nosey bastards." The man chewed his gums and crossed his arms angrily like a small child in a sulk.

"Listen here, I may be old but if you don't clear this up quickly I will kick your arse out of here, pronto." The lady was staring at him too now.

"I'm a real Sergeant, I'm investigating a murder and some information about Jeff Boston may help our inquiries." The lady raised an eyebrow.

"Okay, you have earned yourself a brief reprieve, now tell me how and why."

Harry was feeling a little uncomfortable now; he was used to interviewing suspects – he wasn't used to being interrogated himself.

"Look, I know how this is going to sound but I know your son turned out to be the Butcher but a new murderer has appeared, saying they are the Real Butcher, so to try and get a handle on the new one we need to try and find information on the old one in case there is a connection that will help us catch them." It was a long sentence that was blurted out and hung in the air. There was no other way of putting it really, Harry now just sat and waited for the fireworks. As it happened there were no fireworks, or even raised voices.

"Okay, I'm Sherry Boston and this is John Boston, my husband. What do you need to know?" She sat back and relaxed into her chair. Harry was shocked and it showed.

"No good sitting there with your mouth open, Sonny, we're actually okay people."

Her husband butted in with, "Speak for yourself."

She tutted and continued. "It's just we've had enough of the bloody papers and sickos coming round looking at us, staring as if we're goddamn goldfish."

Harry apologised. "Sorry, but I just need to know as much as you can tell me about your son in the hope something may click into place with our latest case." He continued, "I'm working with Inspector Del Martin who was working with your son and still speaks very highly of him, so we're not after any dirt for the tabloids, just the facts." Harry had gotten a note book out while saying all that.

"Okay, well let's put you right on one fact straight off, and this is not a widely known fact. Jeffrey was our son and we loved him dearly from the moment he was ours, however, he is not our blood offspring. We adopted Jeffrey when he was eight, or was he nine?" she questioned herself. "Oh, bloody brain, I can't remember exactly now."

Harry was meant to write this down but didn't, he just asked another question.

"Who knew that?"

He was told that not many people at all knew the facts. "Jeff knew, we knew and the adoption agency knew, we told no one else."

"Too right, no one else's bloody business," piped in the old man again, still with his thin arms folded with poorly concealed contempt.

"Did he ever try and find his real parents?" said Harry, and actually started to write something down.

"Not a lot of point him trying that, they were dead! Although he didn't know that. Jeff and his parents were in an accident when he was young and they both died. He lost his memory in the car crash and then we eventually adopted him." Harry was scribbling things down now.

"Did he know all this?"

The husband had lit a pipe during the conversation and sat pulling on it. "Not all of it, no," he said, puffing out billows of smoke.

"Old Puffing Billy over there is right, he knew he was adopted and he knew his parents had left him. He was told he lost his memory due to an illness and his parents couldn't cope so put him up for adoption, but other details were never let on."

They continued to talk for a while and Harry found out that the adoption agency had suggested they only let Jeffrey know a little and keep the rest a secret to protect him from the horror of the car crash he was involved in. According to the couple it was a horrific accident that happened when he was eight so he had a rough time. However, they didn't know where in the country it was. Harry thanked the couple for their time and also said, "Oh, and if you have any trouble with any bloody reporters, call me, I will happily come and kick their arses for you." He gave them his card and left.

CHAPTER 6

I.D.

A new day at the office started the same as the last had ended. Del was wading through endless house-to-house enquiry forms and CCTV footage… and was getting nowhere. He had searched through missing person reports and had come up with no matches, so still did not know who the male victim was. It was midday when his phone rang.

"Hello, Inspector Martin. How can I help?" There was the usual silence while someone else spoke. "Okay, what is the address?" Del grabbed a pen and jotted down an address on a note pad on his desk. "Thanks." He placed the phone down. "At last."

It happened to be the address of a female saying that her husband had not returned home. The description matched their graffiti victim. Del rushed downstairs and out of the station and it wasn't long before he was heading towards the address he was given; 74 Bishops Lane was not a particularly high-class area but was not exactly a slum either. He pulled up at the address and it was a well looked after semi-detached house. It had a well-trimmed lush green hedge and a nice lawn with similarly well-kept shrub borders. He checked the paperwork he had, making sure there was no evidence of the crime he was investigating showing. He didn't want to scare the woman unnecessarily. He briefly wondered if it was a little sick that he hoped this was his victim's wife. He approached the nice-looking, red-painted wooden door and rang the bell. Nothing fancy, just the regular dong following the ding. The door opened and a female answered. She was in her forties and had obviously been crying.

"Hello Mrs Hancock, I'm Detective Inspector Martin, can I come in and have a word please? I believe you have reported your husband as missing."

The female sniffed and said, "Yes of course, please come in."

The house was an ordinary place – tidy carpets, clean furniture and walls. Unlike some of the pits he had visited during his time in the service, it really was the case at times where he had wiped his feet on the way out. The times he had seen carpets move under his feet was scary, and not because of the garish patterns, purely because of the amount of creatures running around.

"Would you," she sniffed, "like a cup of tea?" The woman was clearly upset and had been for a while.

"No thank you, Mrs Hancock."

"Hillary, I'm Hillary," she said, wiping her nose with a tissue she took from her pocket.

"No thank you, Hillary, please sit down. When did you last see your husband?" Hillary thought for a moment.

"It was the evening before last, it was Tuesday about 8 o'clock."

Del asked her if she knew where he was going. She told him that he had said he was just going out for a drink with some work mates.

"Okay Hillary, where does your husband work?"

She said that he worked at a printing firm. "But he wasn't in today, I phoned them."

Del asked her to describe her husband to him. Her description was bang on for his victim as far as he could tell.

"Have you a recent picture of your husband please?" It wasn't long before she gave Del a photograph of her husband, it was of both of them at a recent party. Del was 98% convinced he had found his victim's next of kin.

"Will you excuse me for a while? I just need to step outside and make a call, and can I keep this for a while please?" He didn't actually wait for an answer and just walked out. His call was to Police Control and he asked for a female liaison officer to attend his location as soon as possible as he believed he was going to have to inform Hillary that her husband had been murdered. He went back in and said to Hillary that he was waiting for a colleague but could he have that drink after all. She had not finished making it when there was a knock at the door.

"I'll get that, Hillary, it's more than likely my colleague." It was, it was a female PC who Del knew to be a very accomplished officer. They went to the sitting room and waited for Mrs Hancock to return. Del picked out a picture from the autopsy that was the best he had. It was a full frontal but Del held it under a piece of paper to just show his face; the neck had been stitched together a little haphazardly and looked like one of Dr Frankenstein's creations. So he wanted to avoid that part if he could. Mrs Hancock returned with two cups of tea.

"Sorry, I didn't realise, I should have made another," she said, looking at the new officer. Del gestured for her to sit down.

"Don't worry about it, PC Boid can have mine. I have called PC Boid here as she is a liaison officer who helps us in certain circumstances." The PC sat down next to Hillary. "She is here because I believe I'm going to be passing on some distressing news."

"I knew it. What's happened?" She started to well up and her sniffing became apparent once again.

"Mrs Hancock, this is not certain but I have a picture here I want you to look at. Can you tell me if it is of your husband please?" Del stood up and walked across the navy blue carpet towards her. She was sitting next to PC Boid who took hold of her hand and asked her if she was ready. Hillary nodded erratically. Del moved the paper forward that had the picture half covered. It was not a lovely picture of him as he was extremely pale, as he had had all of his blood drained, but Del had eased it as best he could. Hillary burst into tears.

"Yes, that is Eric, wha… wha… what happened to hi… hi… him?" She was stuttering through the tears. Del explained that he believed he had been murdered.

Hillary broke down further at this point and was inaudible in her next statement. PC Boid had her arm around her.

"She asked how, sir." Del was not going to pass on that full horror, not at the moment at least.

"I'm trying to find out why and who by. Can you think of anyone who had a grievance with your husband or would want to harm him in any way?"

She continued to sob under the armpit of the female PC. After a little while more snivels came from her and PC Boid said, "She said she doesn't know anyone that wanted to harm him." Del wanted to speak to Hillary but she needed time to calm down.

"One last question before I leave you alone for a while. Do you happen to know where your husband was drinking last night?"

He got the answer from PC Boid that she thought it would be the Pocket and Shilling on Wellington Road.

"Thank you Mrs Hancock, I'm sorry for your loss and will speak to you again at a later date."

Del nodded at PC Boid and thanked her for her help and left the house. He already had basic details of her husband as Control had completed them when she had called, hence why they put it straight over to him. Del sat in his car and looked at the picture.

"Well, at least we now know who you were."

*

Del pulled up outside the Pocket and Shilling public house. It was a large place and the board hanging outside on the wall had a picture of a coin being dropped into a pocket; it looked tidy and well decorated. He knew looks could be deceiving but it didn't look a dive from the outside. He scanned along the edge of the building to see if he could see any CCTV. There was. It was a dark ball on a white housing and it looked like it covered the main entrance. Del walked in and took in his surroundings. It was the type of place it looked like from the outside, a large premises that was tidy, well kept, comfortable and set up for drinking and a nice meal if that was what you wanted. It had a number of large-screen TVs placed in some of the corners showing the news at the moment but could and would be utilised for any sporting event to draw the public in. There were a few punters in but it was daytime so unlikely to be buzzing. Del was fairly conspicuous, standing a few metres in from the doorway just looking around. He was again looking for CCTV; unfortunately he did not see too many inside.

"Afternoon, can I get you a drink of something sir?" It was the male behind the bar that had spoken. He was a bald man – not receding, just bald. He was not old so Del presumed quite correctly that his baldness was not a matter of nature being cruel, but more of a razor being sharp. He was wearing a plain black shirt and the tidy image was somewhat distorted by his crooked nose. It had obviously been broken in the past. Del walked towards the male.

"Yes, okay, why not? I'll have a lemonade please."

The barman smiled. "Okay, on duty, hay!"

Del smiled back and got out his warrant card. "Am I really that transparent?" he said, showing him his credentials.

"No, I've seen a lot worse, but only certain types of people walk in here and instantly check out the CCTV, and it's coppers, crooks, or someone with something to hide."

"I could be a crook or have something to hide!" said Del, sitting down at the bar.

"No, not likely, if you had something to hide you would be covering your identity and if you were a crook, well let's just say I would be expecting to be pouring more than a lemonade."

Del laughed and said, "Okay, yes, fair enough, I suppose you have me there." The barman put the lemonade on the bar.

"Okay Inspector, that is £1.20 please and what can I do for you?"

Del searched around in his pocket and dragged out the correct change, he then picked up his drink and said thanks. "Well, basically, a man has been murdered and I want to know if he was in here the night he was killed, simple as that." Del handed him the picture he had been given by Mrs Hancock. "Was he in here the night before last?"

The barman looked at the photo for a few moments.

"Yes, yes he was. He actually sat there." He pointed to a stool a few paces away. "He wasn't here long though, he had a couple of very quick drinks before he took a call and left." Del took back the picture.

"Thanks, are you sure?"

"Yep, you get used to noticing people in here."

Del put the picture away. "Okay, can you access the CCTV and show me or do you need the boss or something?"

The man smiled again. "I can do that. I'm the boss, I own the place." He walked away and jutted his head for Del to follow. As he passed a doorway with a solid-looking, black-painted door he opened it and shouted, "Pip, can you keep an eye on the bar for a while? I need to look at the CCTV." He continued to the other end of the bar, moved a bar towel and lifted up the counter top. "Come on through this way." He put his arm out to show Del the way through the second door.

They made their way to a box room that was made into a study. There was a table on the left as they entered, it had a TV screen and what looked like a large Sky box; it was a digital recording device and had quite a few arrows and buttons. The barman was called Desmond and he sat at the desk and turned on the TV unit.

"Okay Inspector, let's see how accurate my memory is, shall we?"

The screen flickered and pinged into action with a four-way split-screen view of some of the cameras. Desmond pressed a few of the buttons and a search bar appeared. He put in the date he wanted and the time of 19:50 and pressed the button. The four screens flickered and changed to the relevant time. The screen was manually spooled forward and at 19:55 Del's victim entered and sat exactly where Desmond had said. The pause button was pressed.

"I think that's your man, what do you think?" said Desmond.

"I think you're right and have a bloody good eye for faces and times. Can you spool it forward visually for me so I can see what he does please?" He was only too happy to oblige and as predicted Eric drank two quick pints. Just before he had finished the second he spoke on his phone, he drank up and then left quickly.

"Can you remember if he dialled out or did he get a call?"

Desmond nodded. "Yes, he got the call because the ring tone was awful, some dance crap."

Del thanked him and asked if he could burn him a copy of the footage. He gave him his card and asked him to call when it was ready to collect. Del left the pub but sat outside at one of the small round tables. He was thinking that if the new Butcher was anywhere near as clever as the original he would not make finding him easy. If he had picked Eric as a victim already it was more than likely the killer that had called him. However, Del knew that when Eric was found he did not have a mobile phone with him. It was a long shot but he would get the phone triangulated to pin an area down. The unfortunate part of that was it would only work if it was on and being used, a long shot at very best. He wondered how far away the killer would have waited and how well he knew them. Del glanced around the surrounding buildings but he couldn't see any with CCTV. He also knew the parts of town covered by council cameras, and this was not one of them. He decided to head back to the station. At least he could update the white boards with some information on the victim. He would have to go back to see Mrs Hancock soon and try and get some more details on her husband's enemies and even friends.

*

When he got back to the conference room Harry was there too. He was writing on the separate board. He looked around at Del as he entered.

"How did you get on today?" Del noted the word that he had written on the board – 'adopted'.

"Never mind that for the moment. Adopted!" He was shooting Harry an inquisitive look.

"Yes indeed, Bos was adopted. His parents were not his biological ones."

Del went and sat down; he did have a vague recollection of this fact. He thought for a while and then remembered a distant conversation with Bos where he had mentioned it. Del remembered it now, it was in a pub and it was the moment he had realised that Bos was not just a great detective inspector, he was a human struggling with other issues.

"Did you get anything else then?"

Harry said yes and put his pen to the board again. He wrote, 'real parents dead – car crash'.

"By all accounts they died in quite a nasty accident and Bos didn't know they had died. He was told they left him because they couldn't cope with the illness he had."

Del was actually impressed. "Where the hell did you get this stuff from?"

Harry sat down now. "From a very reliable source, his adoptive parents. They were extremely prickly at the start but I quite liked them actually. It's not surprising they were prickly though. By all accounts they have been hounded by the press and nutters."

"Excellent info though, so what next for you?"

Harry told him that his next task was to try and track down the details on the accident that Bos and his parents were involved in. "I know the rough dates but not where or exactly when, so it's going to be a bitch."

Del was thinking. "So Bos was in the same accident as his parents but survived, and it was a nasty one?"

"Apparently, yes."

Del went a little quiet for a moment.

"You don't think he had anything to do with it, do you? You know, first Butcher victims or something." Harry was a little stunned.

"I had never thought of that but I suppose it's a possibility, it's possible he killed them and then pretended to lose his memory. Doubtful though, I need to track down what happened."

Both men sat in silence for a while, deep in their own thoughts. Del was worried now. He knew Bos was clever but could he have been killing since he was a boy and gotten away with it. The thought sent a shiver through him. Harry was the one to come out of his internal thoughts first.

"Did you get anywhere today?"

The question seemed to take a while to sink into Del's brain. Most things move slower in the dark and Del was definitely thinking dark thoughts at the moment. Eventually the question did register.

"Oh, yes, not too bad actually. We have an I.D. on the vic now and CCTV footage of him in a pub the night he was killed." Del told Harry to think of his next move. "As I'm putting mine into action now."

Del picked up the phone and dialled.

"Hello, PC Boid? …Are you still with Mrs Hancock?"

Del was told that she was actually still there and that she was able to talk and had her earpiece in.

"Okay, could you do me a favour please? Could you get her husband's phone number from her?" Del waited for a few moments with his pen hovering above his page. He then started scribbling a number down. "Thank you. How is she?"

PC Boid was short with her answer. "Not too bad at the moment, the doctor has given her a light sedative."

Del did not put the phone down, he just pressed the cradle with his left hand and then redialled. This conversation was brief too but very much to the point. He was asking for the number he had written down to be triangulated. It ended with him saying that he would send the form as quickly as possible but would appreciate the wheels being put into motion sooner rather than later. No sooner had the phone hit the cradle than his arse was off the chair heading for the computer. He looked over to Harry. "Our victim had a phone with him the night he died but there was not one at the kill site. I know it's a long shot but if it was taken we may be able to track it down."

The rest of the shift for Del consisted of completing the form to track a phone. Harry, on the other hand, was not as lucky to have something that obvious to cling to; he had gone to his main desk and was searching the computer for something, anything about a nasty crash that involved a young boy and his parents.

CHAPTER 7

A Step Further

Del woke up to the screaming of the alarm and quickly punched it quiet. It was a fast reaction this morning and had resulted in Janice not being woken. Del felt good as he pulled the covers silently off his legs. He was in a positive frame of mind. He didn't know why but he felt like good things were on the cards today. He walked to the bathroom and emptied his full bladder; he looked in the mirror and was actually quite pleased with the person looking back. He smiled.

"Mmm, not too bad this morning." It was one of those mornings where everything seemed to be going right – his toast was perfect, his coffee was lovely and he felt light and alive. He left the house in plenty of time and even the tunes on the radio pleased him this morning. His journey to the station started with 'Jonny B. Good' and ended as he pulled up with the roar of ZZ Top's 'Sharp Dressed Man'. He looked in his rear-view mirror and altered his tie. "Yes guys, you may be right."

He was in before Harry and made a couple of drinks ready. Five minutes later Harry walked in.

"Bloody hell, Harry, you look a little rough." Del was right. Harry looked a little worse for wear.

"Don't, I had an awful night's sleep."

"Never mind, here you go, have a coffee." Del didn't say anything else but something niggled at the back of his mind. During the original Butcher investigation Bos was ill and became worse the further it went along. It turned out it was because he was getting little actual rest due to the fact he was out murdering people. Del was thinking that lightning couldn't strike twice but he didn't like the coincidence. He was sitting in quiet contemplation, looking at the drawn face of his colleague as his phone rang.

"Hello, Inspector Martin, how can I help?" Harry noticed that Del closed his eyes and shook his head while listening to the response. "Okay, we'll go right away."

Del put the phone down and turned to Harry, but before he could say anything Harry asked, "Is that what I think it is?"

"Well that depends on what you think it is. If you think it was an address of a dead body then you were quite right, and the day started so well too!"

Harry asked if it was their man.

"Not 100% sure but the description sounds very much like it, a body with writing on that looks like it has bled out." The two men rose from their chairs and made their way out of the station.

*

The victim was a little further away this time, but Del knew where the place was. It was a garage on the outskirts of town. It took just over half an hour to get to the garage and as before, a marked unit had already made its way to the scene. There was a PC standing at the entrance to the garage and another in the car with what looked like a member of the public. Del went directly to the PC on the door.

"Morning sir."

"Morning. What have we got? Give me a quick rundown please."

The PC nodded. "Okay, well, in our car we have a Jo Bright who worked here with a Tony Slugget. Both have keys to this property and the first in usually opens up. Mr Bright came in to an unlocked premises this morning and found the body of the owner, Mr Slugget, in the back. It's not a pretty sight and he called us. He is understandably a little shocked and my colleague is trying to calm him down in our car."

Del glanced back at the marked car and the gentleman in the back did look a little pale. "Have you called an ambulance?"

The PC looked a little put out. "No sir, I'm no expert but that bloke is dead and an ambulance ain't gonna help."

Del smiled a bit of a pitiful smile. "No, you prat. Not for the victim, for our friend in the car. Shock can do funny things so get one here. Is CSI on the way?"

The PC went quite rightly a little red. "I will radio for the ambulance and CSI are coming when they have cleared from the job they are on."

Del thanked him and also said, "I will need our victim's address when I come out. Can you try and gently retrieve that from our pale friend for me?"

Del walked in through the door. It was a glass panel in a large glass-fronted office space; it was where the public came to book in their vehicles. There was a paying coffee machine on the right and the full-face frontage was covered by vertical blinds that were all drawn so people couldn't see in. Along those blinds were also a row of comfy chairs for customers to wait on. Del walked in behind the counter through a door to the right. This led straight into a working garage area and the sight that hit them was not going to be one that would disappear from their memories any day soon. Del walked slowly forward. In front of him was a vehicle lift. Attached to the lift was a male, a naked male. He had been cable tied to the car lift by his ankles. The ties were the only thing holding him up; this was quite a feat considering the size of him. His body was facing towards the lift so it was his back that faced outwards toward the large lifting doors that were still shut at this time. Hanging like this had given him a waist line that he probably hadn't seen for years, however, the belly that used to reside there was now hanging unabashedly over his chest. An oil drip tray had been placed under the victim and it had been used to catch the blood that had drained from the slit throat. The drip tray was woefully inadequate for the job and the blood had overflowed and had made a large puddle under the car lift. The tray hadn't been cleaned out well so a rainbow sheen of oil glinted off the top of the rich red contents. The male, again, had the red lines drawn on him and the cuts of meat written in.

Del looked closer.

"He was drawn on while hanging." There was only one difference between this and the first body as far as Del could see. The flesh of his buttocks had been removed. There was not a lot of blood around the removed section so it had likely been sliced after the victim had been drained and killed.

Harry was standing back. "How do you know he was already hanging when drawn on?"

Del pointed out that the lines had been made with his belly hanging down. "If he was lying down or even standing as normal, the lines would be on the top of his belly rather than the writing on the bottom of it. I wouldn't fancy lifting that just to draw under it."

Harry walked around a little. "Can you see if he has a note in his mouth?"

Del leant around to see but couldn't quite notice anything sticking out of his mouth.

"I can't see anything."

Del came away and stood a couple of metres from the body. He started looking around the room.

"Okay, this nutter has said they are the real Butcher, the old Butcher left us notes too but he scrawled them on walls and mirrors and things. Let's have a quick look without disturbing anything."

The two looked around but found nothing. They looked for five minutes and Del decided to leave ready for the CSI unit. As they came back into the reception area they noticed the PC was back and there was also an ambulance in attendance now. Harry asked this time, "Did you manage to get the owner's address?" The PC had and handed Harry a piece of paper. "Thank you. Make sure you start a scene log." It was an obvious thing but Harry was taking no chances after hearing of the PC's inept behaviour so far. They walked to the car.

"I don't believe some people sometimes. No ambulance... Did you see the fucking colour of that bloke!" Del was shaking his head. Harry passed him the paper with the address on it.

"I know, it looked like he had less blood than our fucking victim!" Del sat down and looked at the note. "Can you search where Hinkley Road is please? I don't know where that one is."

Harry got his phone out and searched for the address. After a few blue words he managed to get enough of a signal. Seconds later they were off towards their victim's home.

*

It wasn't far away from his workplace and it didn't take them long to arrive; 54 Hinkley Road turned out to be one in a road of semi-detached properties with average front gardens. They all looked the same and Del presumed that they had once belonged to the council but had been privately purchased long ago, as the buildings looked identical but the fixtures and fittings were now the only things the residents could change to make their homes stand out from the crowd. Some were obviously more conspicuous with this than others and Tony Slugget had been happy to be ordinary. Del and Harry approached the main door with nothing standing out to say something untoward had happened here, however, when Del knocked on the door it swung open.

"Fuck, this seems familiar, the Butcher's victims' homes were usually unlocked." Del took a pace into the property and shouted, "Hello, this is the police, is anyone in?"

Predictably there was not a response. Harry followed Del in. The main door led straight into a hallway that ran from left to right. Directly ninety degrees to the right was a door, to the right in front of Del was another door and then there were some stairs directly right. He motioned to Harry to stay in the hallway as he opened the door on the left. It turned out to be a large living room area; it was tidy and void of any people or any trouble. There was not another exit to the room so after looking behind the sofa he could check that room off as clear. Next he zeroed in on the other door on the bottom floor. It was a kitchen. Again, no person to speak of but not exactly a tidy place; he had definitely seen worse but wouldn't fancy eating anything. Del walked out.

"It's clear down here, stay behind me as we go upstairs."

Del walked slowly up the flight of stairs; they creaked and moaned as he did so. There were four doors at intervals at the top all around a central landing. Del motioned Harry to stay at the top and keep an eye on all the other doors as he went to the door on the left. He opened it, slowly. It was a box room and had been utilised as an office but on the floor was a glass tank. To Del's shock it had a piece of paper taped to the front with his name on. He looked at the tank closely and at the top was a shelf with a clear liquid in. At the bottom of the tank was a hole with a piece of string sticking out. The string was attached to a piece of card and also to one edge of the shelf.

"Harry, come and have a look at this."

A second later, Harry walked in.

"What the fuck is that?"

Del shrugged and took off the paper with his name on.

Del, if you want my info you had better be gentle and read quickly.

It made no sense to Del whatsoever, so he passed it to Harry. Del delicately pulled at the string that was coming out from the tank. It moved the card towards him slightly but also tipped the liquid a little so some of the fluid started dripping down the inside of the tank. Del could see a piece of paper under the card that moved, it had 'Del' written on it.

"What the hell is this shit?" He pulled the string a little more; it revealed some more words but more fluid started to run down the tank. The fluid was not water. Del could see it. The paper at the bottom read:

Del, we have or should I say had a mutual friend.

He could not see any more. The liquid had reached the bottom of the tank now and it hit the piece of paper. As it did so the colour disappeared from it and the word 'Del' started to fade.

"Oh shit." Del pulled the string to uncover the paper; this sent a lot more liquid down. He quickly read some more before the paper faded completely.

I know you are struggling to understand his demise hence

your nightmares. I'm going to endeavour to help you understand.

This was the amount he read before it disappeared. If he had have been a little quicker or stealthier he would have read the end. It said:

You named Bos the Butcher, he was only half there, wait and see the Real Butcher.

It was then signed at the bottom with 'The Butcher'.

"I hate this coded shit."

Harry looked on in quiet admiration. "Hang on, how did he know about your nightmares? I didn't think they were common knowledge."

Del stood up. "I don't know but this is all becoming far too fucking familiar. Bos was getting pissed about and wound up during that investigation." Del pulled the string to try and see if he could retrieve anything but the paper had come away. The string in his hand smelt strongly, it was bleach. Now he knew why the liquid ran slowly – it was thick bleach. The paper that the note was written on looked like toilet paper and it didn't last long with the bleach onslaught.

"Yes, but Del, it turned out that he was winding himself up as he was the killer. Call me hopeful but I don't think that is happening again, so who the fuck is it?"

Del lifted the string up. "I don't know but he is a clever bastard. We need to keep our eyes peeled, someone is watching."

They checked the other rooms but nothing else

was there. Del wrote down in his note book what he remembered of the message as they sat in the car.

"We have or had a mutual friend. I'm struggling to understand his demise, then he mentions my nightmares. He must be on about Bos." Del was muttering and writing.

"So the new Butcher knew the old one, at least that is something to go on."

Del just 'mmmmed' at Harry, he was not feeling very comfortable with the intrusion into his personal life. He was starting to understand a little of what Bos had gone through. It was definitely not a pleasant idea that a killer, an intelligent killer, had you firmly in his sights and that they were watching everything you did.

"If this new Butcher is watching you is there anything we can do to throw them off and put them on the back foot?" Harry looked over at Del, he was too preoccupied with the intrusion into his personal life to think of anything constructive but he nodded at that question.

"I like the idea of that but how?"

The two men sat stationary in the car with just the gears of their minds clunking away. Harry was the one that came up with an idea. "Okay, how about this? You publicly fire me and chuck me from the case. However, instead of disappearing I hang about and use my time to keep an eye on you. That way he thinks you are on your own and I can see who the fuck it is following you."

Del thought for a while.

"I need you looking into Bos, I have a feeling this

bastard isn't going to fall for something like that. However, whenever you get a dull moment in your Bos enquiries you could follow me. I would like to see if there is anyone on my tail. Plus, well, you never know, perhaps it's me this time!" Del smiled a very bored cheeky grin at Harry, who laughed in response.

"Yes, okay, but if it's you and you are a real butcher, could you get me a joint of beef ready for Sunday please?"

Del smiled, called him a twat and grabbed his phone. The call was made to Control to ask for a uniform presence and a CSI unit to come to the address. Del doubted they would find anything but had to try. They just sat in the car for a while waiting to be relieved from the house; they certainly didn't want to leave it open without a police presence of some description. It wasn't long before a marked unit arrived to babysit the property.

"I want to go back to the garage. I want to see if there was a note in the victim's mouth this time."

It went quiet and Harry responded, "Something has been niggling at me. Why leave a message in the body and then a separate message in the house!"

Del had been wondering that same thing which was why he wanted to go back to the crime scene now. "I don't know. There is something a little odd about it. If there are two separate messages, I need to find out."

CHAPTER 8

A Wait

The car pulled up at the garage alongside the white van that Del knew to be the vehicle the forensic team used. He climbed out and walked to the garage entrance. The forecourt had been taped off and they had signalled to the PC on guard that they were entering the site. As he stepped through the main glass front door, the rear door was open and he could see flashes of light coming from the back. He walked through and stood in the doorway for a moment. Inside were two CSI staff both dressed in white paper suits. It always made Del shiver seeing that, as it reminded him of being helpless in front of the Butcher waiting to die. The Butcher had worn this type of suit when killing. The attention of one of the men was grabbed by Del waving an arm at him. The one who saw was the person taking pictures of the victim; he stopped and walked towards Del and Harry.

"Hi Del, how's things?" It was Buddy. He had worked on some of the original Butcher scenes.

"Hi Bud, not great. I'm here to ask if you've found

a note on the victim in this one?"

Buddy told him that he hadn't but he hadn't finished photographing it yet. "Once I have all the photos of the scene in situ then I will have a closer look for more hidden aspects."

Del asked how close he was to that part.

"Sorry Del but I can't really say. I'll call you if I find anything though."

Del said that it would be very much appreciated and then, "Do you know if anyone has looked at the premises CCTV yet?"

Bud said that they hadn't. "I know you're chomping at the bit for some info, Del, but we can only go so fast. Once we have finished in here we'll start in the other room. I'll get you any footage after we have dusted in there." It wasn't what Del wanted to hear but he knew Bud was excellent at what he did and if any evidence was there he would find it, he just had to wait.

"Okay Bud, cheers, keep me updated."

Bud said, "Will do," and walked away, back towards the victim hanging on the car lift. Inspector Martin and Sergeant Gorham walked despondently from the site back to their vehicle.

"I think we need to go back to the nick and think on where to go from here, but I think we'll have something to eat first. I'm starving."

*

Del unlocked the car with a bleep from his fob and they headed off. They pulled up to a place called 'The Roadside Diner'. Del marched straight into what looked like an advert for cleaning products, the 'before' shots of one anyway.

"Afternoon Brian, can I have a Bos special please?"

The man behind the counter with a very dubious apron on shouted, "Sure thing, Del. Just a tea for you Harry?" Harry nodded and they both sat down on the nearest table on their right.

"Why the bloody hell do we always come here? It's a shit hole!"

Brian heard the comment. "Yes, but Harry, it's a friendly shit hole."

Del smiled. "He is right. Everyone is welcome here."

"Yes, that is always my worry. On one table could be sat Sam and Ella, the other could be Botcha and Lisem and across the room may be E. Coli. Yes, all fucking welcome in here! But let's face it, there are some people I don't want to mix with!"

Brian brought over two teas. "I will have you know I have certificates for this place." Harry laughed.

"Yeah, but fuck knows what they say."

Del grabbed a spoon and started shovelling heaps of sugar into his drink.

"Oh come on, it's not that bad. Anyway, a bit of grime does you no harm, puts hairs on ya chest."

Harry picked up his drink. "I don't mind them on my chest, I would just much prefer them to stay out of my drinks and food." He picked a hair out of his cup and wiped it on his trousers. Secretly he did actually like the place but he certainly wasn't going to let Del or Brian know, he liked winding them up.

"Okay, where do we go from here then, apart from the toilet as usual?" said Harry, sipping his tea. Del took out his notes and read the message from the glass tank again.

"We have or had a mutual friend. I know you are struggling to understand his demise hence the nightmares. I'm going to endeavour to help you understand." He read it out loud and then sat staring at it.

"I'm now thinking he is talking about Bos, but what is there to understand? He killed people!"

Harry shook his head. "I don't know, it's the tank that I don't understand."

Brian put down a plate piled with a fry-up in front of Del, said, "Here you go. Tuck in," and then walked back to his counter.

"So who knew you and Bos?" said Harry as he watched Del start to demolish the mountain of food on his plate. Del thoughtfully chewed through a mushroom.

"Well, as far as I can tell just staff in the police, but I refuse to believe we have another killer among us." It was silent minus Del's knife and fork bashing about like some miniature fencing tournament.

"Do you think someone is hacking into our systems and files?"

Del thought on that for a moment too.

"It is always possible, but my nightmares are not in any of that info."

Back to the quiet again. Then Del's phone blurted into action. He swallowed the bacon he was chewing and answered it.

"Hello, Inspector Martin, how can I help?"

In the quiet of the shop Harry could hear the person on the other end.

"Hi Del, it's Bud, just wanted to let you know there is a note in the victim's mouth."

Del asked what the note said but was told that it had been bagged for evidence and would be inspected properly at the lab. "I just wanted you to know it was there."

Del thanked Bud and hung up. "I don't get why they would leave two separate messages."

The food was polished off and two more drinks drunk before they headed back to the station to finish off their day. It was not a productive last hour as thoughts on the notes had turned to frustration at having to wait. During their conversations they decided that tomorrow was going to be a day for Harry to continue to look into Bos.

CHAPTER 9

Home

Del was glad to get home; at the back of his mind as he tried to come to terms with the Real Butcher and Bos, he knew he was in a much happier position than Bos was. Del had his wife to come home to whereas Bos was on his own, his wife had died in a car accident. At that moment as he walked in the door he felt a cold finger run down his spine.

"Holy fuck." Janice came round the corner at that moment.

"You okay, babe?" Del walked towards his wife and gave her a kiss.

"Sorry, I'm fine, it's just I've had a thought slap me in the face."

Janice took him by the hand and walked him to the living room. She sat him down and said, "Wait there, I'll be back in a second." She did come back in a couple of seconds and she was carrying two glasses of red wine. She sat next to him. "Well, what's up?" she asked, handing him a glass.

"Remember last night me telling you that Bos was adopted due to a car accident?"

Janice sipped her wine. "Yes."

"Helen, his wife, died in a car accident too. Now I know that may be a coincidence but I don't like coincidences. What if they are linked!"

Janice initially did not say anything, she just sat back in the chair.

"But they were years apart, and you said he didn't know much about the accident."

This time it was Del that sat back. He hummed at her statement. "I still don't like that link."

Janice told him that tea was nearly done. "Oh, and I met up with Sue again today and she has invited us to hers for a meal tomorrow."

Del swallowed hard; he was uncomfortable around Sue, not just because her looks made his underwear elastic seem tight, but it was her flirty behaviour in front of Janice that made him feel very naked and vulnerable. He didn't voice this, he just agreed and said, "That will be nice."

Janice chuckled. "She doesn't mean anything by it," and disappeared from the room.

She might not but it still gets me hot under the collar, he thought, and took a large gulp of his wine. The meal was lovely, Janice really did know how to please a man's belly. She also looked lovely tonight. He sat back in his chair at the dining table and told her how good the food was. "You look lovely too."

She smiled and leant forward and kissed him. "Thanks babe, you wait until tomorrow then. Sue is fab in the kitchen."

Del's mind wandered for a second but shot back into focus when Janice stood up and sat on his lap. She kissed him gently on the lips. "Don't get too muddled with this new case, I don't like the idea of your nightmares getting worse."

He smiled at his wife. "They're just dreams, babe. They can't hurt me." He kissed her harder and placed his glass on the table. He grabbed the back of her head with his right hand and pushed it firmly into him, his left hand lifted to touch her neck. Janice sighed a contented sigh and put her arms around Del's neck. The embrace quickened and it wasn't long before Del's right hand found its way up the dark blue blouse and was pressing firmly onto the front of her bra. Janice leant back and adeptly, with her right hand unclasped her own strap and freed her breasts. Del was leaning her back and supporting her with his left hand while gently fondling her with his right. She moaned with anticipation. He then stood up with Janice still in the sitting position; she straddled her legs around his waist and they joined with their lips once more. It was a passionate embrace that continued as Del walked her into the bedroom and laid her on the bed. It was a warm evening which turned into a long, hot night.

CHAPTER 10

Adoption

Harry started early and without Del, he wanted to find something on the crash that Bos was involved in when young. The unfortunate thing was, he didn't know a lot about it. None of his searches online had revealed anything. He decided to call up Sherry Boston.

"Hello Mrs Boston, it's Sergeant Gorham here. If you remember I spoke to you the day before yesterday about your son." Sherry remembered and told him that she wasn't bloody senile and of course she did. Harry grinned; he had forgotten how feisty the couple were. "I wonder if you can answer me a quick question. What adoption agency did you go through?"

She told him that it was Essex County Council that arranged it all. "We had to travel down there a lot for what seemed like forever."

Harry thanked her. "I don't suppose you remember the name of the person you dealt with, do you?"

"Ha, no, I'm not senile but my memory ain't that good. All I remember is she had a bloody great nose on her." The call ended and Harry looked online for the number for Essex County Council Adoption Services. It didn't take him long before he was dialling the number. The call went through the usual rubbish. 'This call is being recorded for training' etc., then press this button for this, that button for that, another button for something else.

"I just want to speak to some bugger." He kept pressing buttons until he found an option that said he could speak to an advisor. After listening to some God awful tune for a while, a voice spoke to him. It wasn't who he wanted.

"Look, I'm sorry but I'm Sergeant Harry Gorham. I'm urgently trying to speak to someone in the adoption department." The female on the other end was actually quite helpful; Harry found that it was usually the case once you finally got to speak to someone. She put him on hold for a few seconds.

"Hello Sergeant Gordon, I will just put you through." Harry was going to correct her but thought better of it. What was the point? He was getting through to the right person now. The phone rang and then kicked in with the bloody awful tune again.

"Jesus, haven't they got another tune!" Harry said, looking at the receiver for some reason. This time it wasn't for long.

"Hello, Essex County Council Adoption Department, this is Harriet. How can I help you?" Harry thought it was quite a pleasant phone manner.

"Yes, hello, I'm Sergeant Harry Gorham and I'm

investigating a number of quite gruesome murders. One of the murderers was adopted when young and I believe it was your department that dealt with it."

The lady on the other end was still pleasant but did have an edge to her answer.

"Okay sir, but we're unable to give personal information like that out over the phone. It is against our policy." Harry was not unsurprised to hear that reply, in fact he would have been shocked and quite appalled if they had readily given such info at the drop of a hat.

"Yes indeed, that is quite understandable, however, could you tell me if details from thirty-three years ago would still be available?"

The lady said that they did keep all those records and that they would be retrievable.

"That is excellent, could you tell me how I can go about obtaining the relevant information please?"

Harriet described what needed doing. It involved filling in an information application with relevant stamps. This had to be sent to Essex County Council for authorisation. He would then later hear if successful and would have to come in person to retrieve the details. He was then told it would take about five to ten working days.

"I'm sorry but this is rather more urgent than that, people are being killed and I need the info as soon as possible to try and stop it."

The line went quiet for a second.

"Okay Sergeant, you could try a personal visit and see the Head of Department, but I suggest you bring the completed form with you at the same time. Have you an email address I can send the form to?"

Harry was ecstatic to hear that response he thought he was going to have to pull teeth to get this far. He gave Harriet his email address and thanked her.

"No problem, Sergeant, I'll put the department head's details in the email along with the address of our headquarters."

Harry hung up and just waited for the ping of the email system. It was a pain waiting and it seemed like an age, however, that age was really only eight minutes. He was swinging around on his chair as the tell-tale ping of an incoming email sounded. He spun back and tucked his legs under the desk. It was the email he wanted; he opened the attachment and scanned the document. He was quite surprised at its simplicity and printed it immediately. He jotted down the details of the person he was to speak to and completed the form. It didn't take him long and he was soon up and heading for the exit for the journey to Essex. It was two hours' travel time according to his satnav and the traffic and weather were on his side.

*

It was 12:14 when he arrived at his destination in Essex. However, 13:25 and he was still in the waiting room. He stood up and went to the desk where the female receptionist was.

"Look, I know it's a pain but have you any idea how long Ms Doors is going to be? This is an urgent case I'm dealing with."

The lady with the hair drawn up into a bun so tight it looked like her face was being pulled up shook her head slowly. "I'm sorry, sir, but she is in a meeting and as you had no appointment she is fitting you in as soon as she can. I will call you as soon as she is able to see you."

Harry nodded his reluctant thanks and sat back down. The minutes ticked by with Harry tapping his feet in mounting frustration. It was 13:50 when the receptionist spoke up again.

"Sergeant, Ms Doors is able to speak to you now, she is on her way down to see you."

Harry stood up and thanked her. He stood waiting for what he presumed would be a large woman in her fifties to appear. An attractive woman in her thirties came out a door on his right; she wore a mid-length white skirt with a pale pink top. She had long brown hair that was perfectly straight. Harry glanced at her and then continued to wait for the head of adoption to come and meet him. He paid no attention as the woman he saw enter went to the reception desk and spoke briefly to the receptionist. After around thirty seconds she made a beeline directly towards Harry.

"Hello Sergeant Gorham."

Harry looked at her. "Hello, yes, how can I help?"

She held her hand out to shake his. "It is more apparently what I can do for you, I'm Ms Doors, the Head of Adoption Services. I believe you are wanting to see me?"

Harry was a little stunned but rallied well.

"I'm sorry, I was miles away. Pleased to meet you

and very happy you agreed to see me."

It wasn't a surprise to Marrie, it always made her laugh how she was perceived before people met her.

"Yes, okay, nice save. Follow me and we can have a chat."

Harry knew at that point his attempted recovery had failed and he had been sussed. He followed behind through the doors she had walked through and up a couple of flights of stairs. They eventually reached an office that was one of those that could be seen through as it has glass walls.

"Come in, Sergeant, take a seat." Harry took a seat opposite her. "Tell me what this is about then."

Harry smiled at her. "You don't mess about, do you?"

"No, Sergeant, I find there is no point. I will be able to help or I will not. Any pissing around in the middle is quite a waste of time." Harry was quite taken aback with that; she was perfectly right but you never usually hear things put quite that simply.

"Well with that philosophy in place I will be as direct as you. It's simple – I'm trying to catch a killer and information you may have could help with it."

Marrie stood up and walked over to Harry. "Before I go any further I need to check you out, you're in normal clothes. Could I see your warrant card please?"

Harry took out his card from his inside pocket and gave it to her. "Who is your boss, Sergeant?"

Harry told her that his inspector was Inspector Del Martin. He sat in stunned silence as she walked away and went straight to her computer. She typed for a few seconds and then dialled out on her phone. He waited and heard her.

"Hello, could you put me through to Inspector Del Martin please?" She waited for a few seconds. "Okay, this is rather urgent. Could you put me through to his phone then please?" She waited a little longer this time and stood up. "Yes, by all means. However, please point out that I have a Sergeant in front of me after information and I will not be passing on anything until I'm certain he is who he says he is."

Harry sat there thinking, *This is some hard-nosed bitch, but no one is going to pull the wool over her eyes.*

"Oh, hello, thank you for taking my call. I'm Marrie Doors, the Head of Adoption Services for Essex County Council. I have a man here saying he is a Sergeant Gorham and that you're his boss. Could you verify that fact for me, with a description of him please?"

She looked directly at Harry and said nothing, just listened.

"Thank you, Inspector." She hung the phone up and sat down.

"Sorry about that but as we're not going through the correct procedures in this case I needed to make absolutely sure any information I'm to pass will be going to the correct authority."

Harry raised his eyebrows, nodded and said, "No problem, I just hope you can help now."

She said that she would be happy to if she could.

"So tell me what it is you're after."

Harry explained that there was a serial killer named the Butcher a year ago, who was caught and then killed himself. "Unfortunately we have a new killer now who is saying he is the Real Butcher and he says he knew the original." He went on to say that the original was adopted through Essex County Council to a couple called Sherry and John Boston. He told her that he was adopted at the age of eight after some kind of accident where his parents were killed. "I'm after any and all the info you can give me on that young boy."

Marrie listened intently and then asked if he knew the year he was adopted. Harry told her and also pulled out the form that he had been sent and had completed. She smiled at him. "Thank you, this will help greatly in keeping a paper trail of information sharing." Marrie sat at her computer and put some glasses on. It was a few minutes before she moved anything apart from her typing fingers and she had not said a word either. Suddenly she looked over her glasses at Harry. "Was the man you're talking about called Jeffrey BOSTON?"

Harry stood up abruptly. "Yes, yes it bloody was! Have you got it?"

Marrie pushed her glasses closer to her eyes. "Yes, Sergeant, I believe I have. I will collect some appropriate data and print it off for you, I will then collect your signature for the info and this will be kept on this file as evidence of data sharing." Harry was absolutely ecstatic, he did not give a shit what he had to sign. It took her about ten minutes to get a printout and she had Harry sign the bottom of the page and then scanned the signed page.

"I know it is delicate and I'm very grateful for your assistance but was all that necessary?" Harry asked her this as he was ready to leave.

Marrie put out her hand to shake his again. "Honestly, Sergeant, no, more than likely not, but I have worked hard to get where I'm and I know some people would like nothing more than to get me removed. So I make sure I do not give them the ammunition to try."

"Well that I can understand, thank you for your help."

Marrie let go of his hand and showed him to the door.

"Not a problem, I hope you catch this new killer."

Harry left with a healthy admiration for the woman he had just met. She didn't look like he expected and turned out to be so much more. He left the building and as he sat down in his car he started to read the information on the sheet for the first time. He shook his head slowly.

"Jesus Christ, Bos. No wonder you were fucked up."

CHAPTER 11

Note

Del woke with the sound of his alarm. He was feeling on edge. He was concerned about the case. All cases of murder concerned him but this one had far more worrying elements to it. He had fallen asleep late going through it all again and again; he wanted to switch all his thoughts off but they just niggled him constantly. He dropped off about 03:00 and once asleep he did go right up until his alarm woke him. He got ready for work in a bit of a daze, trying to wake from a poor night's sleep. He left the house with a kiss and a reminder from Janice that they had a meal with Sue tonight. He wanted that like a hole in the head but he knew how much it meant to Janice.

The drive to work was uneventful as he listened to the radio. He didn't go to his desk when he reached the station, he went straight to the conference room. The boards were as he had left them; he knew he had to update them and was going to do that once he had checked his emails. The monitor was switched on and he logged in. He had seventy-six emails overnight.

"How the hell did we cope without it?" he said and tutted. He knew that 95% of them were going to be entirely irrelevant to him so just scanned them for the moment for ones that may grab him. One he noted quite quickly was titled 'phone request'. He clicked this the second he saw it. It had an attachment that he opened, it was not good news. The victim's phone was not on and was untraceable.

"Fuck it, you bastard!" Del stood up, half pushing, half throwing the computer mouse across the desk. He wasn't expecting it to come to anything but it was still a pain in the arse being proved right. He walked to the white board and picked up the blue pen. One of the lines led off from the first victim and was labelled 'mobile phone track'. Del snapped off the lid of the pen and drew a cross through the phrase. He snapped the lid back on and threw it onto the rack on the bottom of the board. He thought for a moment about the original murders; they were particularly gruesome by the end and the victims were bled and cut up, not in any way connected to the butcher profession, but the new victims were drawn on as if they were animals in a butcher's shop. He had made a decision. He collected the pictures of the first new Butcher's kill and headed out of the station. He didn't go to his car, he walked right past it; he went onto the main street and headed towards the high street. He walked with a purpose of a man with an idea. He made his way up the street along all the shops of various types and then suddenly stopped outside one and looked in the window. It was a butcher's. It was the best and most well-known one around. In the window was a body and it was hanging from its feet, well, trotters. It was a pig, or to be more precise half a pig. It did not have its head but was hanging in full view. It struck Del as odd how similar it looked to the victims he had seen, however, people were walking past this as if it was perfectly okay. He shook the image of a person hanging in the window out of his mind and entered the shop. The smell hit him, it was the smell of all butcher shops and it was an aroma that he had never quite been able to stomach much. He was a meat eater and to be honest loved the taste of a good pig but he didn't like to see them hanging in their natural shape, he preferred to see them cooked on his plate. The man behind the counter with an apron that had smatterings of blood over it, looked at Del.

"Hello, good morning. What can I get you?"

Del took out his warrant card and showed the man. "I'm not here to buy anything but I do need some help, could I talk to you or whoever is in charge for a few minutes?"

The man looked at the I.D. "Yes, sure. I'm just an employee, the owner is out the back in the office." He turned to one side away from Del and yelled, "Vince, Vince! Someone here to see you."

A second later a large male poked his head around the door. "What's up, John?"

John pointed to Del and said that a copper wanted a word.

"Oh, okay." Vince walked out and lifted the counter for Del. "Here you're, we can talk back here."

Del walked through the gap in the raised top and went through to the back room. He was hoping it wasn't some kind of freezer or a preparation room. He was delighted to see that it was a normal office.

Vince sat down at his desk and pointed to a chair in the corner. "Here you go, pull up a chair. What can I do for you?"

Del sat and told him that it was a little delicate as he had an issue with a murderer saying they were 'the Real Butcher'.

"I do have to point out that we had a killer last year who was named the Butcher; he wasn't an actual butcher but was named that due to the mutilation of the bodies."

Vince didn't say anything, he just sat and nodded slowly to what he was being told.

"That man was caught but now we have our new man." Del took out the picture of the victim, Eric Hancock. "If I show you the picture I have of our victim could you give me your opinion if you think it could be the work of a professional in your area please?"

Vince thought for a second. "Yes, I'll take a look."

Del handed over the photo and waited for the response.

"Well, I'm an expert at what I do but I would say that the person who did this is not a butcher by profession."

Del was grateful for the immediate response but wanted to know why. "Okay, thank you, but why that conclusion?"

Vince explained that by the look of the victim in the picture, he had had his throat slit from one side to the other. "That is not an efficient way of bleeding an animal. With pigs and cattle they need to be stuck closer to the chest as that is where you get the major arteries running together, other animals can be bled nearer the neck but the slice is still an inefficient way to achieve a quick bleed."

Del was impressed in the man's attitude but he had asked him to view it as a butcher. "So you think this is a beginner?"

Vince handed the photo back. "No, I wouldn't say that, I doubt very much this is their first cut."

The photo was put back away and Del leant back in the chair, intrigued by the conversation. "Why do you say that?"

"If you look at the picture again, that cut was one incision and it was smooth and deep. I have trained plenty of people up as butchers and abattoir workers, and I know how it goes. The first cut is a big deal, the first is tentative and sloppy. That one was neither. I would suggest they have done this more than once."

Del nodded in approval at his conclusion.

"Oh, and the markings. A professional will not draw those markings, we don't need to, we know what we're doing. I think that is either someone drawing them because they think that is what is done or they are just making a statement." Vince stood up. "Come on, I take it as you're investigating this type of thing you have a stomach for it." He walked out of the office and Del reluctantly followed him. They went through a doorway that had large, thick plastic flaps hanging down. It led to a carving room. Surprisingly to Del it was clean and void of lots of blood.

"It's clean in here."

Vince looked round. "Did you expect gallons of blood everywhere? That doesn't happen, I wouldn't be open long if it was like that in here. Contrary to what most believe, there is not that much blood about in a butcher's shop. The reason being, the topic we're talking about, bleeding them out." He walked over to the other side of the room and opened a large door. It led to a walk-in freezer. "Here you're, look at this." He went in and Del followed. Along the right side of the freezer was a whole half of a pig like the one in the window. It was skin out so Vince went to it and swung it round so the inside was facing Del. Vince picked up a large eight-inch knife.

"Look, see here." He pointed to the area that was the chest. "Around here is where the incision would go." He placed the knife next to the body of the pig and then moved the knife inwards. "This is the direction the blade would go to bleed it correctly, and after the first thrust the knife is lowered like so." He moved the hilt of the knife downward.

"Your so-called butcher just sliced along here." He pointed the knife sideways along where the neck was. "Very inefficient. I mean, it will do the job eventually but not quickly." Vince then made movements along the body; they made no sense at all to Del. "They are the different cuts of meat; we don't need lines to guide us. Next time you're surfing the web, search for a plan of meat cuts on a pig or cattle, you will find them easy enough."

Del was finding the meeting extremely interesting when his phone rang.

"Excuse me. Hello, Inspector Martin." It was Control, asking if they could put through a woman from Adoption Services. "Not now, I'm in the middle of something."

He was told that she had a Sergeant with her wanting information and she would not pass any information until she verified who he was.

"Oh for Christ's sake. Go on, put her through," he said.

"Oh hello, thank you for taking my call. I'm Marrie Doors, the Head of Adoption Services for Essex County Council. I have a man here saying he is a Sergeant Gorham and that you're his boss. Could you verify that fact for me, with a description of him please?"

Del listened to this and sighed. "Hello Miss Doors. I'm Inspector Martin and I do have a Sergeant Harry Gorham investigating an important murder case, and to help with this we're trying to find information regarding an adoption. As far as a description goes, he has short, dark, curly hair, around five foot ten in height, slim build and quite frankly as ugly as sin. Does that help?"

The answer was short and sweet. "Thank you Inspector," and the phone went dead.

Del put his phone back in his pocket. "Yes, goodbye," he said sarcastically.

"Can I help any more, Inspector?"

Del said no, he had been very helpful and extremely informative.

"No problem, I will show you out. If you need any more help just pop in, but you must remember everything I have said is the view of a butcher. I don't really know the anatomy of a human so am not up to scratch in the best way to bleed them out." He smiled and added, "If I was I'm sure I would be of more interest to you."

Del left to head back to the station.

*

He arrived back in the conference room and went straight to the white boards. He wrote: 'not an actual butcher, but well versed in the act of killing'. He sat down at the desk and stared at the board, swung his legs round and saw for the first time an A4 envelope sitting on the desk. He picked it up and read the front. It was the preliminary report on the second victim. He opened the envelope and took out a number of photographs and then started to read. He scanned it for major points. First of all, this victim had an identity as the male had been arrested before. He had an arrest for drink driving seven years previous and his name was Tony Slugget. His last known address was 8 Hymn Road, although Del knew this to be out of date. He was like the first victim, well tanked up on alcohol. He had a note inside his mouth and in brackets the report said: 'See photographs'. Del fumbled quickly with the pictures to find the one taken of the note. He got it and looked at it intently. It said:

I started slow, now watch me grow, this is a taste of things to come. Bos was a good man on the inside, a claim I do not make. I will however show you some good insides of some others.

*

And it was signed, 'The Real Butcher'. Del sat back and read it again.

"I knew this was going to be bad, he is telling us he is going to continue. Not threatening, it's a fact and I believe him. We really need to find this bastard." He was talking to himself. He wanted to go back to the victim's address but he was not going to today, he would wait for Harry and they would both go in the morning. He continued to add the relevant details from the prelim report to the board. The boards had a lot of areas blank, in fact there were whole boards still empty. He had deliberately done that as he suspected there was a lot more to follow. Eventually his shift came to an end and he realised, "Oh shit, now I have to go for a meal with Janice's man-eater friend."

CHAPTER 12

Meal Out

Del walked into the house and shouted for Janice.

"Babe, I'm home." There was no reply.

"Babe?" He walked in to the kitchen and there was no trace of his wife. He walked into the dining room and this too was empty.

"Babe?" he shouted again. This time there was an answer from upstairs.

"In the bedroom, honey."

Del walked slowly to their room. It had been a tiring day. He entered the bedroom and Janice was standing with one leg up on the bed smoothing out one of the stockings she was putting on. Apart from that and a pair of quite skimpy knickers she was naked. Since her yoga classes she had slimmed down quite considerably, not that Del thought she was fat before. He walked over to her and stood behind her; he took hold of her left breast with his left hand and held her bottom with his right and kissed the back of her neck.

"Hi babe, how was your day?" he mumbled while kissing her.

She put her leg down and turned around to face him. "Mine was fine, better now though." She kissed him. "Do you want a drink before we go out?"

Del asked her what time they were going as he was starving.

"About seven thirty."

He was back at her neck, but this time from the front.

"You certainly seem hungry," she said playfully.

Del chuckled. "I can't help that, babe, you're gorgeous." She kissed him again.

"Thanks honey, but that hunger will have to wait until we get home." She asked him to go and pour them both a drink and she would be down in a few moments. Del walked rather uncomfortably downstairs, into the kitchen, poured two generous measures of wine and sat in the living room waiting for Janice. He was halfway through his when she came in looking wonderful.

"You look fab, babe," he said, and handed her the wine he had poured her. She took her glass and looked at his.

"Bloody hell, slow down, I haven't been long."

The truth was that Del was not looking forward to tonight, he was only going because he knew Janice was very fond of her friend Sue. He also knew that she was coming to pick them up so he could have a drink before leaving. They would be calling a cab to come home in. Janice bent down and kissed him.

"I know she makes you a little nervous but she doesn't mean anything by it and she does have a heart of gold." Del smiled and then lifted his glass and took another swig. There was not a lot he could add to that; she was right, he did get nervous and a little flustered around Sue. He didn't know why but it worried him that it may be because he fancied her and he was a loyal husband. Her flirting didn't make it any easier to deal with. He finished his glass and Janice was nowhere near the end of hers, not even halfway through.

"Go on, pour yourself another. Dutch courage, is it?" she said, winking at him.

He stood and started towards the kitchen, but the doorbell stopped him in his tracks. He looked at his watch and it was only four minutes past seven. *Holy shit,* he thought, *that can't be her already!* He turned away from the kitchen and headed for the front door. The front door had an arch of glass in the top quarter and he could see that it was indeed Sue calling early. He opened the door; Sue was standing in front of him with the same long, straight, brown hair. This time she had a paler lipstick on but again not a lot of other makeup. She had an electric blue dress that was stunning. It hugged her slim build and had an open diamond area that showed off her perfectly flat stomach and navel. The top of the dress came around her neck and crossed across her breasts. Her cleavage was very apparent and the material flowed across them and ran down around her waist. She did not have a bra on and the dress was not in any way designed to keep her chest secure so any movement on her part and the dress would provocatively flash glances of her well-formed assets to anyone wanting to see. He stood with his mouth open for a split second, for him it felt like eternity so he quickly tried to recover.

"Erm, hi Sue. You look stunning, come in." She flashed a beautiful white smile and stepped forward. She grabbed his face and kissed him hard full on the lips. Del couldn't move, well, most of Del couldn't move! It was hard for him to react in more ways than one and as she pulled away she looked down towards the now quite obvious bulging in his crotch area.

"Oh Del, you're pleased to see me." Sue then stepped past him and headed into the living room and as she did so she gently let her arm float down and brushed across his bulge with her hand. She wasn't even looking at him but it was a deliberate movement that stuttered and took a slight squeeze at the appropriate place. Del let her pass and then moved back and stood against the side. He leant his head back to hit the wall.

"Holy fuck, what the hell is she doing to me!" This was not something he was used to and frankly he did not know how to handle it. He stood still for a second or so, trying to concentrate on being able to nonchalantly walk into the living room without looking like he was trying to smuggle a banana in with him. That wasn't easy, that dress was phenomenal on her and kind of stuck in the visual memory. It reached the point where he was going to have to walk back or make some excuse as to why he was still out there. Sue had walked in and greeted Janice in very much the same way. Janice stood up to greet her and was treated to a full-on kiss.

"Hay Janice, your husband is such a sweetie, it's nice to have a gentleman stand to attention when you come in." This remark went over the head of Janice who was oblivious to what had actually gone on.

"You look lovely, honey," said Janice, holding Sue's hand and standing back to admire her friend's dress and figure.

Del walked past the door and said, "Just going to the loo before we leave," and scuttled past the entrance.

Sue laughed. "Bless him, he is excited." The two girls sat down while they waited for Del to calm himself down. Sue's dress was short too and showed off the top of her thighs; they were not thin sticks, they had ample flesh that had been toned by her yoga and well-tanned by either false methods or regular visits to hot places.

"What are we having to eat then, Sue?"

Sue took hold of Janice's wine glass and took a sip. "Oh now honey, that is a surprise. I never tell anyone I cook for what they are eating, I always want people to make up their minds and enjoy the food by the taste, not by the label. It's more genuine that way." Janice took another sip.

"Okay, yes, that makes sense, can't wait."

Sue commented on how Janice was dressed while they were waiting. "Are they stockings you have on?"

Janice smiled a coquettish smile. "Yes, I do like them sometimes."

Sue stood up and grabbed Janice by the hand. She stood her up too and bent down. She was facing

Janice and as she bent down she looked up at Janice's face. She took hold of each side of the dress hem and slowly lifted it up. Janice never moved and Sue continued to lift the dress until it was just above her pubic line. Sue stood back at that point and looked at Janice standing with a near empty glass of wine, one leg slightly bent forward so her weight was on that one more than the other, and her dress lifted up to show her panties, stockings and suspenders.

"Wow, babe, that husband of yours is a lucky man." She walked forwards and kissed her again. Then sat down as if everything was perfectly normal and they were just talking about something like the weather. Janice finished the little drink that was left and then smoothed down her dress.

"Thanks, you look wonderful too. Del doesn't know how lucky he is."

It wasn't long after that when Del came back in. "Are we ready then ladies?"

Janice and Sue stood up in tandem.

"We're, you lucky boy."

*

They left the house and Sue drove to her place. Del was expecting a flash car but it wasn't. It was just an ordinary run of the mill Renault Cleo. Her house, though, was anything but run of the mill, it was lovely. It was detached, in fact it was more lonely than detached, it was on its own down a lane that led just to that one property. It had a cottage feel to it and was big. Del and Janice followed Sue in through the front door into a large open living room.

"Here you're. Take a seat and I will get us all some drinks. Do you want to continue with the red wine?" They both agreed and Sue disappeared for a while. Janice sat next to Del on the large couch.

"Thanks for coming babe, I know she makes you a little uncomfortable." Del moved his sitting position and thought, *If only she knew how uncomfortable!* Sue walked back in with some glasses that Del was sure were not real wine glasses, they must have held about half a bottle each. She handed them to the couple and turned immediately and left. It was only seconds later she appeared again with a plate full of nibbles.

"Here you go, just something to get your juices flowing." She looked directly into Del's eyes as she said it. She slowly bent down and put the plate on the table in front of them. As she leant forward the loose-fitting straps of her dress fell forward and gave Del a full view of her breasts. She stayed in that position briefly, turning the plate around. She then lifted her head up and looked directly at Del and winked with her left eye which Del knew would not be seen by Janice. Janice was either oblivious to it or just didn't mind. She leant forward herself and picked up a bite-size morsel and placed it in her mouth.

"Oh wow, this is lovely," she said, covering her mouth with her right hand. Del dragged his eyes away from Sue and looked at his wife.

"What is it?"

Janice told him that she didn't know. "Sue won't tell us anyway, she always wants her meals to be a surprise." Del picked one up if just to distract himself. He was impressed too, it was lovely.

"Did you do all the cooking yourself tonight, Sue?"

"Oh yes, I know you may not believe me but I'm very particular with who or what I put in my mouth." She smiled and walked back out of the room. Janice burst out laughing.

"She really is so naughty."

Del thought to himself, *For fuck's sake*, and swallowed the other piece of food he had placed in his mouth. *I'm never going to get through tonight,* he thought.

Del and Janice sat in the sitting room with just the tick-tock of a large cuckoo clock on the wall – it did seem unreasonably loud. It was only a little after the plate in front of them had been emptied that Sue came back in.

"Come on in to the dining room, the food is ready."

The dining room was lovely and the lights were set lower than normal. Janice was led to one side of the table and Del was guided in opposite her. On the table were a couple of large silver bowls with lids on and a couple of silver trays which contained vegetables. They had plates in front of them and Sue sat down to Del's right. He noticed directly as she sat down that she sat side saddle on the chair so that her legs pointed directly towards him and away from Janice.

"Okay, I don't know what vegetable you prefer so please help yourselves and I'll serve up the rest after." The smells were terrific coming from the bowls and from the kitchen. After they had all loaded up with some vegetables Sue stood up and walked around behind Del; this made him nervous and very hot. She leant forward and removed the lid from the silver bowl. Inside were a pair of serving tongs; she picked them up and picked up a few pieces of meat from the juices it was marinating in. The meat was obviously red meat and was dripping with brown juices from the bowl. It was laid on the bed of veg and another amount placed too. Then another bowl was uncovered and it contained a ladle. She ladled some sauce over the meat.

"Hope you enjoy it, honey." She moved away from Del, stroking his shoulders as she went. She dished out the same for Janice and then for herself and then sat back in her side-saddle position. She watched Del cut up and place some of the meal in his mouth. She waited until she had his gaze.

"Del, how is my meat?" As these words were uttered her legs opened a little and as a result her dress moved a little further up to show more of her legs. Del coughed a little as if choking.

"Erm, yes, it's lovely actually."

Sue smiled and asked Janice.

"Oh, it is beautiful. I know you won't tell us but it has a sweetened beef taste and is very tender."

Sue placed some food provocatively in her mouth, making sure that her tongue came out and wrapped around it before entering her mouth. As she placed the food in with her right hand her left disappeared below the table line and gently lifted her dress a little more while parting her legs imperceptivity further. Del was becoming very warm and could feel himself starting to stir. The wine flowed and the meal continued with conversations about shopping, yoga and then Del's work. It was coming to the end of this course when Del looked across and Sue's dress had fully uncovered her pubic area and her legs were far enough apart for Del to get a clear view of her. She was not wearing any knickers at all and her pubic hair was trimmed to a tidy inch width and was hovering just above her tidy cream-coloured lips. He really didn't want to look, he was feeling guilty that his wife was sitting opposite him enjoying the food, but he just couldn't look away. She moved her left hand down as he watched and started rubbing herself slowly up and down.

"Was it juicy enough Del?" As she said this she parted herself with her fingers and she glistened in the light. It was at that point Del dragged his eyes away and stuttered a response.

"Err, err, yes, definitely. Yes, just right, lovely." He was struggling with getting his brain to work but then again, it was obviously not getting as much blood as usual as his body had decided to send that elsewhere. She snapped her legs shut and turned to Janice.

"How was yours, honey?" Janice told her that it was lovely. Sue stood up.

"Have we all finished with the main?"

Del just nodded like a fool and Janice said that she had.

"Excellent, I'll get the pudding." She leant towards Del and lifted her left hand and moved towards his face. "Tongue out." Del stuck his tongue out and she slowly moved her finger across it, then rubbed his cheek. "Sorry honey, you had a little mark on your face."

Del could taste her now and it made things ten

times worse. *Jesus Christ,* he thought, *I'm going to fucking explode in a minute.* He tried to calm himself down but this was difficult with the taste of Sue still in his mouth. He grabbed his drink and took a couple of very large mouthfuls. Sue came back in.

"This is a very simple light dessert after that meal."

It was a brownie, about an inch and a half square, and a scoop of dark chocolate ice cream. For the rest of the evening Sue kept her dress up and the conversations continued. Del slowly became able to think with his main brain again and the time edged towards midnight. It was eleven forty-five when Janice asked if Sue could call a cab for them, and twenty past midnight when they left. Del was given a full kiss goodbye as he was becoming accustomed to and watched as Janice received the same.

"Thank you for a lovely evening you two. I'm glad you enjoyed the meal, see you soon." Sue blew them a kiss and as they entered the cab she shut the door. The conversation home was about the meal and Del didn't mention anything about Sue's antics. They did both agree that the meal was perfect and both agreed that for all her secrecy they had just eaten plain beef but done with some very special sauces. It was twelve thirty-six when they arrived home but past two o'clock before any sleep was on the cards. At that time Janice was panting and sweating and very happy with her husband.

CHAPTER 13

Catch Up

Del was a little tired as he arrived at the station the next day, nothing to do with the case burden but all to do with the amount of sleep he had. He could still see the image of Sue next to him but what she did do was build up his desires to bursting point. However, he soon opened that pressure valve when he got home with Janice. He sat down in the chair in the conference room with a cup of coffee and waited for Harry to arrive. Two minutes later Harry walked in carrying two cups of coffee.

"Thirsty this morning, are you?" said Del, lifting his cup.

"I didn't think you were in yet, I never saw the car." There was a very good reason he didn't see the car, that was because he didn't drive in. With the wine he had the night before he wasn't going to risk driving and still being over the limit.

"I took a taxi in, I was drinking last night and left Janice to sleep."

Harry sat down. "I had an interesting visit to the adoption agency yesterday."

Del smiled. "Yes, I know. I got a call about it, I just said you was an ugly bastard and that seemed to placate her! Believed it was you right away after that. What did you get from her?"

Harry dug in his pocket for the paper she had printed for him. "All in all it is a bit of a shocker and not surprising that Bos was fucked up."

Del put his cup down. "What do you mean?"

Harry said that Bos was involved in a horrific accident along with his parents. Both parents were killed, one of them decapitated in the seat in front of him. He also said that he doubted Bos had anything to do with that accident so would not be linked to the death of his own wife. His name at the time of the accident was Ben Oscar and his parents were Mike and Madison. They lived in a large manor house called Oakwood Manor and—"

"What? Oakwood Manor did you say?" Del butted in.

"Yes, do you know it?"

Del shook his head. "No I don't, but the first set of The Butcher's murders all took place in Oak trees, may be a coincidence."

Harry went on that the house was rented to the family and paid for by their employers at the time. "They said he had no memory of events before the accident but it must have been horrendous in that crash." Del immediately turned to his computer.

"What was the address of that house?"

Harry read it out and Del typed it in the search bar. He pressed enter and a number of sites came pinging up. He clicked on one from a newspaper and the picture was an awful twist of metal with branches sticking though the screen area. The heading was: 'Tragedy at Oakwood Manor', the subheading was 'parents dead and their only son critical'. They read the article through and it was an awful tragedy of a relatively new and young family cut off in their prime by a freak accident.

"I think we need to visit this house," said Del as he pressed the print button.

"It may be an idea. How did you get on yesterday anyway?" asked Harry. Del sat back in his chair.

"Okay, well, to start with I went to see our local butcher and found out that according to him our murderer is not a professional butcher but has definitely killed before."

Harry was nodding his head with a surprised look. "And how does he come to that conclusion?"

Del explained about the correct incision to bleed an animal out and the smooth, deliberate cut on their victim's neck. Harry looked satisfied with that.

"Yeh, okay, I can see that as a theory."

Del then went into the drawer in front of him and took out an envelope and passed it to Harry.

"We also got that, the preliminary CSI report on our second vic." Harry did virtually the same as Del, scanned the main points and then looked for the picture of the note. Del could see the frown on Harry's face. "I know what you're thinking and I'm thinking the same. Why two fucking notes?" Harry looked at the boards and again at the note.

"Have you updated the board with this one?"

Del said he had and Harry stood up and walked over to them. He stood looking for a moment. "I can see a small pattern here but we're not going to know unless we get any more." Del joined him at the boards.

"What have you seen?"

Harry pointed to the first and latest note. "These talk about Bos as a kind of friend or something, but the other, it seems to be directed personally at you!" Del looked at the board again. There did seem to be a bit of a different tone about the tank message, it started with his name for a start.

"Yes, but do you think I will get another one?"

Harry said that they needed to keep an eye out for suspicious-looking fish tanks in the middle of places and smiled.

"No shit, and there was me going to ignore the next one." They sat back down and drank more of their coffee.

"So Mr Slugget was pissed as well. Do we know where he drank yet?"

Del said they didn't. "But we're going back to 54 Hinkley Road in a few minutes so drink up."

Harry asked why and Del said that he would explain on the way and stood up ready to go. Del walked out purposefully and Harry followed. Once Del had entered and started his car Harry asked again, "Go on then, why are we going back?"

"Because I fucked up," said Del and then explained further. He said that they didn't really have a good look around as the tank find with the message had kind of put a stop to things. "I'm after some info on the man now, some clues as to what he did and where he went."

＊

They pulled up at the address. Unfortunately since their initial visit the place had been locked up and secured properly. No windows were open; the front and back doors were shut.

"Okay, what now?" said Harry. Del wasn't going to give up quite yet.

"Right, we know he was a drinker and they tend to forget or lose their keys, don't they?"

Harry said that he would take his word for that as he was not a piss artist.

"My point is that they often keep a spare key about to let themselves in." Del went and lifted the door mat that was near the front door, it was empty. "Oh well, first try no prize." He looked around and lifted a plant pot, nothing. He put his hand in the letter box to see if the owner was stupid enough to keep a key on a piece of string on the inside but he wasn't. He sat on the doorstep and looked about. There was nothing out of the ordinary until he saw a couple of large stones to his right and remembered seeing something similar in a shop a few years previously. He stood up and walked over to the rocks and picked one up.

"You're not doing what I think you're doing, are you?" said Harry suspiciously. Del looked over.

"Well that depends on what you think I'm doing."

"You're not gonna chuck that at the window are you?"

Del laughed. "Of course I'm fucking not, you prat. I'm a copper, not a robber." Del put the rock back down and picked another one up. He looked at Harry and grinned a huge grin; he held out his hand with the rock sitting on top.

"Well?" said Harry, a little perturbed at his inspector's odd behaviour. Del flipped the rock over and it had a screw on the bottom.

"It's fibreglass with a compartment hidden in the bottom to store a spare key."

"How the bloody hell did you know that? You lucky bastard." Del threw the fake rock to Harry after first removing the key.

"It's not luck, I remember seeing something like that in a shop a few years ago." Del opened the door and turned left into the living room.

"So what is it we're looking for?" asked Harry. Del didn't really know, he just said anything that may help understand what he was doing in the last day of his life. They started rummaging around in the drawers of the cabinets and desk that was in the main room. One of the cabinets had a lot of booze in – whisky, vodka and rum, a few bottles of each and at least one of each type was more than half empty.

"So being sloshed does not look like it was a rare occurrence, all these bottles look quite new so he was used to a drink or two." Harry lifted a magazine from a drawer and held it up.

"So he liked his drink and his women, this drawer is full of these." It was a pornographic magazine and Harry riffled through a few of the pages.

"I think he got these from under the counter somewhere, ordered specially, you won't get this stuff from your local news agent's top shelf!" He put it down and continued to search. Del shut the latest drawer and started to walk out.

"You carry on in here, I'm going to the kitchen, let me know if you find anything." He walked out into the hall and turned left. He had an idea, not an enjoyable one but it was a chance. He looked around and spotted what he was after. He took the lid off the bin and had a look in; it stank and had a light covering of old curry on the top. He went to a drawer he presumed would be the cutlery drawer and picked up a fork. He walked toward the bin.

"Jesus, are things that hard at home? Janice not feeding you!" Harry was standing at the door looking at Del near the bin with a fork.

"Just a little peckish, that's all!" Harry walked across the room to the bin too.

"There is nothing in there that is of any use."

Del tilted the bin slowly and started trying to sift through the rubbish. Quickly Del realised that this technique was not going to be thorough enough.

"Sod this." He tipped the bin on its side and slid the contents along the floor. He put the bin to one side and started to fork his way from the curry end onwards. There was obviously a lot of 'rubbish' as far as Del was concerned but there were a few pieces of what he was after; receipts and letters. Whenever he found a piece like that he would just put it to one side and carry on. At last he scraped the last piece of filth away and his search was complete. He left the shit all over the floor and went to the sink to wash his hands. He shook his hands dry and walked back to the papers he had rescued.

"Right, let's see what we have." He picked up the first one that was stained with something undesirable.

"Oh." He threw it back with the other detritus over the floor. A shopping list with four items on. The next piece had tomato ketchup smeared over it but between the red stains Del could see some light of hope flicking across his brain. It was a credit card receipt for a meal and drinks at a pub. Del read through what he could and it seemed like a bill for one meal. He waved it at Harry. "This is hope."

Harry took it from him and looked. "It's a bill receipt."

"Yes, but my hope is it's a receipt from a place he frequented on a regular basis."

Harry passed it back. "A bit of a leap of faith isn't it?" Del shook his head.

"No, not entirely. That receipt says it was a meal. **A** meal, which it means he was on his own. That does suggest it would be a place that he is comfortable to be in on his own, and for that to be the case he will have been there a few times. However, we shall see." Del looked at the other pieces of paper he rescued but the other bits showed no promise. Del left the house with hope; he shut the door and replaced the key inside the fibreglass rock. Nobody would know they had been in, well, unless they visited the kitchen with the shit covering the floor! They headed off to visit the pub on the receipt, The Globe.

*

The Globe was a trendy new pub, clean and tidy. It sold food and did bed and breakfast. They walked in through the double glass doors; it wasn't very busy, it had a few couples eating and a male sitting at the bar. There were a few members of staff milling around serving food and cleaning. There were also two staff behind the bar. They were all wearing a kind of beige and yellow uniform. Del walked towards the bar and noticed that they were all wearing name tags; one of the bar staff had 'Manager' under his name. As he approached he read his name as Ryan.

"Hello Ryan, I'm Inspector Martin and this is Sergeant Gorham. Could we have a minute or two of your time please?"

Ryan put his cloth down and said, "Of course, how can I help?"

"Thank you. First of all it's nothing to worry about, we're just doing some enquiries and hoping that you or your staff may be able to help us." Harry moved forwards and took out a picture from his pocket, it was one he had picked up from a drawer in the victim's house.

"Do you or any of your staff recognise this man at all?" Ryan looked at the picture and it didn't take him long to reply.

"Hah, yes, that's Tony Slugget, known as Slug to the staff here." Del was overjoyed at that response.

"That is fantastic news, how often did you see Mr

Slugget in here?"

Ryan said that he was unfortunately one of the regulars but the last time he had been in was the night before last. Del looked around the place but couldn't see what he was after.

"Why unfortunately a regular?"

Ryan looked around the pub. "As you can see we have some female staff here and due to his attitude towards them he is not the most popular customer, hence the nickname Slug." Del thought that his womanising days were over now.

"Have you any CCTV here?" The answer was not what they wanted to hear.

"We have two covering the door, they catch people in and out but that is all; the owners do not want to have more, they think it would be an intrusion into people's lives."

Del was not particularly happy with that viewpoint but it was one that he had heard before.

"Do you think that they would have caught Mr Slugget coming and going three nights ago?"

Ryan again answered quickly, he seemed an intelligent man.

"Yes they would but I can tell you when he came in and when he left as I was in on that night."

"It would be great to hear your account of his night but could we have the footage of his entry and exit and freeze frames of all the other customers that night please?" Ryan nodded at Del.

"Of course, I will get the CCTV burnt off and call

you when it's done. He came in at 18:00 because he asked me to turn the telly over to the news. He did that quite often. He left at around 20:10 after a phone call." Del was again impressed.

"How do you know that he left at that time without checking?"

"Because it was the night of a game on the TV and he was here to watch it, it was only ten minutes into the match when he asked to pay his tab. I spoke to him about watching the match and he just winked at me and said something had come up."

Del asked if he had said anything else about where he was going but Ryan told him, "No, he was in a bit of a hurry after the call." Del gave Ryan his card.

"Thank you for your help Ryan, could you give me a call when the footage is ready please?" Ryan took the card and put it in his pocket.

"Yes of course, do you want me to call you when Slug comes in next?"

"That won't be necessary, thank you. Unfortunately we're investigating his murder." Ryan's face dropped like a stone and he went a little pale.

"Er, er, we called him that but we wouldn't have done anything to him, none of us, he was a good customer really, just a bit slimy to the females." Del reassured Ryan that they had no evidence to suggest any wrongdoing on the part of him or his staff, they just needed to get as much information on his last moments that they could. The two policemen walked out of the pub and Ryan was static watching them out; he was shocked to say the least. He had not known anybody who had been murdered before.

They stood outside and looked around; there were a few other shops and businesses about.

"We need to get house-to-house done around here and if any of these buildings have CCTV we need to get hold of it." They headed back to the car and Harry drove them back to the station.

*

When they arrived back in the conference room there was another envelope on the desk. Del picked it up and it was marked as CCTV from Mr Slugget's garage. Del opened the envelope and pushed the disc into the computer. The system started the footage and both Del and Harry watched in anticipation. The footage showed Tony unlocking his door and unsteadily coming in. The time on the system said 20:29. He was on his phone and speaking but the CCTV was visual only and could not pick up what was being said. He walked through the main reception and another camera picked him up going into the cupboard before the main garage area. Seconds later the footage stopped.

"What the fuck happened?" Del rewound the image and played it again. Harry looked on.

"He turned it off, he turned the bloody system off himself." Harry had picked up and read the piece of paper that was included with the disc. It said that the CCTV recording equipment was housed in the cupboard that Tony went into and when they went in to view it, the entire system had been unplugged.

"What? Why the fucking hell would he do that?"

Harry shook his head. "I don't know but I suspect if we knew we would be a bit closer to catching this fucker."

They rewound it again and watched; although they could see him come in and could see he was on the phone the quality was too poor to see what was being said. Del was frustrated.

"Harry, can you get uniform to do extensive house-to-house around The Globe? I want any info on what people saw and copies of CCTV from 20:00-21:00 whether they think it contains anything or not."

Harry knew that Del was irritated. "Sure thing," he said, walking to the door.

"I want to see who was around the streets when Tony left that pub; he was meeting someone and I want to find out who the fuck it was."

It was a long day. Del had taken the disc to the I.T. boys and they had cleaned it up and sharpened the picture as best they could but in the words of one of them, "You can try and polish a turd but in the end you still end up with shit." He then found some experts in lip reading but the only part of the conversation they could get was, "I'm doing it now," as he walked under the first camera. Before they left for home they decided that tomorrow was going to be spent apart with Harry looking into Bos again and Del looking at the info from the house-to-house that had already got underway. Del left for home despondent and frustrated.

CHAPTER 14

Confession

Del entered the house and Janice was in the kitchen. He was glad, it looked like it was just the two of them and it was not anything special. He was not in the mood to socialise with anyone else apart from Janice. She saw him come in and smiled at him.

"Hi babe, how was your day?" He walked over and gave her a kiss.

"Not fantastic, let's put it that way."

"Oh no, you didn't get another murder did you?"

He told her that there wasn't another body but they were not any further on catching the new Butcher. "It's all just dead ends at the moment. Wherever we go they seem to have covered it." He then explained about the last victim going in and cutting off his own CCTV.

"What? Why would he do that?"

Del dipped his finger in the cooking pot and brought it out quickly into his mouth.

"That, babe, is the key. I'm thinking there are only a few reasons for it and I want to find out which one. It's either he was threatened to, he was asked to, or he was up to something himself that he didn't want to be seen doing." He told her that the sauce was nice, whatever it was, and said he was going to have a shower and get changed. He walked off and headed upstairs. On the way up he undid his tie and took off his jacket. He couldn't wait to get in a hot shower; he was feeling extremely tense after today's setbacks.

By the time he entered their bedroom he was naked on the top. He threw his jacket, shirt and tie onto the bed and within seconds had stripped naked. He left the clothes where they landed and walked into the shower. He turned the water to between warm and hot and stood leaning against the wall. It was a cold slap at the start but that didn't last; before long he was being hammered by hot droplets pounding him under the pressure of the shower. He let out a sigh as the steam engulfed the cubicle and just stood there letting the tension in his body slowly melt away. The frustrations of his day at work slowly dispersed and other thoughts started popping into his mind.

The shower was hot and thoughts of Sue came into his head. The image of her next to him fondling herself was the first one, and with that image in his head it didn't take long before muscles stirred. Well, one muscle, and within seconds he was as hard as he ever had been. He could see it all as if it was all happening again. He tried to think of something else but each time she came into view, either flashing her breasts or kissing him. This was not good. He washed his hair while standing to attention. He then washed his body with some kind of orange scrub that was in the shower. This reminded him of Janice; he loved his wife. He breathed in deeply and took in the scent of the scrub his wife used. He thought of her and slowly his erection dissipated. *Thank God for that,* he thought. Then started to think a bit further. Was that right? Was that good? Surely that was not the right way round. He was starting to worry now. He rinsed himself off and walked out of the shower. He grabbed the towel from the door and started to dry himself as he walked out of the shower back into his room. He looked down at his now flaccid penis.

"I think of another woman and get as hard as I ever have then lose it when I think of my wife!" He sat on the bed shaking his head. He was an honest man and a loyal husband. Well, up until now anyway. He was feeling guilty for his lustful thoughts toward Sue. He didn't want to have an affair, he didn't want the temptation of being around her, but he wanted Janice to be happy and she was, with Sue as a friend. He sat wondering what to do and not finding an answer.

"Babe, food is ready." Janice shouted this up the stairs. He had been sitting on the bed for quite a while and didn't realise how long. He quickly dressed in fresh clothes and made his way toward the dining room. As he entered, the room smelt lovely with the spice of the dish grabbing him by the nose and dragging him in.

"Oh wow, honey that smells lovely," Janice was already sitting at the table.

"You were ages babe, have a good soak?" As he sat down she caught the scent from him. "You smell good too. You've been using my scrub, haven't you? Cheeky." He leant forward and gave her a kiss.

"Only so I can smell as good as you." The food was as good as it smelt and Del was loving it.

"Do you think the murders have stopped now as you haven't had a new one for a few days?"

Del did not need to think much about his response.

"I would put any money I had on that not being the case. I don't know why the intermission but I don't think it will last long." Janice put her hand on Del's.

"I was with Sue today and we were talking about it, we hope it stops soon because we don't want to see your health affected like Bos's was." Del put his left hand on top of hers.

"Yes, but babe, I think he was ill because he was doing it all himself."

But with Sue's name hanging in the air it made him think of her body again. *It's no good,* he thought to himself.

"Babe, I have a confession to make." Janice looked at him and waited. He wasn't really sure on what to say or how to put it, the air was silent for a while.

"What's the matter Del?" she said, holding his hand tighter.

"I erm, I don't know how to say this really. You know I said I get uncomfortable around Sue?" Janice smiled and nodded. "Well a part of that uncomfortableness is I, I…"

Janice put her head on the side like a little puppy

and waited. Del sighed.

"Look, I find her very attractive and when she flirts with me," he looked down at his lap, "things happen!"

Del was waiting for shouts but certainly wasn't ready for her actual response. Janice burst out laughing, real belly laughs. After a little while and noticing his indignation at her laughter she tried to stop. She leant forwards and held his face with both her hands.

"Oh honey, she is a stunning lady and is very aware of what her body does to people, she enjoys seeing people's reactions. Particularly if they are uncomfortable and don't know how to deal with it," She kissed him. "I know you, and I'm so happy that you were strong enough and brave enough to come and admit something like that to me." She then looked down at his lap too. "And I don't mind if things stir down there as I know I'm the one that benefits."

He was relieved at his wife's sentiments and happy that he had got it off his chest. He was though, still a little concerned that she may not know the extent to which the flirting reached, however he did not want to ruin her friendship because he knew she was besotted with her friend. That night Del was relieved to find out that a flaccid state was not permanent as far as being with his wife was concerned, and on Janice's part she found the night more of a turn on knowing that her husband could speak to her about his problems.

*

It was 23:20 and Janice's phone started juddering across her side table. Del and Janice were lying in a comfortable embrace, just starting to drift off after the exertions of a couple of hours enjoying each other. Janice stretched out her arm and grabbed the phone. She looked at the screen.

"It's Sue." She pressed the button to speak "Hi Sue," said Janice, a lot more jovially than Del was thinking. After a second she sat upright. "Oh that is awful, are you okay?" There was a break while Janice listened to her friend. Del could hear talking but couldn't understand what was being said. "Oh honey that's fine, I'll wait for you," Sue had said something else and Janice responded, "No, don't be silly, come, it's fine."

The phone was put down and Janice swung her legs out of the bed.

"What is going on babe?"

Janice turned and leant across her husband and kissed him. "You get some sleep ready for work tomorrow, Sue has had a bit of a bust up with her mum and is upset. Her mum is a bit of a controlling witch so she asked if she can cool off here." Del looked at her.

"Really?"

"Oh babe, I know how she comes across to people but she is not like she seems, she is very sensitive and her mum sounds awful. I'll look after her tonight, you get some sleep." She kissed him long and gently. "Night babe."

Janice walked out of the bedroom, collecting her clothes as she went. Del lay awake for a while and it was about twenty minutes later that the front door opened and he heard Janice and Sue talking. It was not a comfortable couple of hours for Del; he was on constant edge waiting for Sue to pop in. This never occurred and Del finally drifted off to sleep in the early hours.

CHAPTER 15

Three

As agreed the day before, Harry was going to look into Bos's past today. He was intending to do this by visiting Oakwood Manor, the site of the accident that killed his parents. It was quite a drive away and he set out first thing in the morning. His satnav said he was due to arrive at about 10:20. Unfortunately at 08:40 he had a call on his phone. He pulled over and answered the call from Del.

"Hi Del, what's up?"

"Change of plan, get back here as soon as you can, we have another body, see you at the nick!"

The phone went dead. Harry threw the phone on the passenger seat and drove off to the next roundabout and headed back the way he had come.

By the time Del arrived at the station some of the house-to-house enquiries had been done. He sat at the desk in the conference room looking through some of the forms. There were a few with discs attached, so they were put in the computer and played. The first two showed nothing of interest at all, in fact one had no people in at all and one saw one person walk past at 20:06. The next CD did show something of interest. The timer on the system said 20:13 and it showed Mr Slugget walking hastily past with a huge grin on his face. Del rewound it and paused it on the frame as he walked past. As before, it was not the best quality but he could see enough to say that this man was not being threatened. He was off to somewhere he wanted to go. Del stood up and went to the board; he looked at the difference between this time and the time the garage footage shut down.

"20:29 and 20:06, so twenty-three minutes after this is when he shut down his own camera." He sat back down at his desk and looked in closer at the smile on the face. "Where the fuck are you off to?"

As he said that the phone rang.

"Hello, Inspector Martin, how can I help?" It was a call that he had been expecting for days. "Okay, I'll get there as soon as I can." He kept the handset to his face and cut the call off with his finger; a second later he was dialling.

"Change of plan, get back here as soon as you can, we have another body, see you at the nick!"

*

09:15, Harry walked into the conference room and Del was sifting through papers.

"What do we have then, Del?"

Del looked up from the paper recycling plant that was his desk. "Thank fuck for that, come on." On the way out of the station Del did actually answer the question. "As of yet I don't know much, we have a naked body in an office."

"Office parties can get a bit rowdy."

Del looked at him. "Yes, I've been to a few of them, but I have never been found in the morning strapped to a board and drawn on."

"Well you haven't been to some I have then." Harry climbed into the car at the same time Del did. Del started the engine.

"Sounds interesting but at least you didn't wake up dead."

*

Again, it was a relatively short journey to victim number three. It wasn't a huge office, it was a local business run in a small shop premises. It was a recruitment agency. At the front of the building stood a PC looking rather bored with his lot. Del signed in and walked into the building. In the front of the place was a couple of computer desks, some settees and a few comfy chairs dotted around. There was a door at the back that led to a small kitchen area and nothing else apart from a flight of stairs. Del walked up the steps and came into an open space. It was the entirety of the bottom floor and had plastic chairs stacked up at one side and a few tables stacked too. At the opposite end to the stairs was a large flippable white board. The floor was red with blood. There was a body hanging upside down on the board.

"Well fuck, that is different!"

Both were a little taken back by the sight. It was a

female; for the first time in all the killings, it was a female. She had been cable tied to the board in a most surprising manner. Her left hand as they looked was on the bottom left corner and her right hand on the other side. Her feet were at the top of the board. Each limb had been cable tied around the corner of the board and then cross secured around the back. The effect was to straddle the woman in a star shape over it in such a way that when the board was flipped she would stay in the same place. They walked closer and could see that there was a piece of paper sticking out of the mouth but they did not move it. That would be the job of the CSI unit. There were red lines drawn over the body, as with the previous two.

"Do you think her rump has been removed like the last one?" Harry tried to look without stepping in the blood that had spread across a major percentage of the floor.

"I don't know but that leg must have taken some time to do!"

The victim's left thigh had been stripped of flesh – just above the knee to a few inches below her crotch was clear of flesh. It was not exactly clean to the bone but there was not much left of it. Her throat had been cut and Del made a point of looking to see how smooth and deep the incision was. It was again, like Vince from the butcher's shop had said, clean and deep, consistent with a practiced killer.

"Do we know who she is?"

Harry went downstairs and came back a few minutes later.

"Yes, she was found by the owner of the business,

unfortunately this was her civil partner and she has gone to hospital in shock." Del shook his head.

"Shit, that isn't good. I've heard of hard-working people being tied to their desk night and day but this is taking that a bit far. Who is she then?"

Harry said that her name was Natalia Horinski, age 27. Del really wanted to read what was on the note in the victim's mouth but resisted the temptation of pulling it out. He looked about; there was no CCTV up here.

"Is there CCTV downstairs?"

Harry again walked down, when he came up he said, "No but there is one outside, it's next door's but does cover the path if she came in from the left." He waited for a second and then added, "What do you think went on here?"

Del looked at the female with her long dark hair dipping in the blood. She was fully naked with muscular arms and chunky thighs – well, one anyway. She had average but pert breasts and a completely trimmed pubic area that had not been mutilated as far as Del could see.

"I'm not sure, but I think she was killed when upside down and I think she was willingly tied up!" Harry glanced towards Del.

"Why?"

"Why is a mystery, but I think it because to tie an unwilling person like that would take quite some doing unless you have a handful of people, and the majority of blood spatter was made from low down. If he had cut her upright we would see blood cast further afield."

Both men stood and stared for a few moments. It may have looked like they were just staring at the naked woman, however, both men were thinking that it could have been sexually motivated. But as far as they could tell no sexual activity went on.

"Did you say she had a civil partnership? With a woman?"

"Yes, she's in hospital."

Del looked back at the victim. "So we know she was gay, but was she bi?"

Harry was thinking. "I don't know, Del, but that would not be a question I would want to be asking her partner any time soon." Del nodded and walked towards the stairs.

"Come on." Harry followed Del down and then out of the building. He went directly next door and walked straight in, it was a travel agent's.

"Hello, I'm Dawn. How can I help you?" said the Barbie lookalike behind the desk.

Del thought, *Oh fuck, that's all I need, a bimbo with the brains of a pea.*

"Hello Dawn, I'm Inspector Martin and this is Sergeant Gorham. We're investigating a murder next door." She did not seem shocked.

"Yes, I did see the PC out front and I presumed something horrible but murder, that's awful. I presume you will be after viewing our camera then?" She stood up and started walking towards the rear of the room.

"Yes please. Could you get the owner to burn a copy off for us?" She turned around and shot him a smile.

"Well Inspector, I could get him to, but I thought you would want it as soon as possible so if that is the case I'll get little ol' me to struggle through with it, shall I?"

Harry chuckled. "Oh yes then, okay, if that's possible."

Del followed her into the back and she sat down at a desk under the camera equipment. She turned on the monitor.

"Do you know what time you're after?"

Del shook his head. "No, not yet, sorry."

She tapped a few thing in on a pad. "No problem, I can search the footage digitally to show me any movement to start with. I'll show you the stills of any movement and you can tell me when you want me to expand on that time." Harry had lifted his eyebrows and was nodding in admiration. Del was impressed and more than a little embarrassed at his first assumption. As the stills flicked across the screen Del watched.

"Look, I'm sorry but you have seen the staff next door, if you see one of them can you stop the still image on them?" Dawn looked round at him.

"Yes of course but haven't you seen her then?" Del nodded.

"Yes I have, but I'm sorry to say the view I had would not be how she would normally look!"

Dawn said, "Oh dear," and continued. It was

about thirty or so images later when she stopped the search.

"That is Natalia." Del looked at the still; she looked a little different from that view.

"Could you play it for me please?" Dawn tapped a few more keys and it started to play. As a matter of fact the footage didn't last long. It showed Natalia walk up the pavement towards her shop and quickly disappear from view, she was on her phone and she was smiling just like Tony was when he was caught on his CCTV.

"Do you want me to burn that off for you, Inspector?"

Del said, "Yes please, but can you burn that on disc as well as all the other still images of people who passed that night too?"

Dawn said that it would not be a problem and started tapping again. It was ten minutes later that he had made an entry in his note book and taken the disc. They walked out and five yards up the road and Harry spoke.

"Bet you felt a prat then, didn't you? That Barbie had brains!"

Del had actually been very impressed with her skills with the CCTV.

"She was bloody good wasn't she?"

*

They made their way back to the car. Del started it and headed back towards the station. Back in the conference room Del added a few pieces of information to the boards. He sat down and was still for a while; Harry was sat on a chair on the other side of the room.

"What are you thinking then Del?"

"I'm thinking why the sudden change from male to female? We have notes to compare between the Butcher and this new one but Bos never killed a female, all his victims were male. And so were the first two of our graffiti artist." Harry didn't know either.

"Hang on, is this one called the Graffiti Killer now?"

Del shrugged. "As good a name as any; he wants to be the Butcher so I'm not calling him it."

"Bos had a particular pattern with his kills, they were all criminals that he knew had got away with things, right?" said Harry, and Del nodded. "Perhaps we have been too hung up on that. What if our Graffiti Killer is purely just an opportunist and will take anyone no matter what sex, nationality, colour, religion or whatever?"

Del thought. "To be honest it's as good as anything else we have, I can't find a pattern to the victims apart from they all seem to be happy before they go." They were both silent for another minute or so.

"Okay, so what about the other aspects of the killings? Why the markings and why carve and remove pieces?" It was Harry asking the question again. Del was certain about one fact.

"I believe the markings are to give the impression that he is a butcher and nothing more sinister than that." He shook his head for a second. "However, the other part I don't know. Bos removed parts of the body but then nailed them to the trees so never removed anything from the scene."

"Yes, but with that we're doing what we did before, comparing the old to the new, if we treat the Graffiti Killer as a separate entity entirely what would you be thinking?" This was the reason Del liked working with Harry, he pushed him to think and think in different ways.

"Right, if this was a new case and a person came on the scene saying they were the Butcher, killed people, drew on them and carved up and removed pieces of the bodies, what would we be thinking?"

Silence for a while but then Del spoke again.

"I have something but to tell you the truth I don't like it much!"

"Go on," said Harry.

"What does a butcher do? He cuts up carcasses. Why?"

Harry sneered and said, "No, you don't think. Eeew, that's nasty."

Del nodded grimly. "That's the explanation I can think of and to be honest not a lot else makes sense of it. He is cutting them up and eating them!" It was a nasty thought for both to take in and one that stunned them too. How would you go about finding a recipe to eat human flesh? The two men started to look through all the house-to-house enquiries and CCTV discs; there were quite a few and it was a mountain of a task to try and match up any people ·from the travel agents to any of the businesses near the globe. Harry remembered something.

"Del, did you ever get the CSI report back from the tank?"

He thought for a few moments. "No, actually I don't believe I did." Del picked up the phone and called the crime scene investigation unit.

"Hello, this is Inspector Martin here, I'm trying to track down a report that I was expecting a while ago." He waited and then added, "Yes, it was from a glass tank with bleach in from the new Butcher case."

The person on the other end asked Del to hold while they went and looked. Half of a dreary hold song later, the woman came back and told Del that it had been delivered already. She said, "I have it on screen here that Terry Newell delivered it at 14:33 yesterday to you at your office."

Del was about to say that was ridiculous when he realised the mistake.

"Okay, thank you for your help." Del put the phone down. "I'll be back in a minute, I think they put it in my office instead of here." That was exactly what had happened; in his metal tray lay an A4 envelope with the details of the job and Del's name on it. He collected it and walked back to the conference room. He went in and sat down where he was before.

"Fingers crossed then." Del opened the envelope and pulled out the sheet of paper and a couple of pictures. The pictures were quite mundane, there was not a lot to capture, particularly as the writing had disappeared.

"It says it was normal household bleach, nothing special, but on the tank was a clear set of prints."

Harry said. "Yes!" and punched the air.

Del was emotionless. "Mmmm." Harry frowned.

"Why so glum? That's a break for us at last." Del shook his head.

"Well I wouldn't be too sure of that, a full set of prints after being so fucking awkward up until now…"

Harry was still feeling positive and said that they all make mistakes eventually.

"Yes, but I remember the first case with Bos, every time we thought we got somewhere it was some kind of fucking wind-up and we were sent down some blind alley." Harry shook his head and raised his voice.

"Look, there you fucking go again, stop comparing this to the first one, the first one was done by the copper trying to catch himself for fuck's sake!" He was right and Del knew it, he had to start treating this case on its own merits and not as a part of the first ones.

"Okay, you're right but it still says here that there is no trace of the prints on our criminal database."

Just then the phone rang.

"Hello, Inspector Martin speaking, how can I help you?" It was Bud from the CSI unit, he was phoning from the scene at the travel agents.

"Look, I know you're keen for this info so I'm calling you a little bit now. I have just bagged the note from out of this young woman's mouth, if you have a pen I will tell you what it says." Del quickly rooted around for a pen and a piece of paper.

"Go ahead Bud."

"Okay, it says, 'Bos was the boss but I own this title. He made you chase the Butcher's tail, I'm the tale. He was nothing without me.' It was then signed 'The Real Butcher'." Bud waited for a bit. "Did you get all that Del?"

Del finished off the last part. "Yes, got it all now. Thanks for that, Bud. You're a star, you really are." Del put the phone down and looked over to Harry. "We have what was on the note in Natalia's mouth." Harry urged him on. Del read out what Bud had told him and sat back. Harry's face twisted with thought.

"This bloke really is a fucking psycho. 'Nothing without me', Jesus Christ, you would think they created him by listening to that." Harry suddenly stopped. "Do you think his parents really did die in that crash? You don't think it may be one of them getting their revenge on his death?"

It was Del's turn to raise his eyebrows again; it was an interesting thought but if it was one or both of them they would be in their late fifties, sixties or even seventies.

"It is possible I suppose. I mean I wouldn't rule anything out in this bloody case but I do think it more than a tad bloody unlikely."

"Yeah, I suppose a geriatric graffiti artist is a bit much to picture!" Harry chuckled at the image in his head of a seventy-year-old with a can of spray paint, trainers and a baseball cap on back to front.

CHAPTER 16

A Match

It took a while to go through the images but after a few hours Del called Harry over.

"Harry, have a look at this." Harry sidled over and looked over Del's shoulder at the screen.

"This is an image from the travel agents from 21:34." He framed it in a window in the corner of his screen.

"This is from a property a little way up from The Globe, which was taken at 20:17." He framed this in another window and sat it next to the first. The view from the travel agent was front left and the other caught the man's right side.

"What do you think?" The pictures were not wonderful.

"Not sure, he is wearing different clothing but it does seem like the same person."

Del immediately screenshot the comparison. He typed out an email to all police asking if they knew the identity of this male. He pinged the email out and then continued to trudge through the footage. It was only a matter of ten minutes after he sent it that he had a response; in fact after half an hour he had several and all suggesting the same male. Del read out the emails and sighed. "Oh fuck." Harry looked over.

"What's up now? We haven't got another body have we?" Del shook his head.

"No, that male on the footage, we know who he is, he has been IDed by quite a few officers local to the area."

"Well that's good, isn't it? I wouldn't class that as an 'oh fuck' moment." Del smiled back.

"No, ordinarily you're right, however he is very well known to be, erm, eccentric, should I say!" Harry leant back in his chair.

"You mean nutty as a fucking fruit cake, don't you!"

Del told him that they were not the exact words that had been used but definitely implied.

"Ah, have we an address for him?"

Del showed Harry a piece of paper; he had written an address down from an email. Del stood up.

"Come on then, let's go and meet Ben Garrick."

*

The car pulled up to 15 Station Lane, it was an unassuming terraced house with a small yard garden in the front. Del knocked on the door, it sounded very hollow. He waited for a moment and then knocked again, still no response. He looked through the post box and saw why it sounded hollow, the place was empty. He could only see the hallway and into a part of the kitchen but it was void of anything, including carpet. The stairs to the left held no carpet either. Del shouted through the letterbox, "Hello, Mr Garrick?"

A voice came from Del's left.

"Hello, are you alright? He won't be in, you know." He stood up and looked at the person speaking. It was an elderly lady and she was smiling at him.

"Hello, I'm Inspector Martin and this is Sergeant Gorham. Do you know when he will be back please?"

"Oh yes dear, that is easy. He will be back," she looked at her watch, "in twenty-eight minutes." Del was a little surprised by the accuracy of the answer.

"That's excellent but how do you know it will be," he looked at his watch then, " 15:57 when he comes back?" She shook her head.

"I'm sorry, my watch says 15:32 at the moment. He will be back at 16:00, he always is. That's when he is home. 12:00 until 12:30 midday, and 16:00 until 17:00. After that God knows what time he comes back in." Del was intrigued and then listened to the lady explain. Ben was a young man with rigid habits, he ate at 12:00 and at 16:00; the rest of the time he liked to walk, he walked everywhere. Del looked at Harry.

"That could explain the images." Del thanked her for her help and said that they would wait in their car for him. He was interested to see if Ben did arrive at four. At three fifty-seven he walked up his path to the house. Del got his phone out.

"Well, bloody hell, it is 16:00 and my watch is wrong. Come on." They exited the car and walked back up the path. By this time Ben had already gone in. Del knocked on the door and waited. About twenty seconds later a red-faced male in his thirties answered the door.

"Hello, I'm not in you know." Del was speechless for a fraction of a second.

"I'm sorry, I'm Inspector Martin, could I speak to you for a few minutes please?"

"I'm doing my food, I will be in after I have it." Ben walked away down his hall into the kitchen. Del walked in after him and Harry followed and shut the door. They had never seen a place so bare but inhabited before; even the squats they had seen had more in. When Del entered the kitchen he saw a loaf of bread, a knife and a jar of chocolate spread. There was a microwave and that was it. Ben continued to make a sandwich as Del spoke to him.

"We're looking into a murder and want to ask you if you know anything about it. Were you near The Globe public house at around 8 o'clock on Tuesday just gone?" Ben stopped spreading his chocolate spread and stood still.

"Yes," he said, and then continued to prepare his food.

"How do you know you were there at that time? I believe you like to walk a long way." Ben looked around at Del in confused astonishment.

"I was there because I was there. You know you're here, don't you? I know I'm here and I also know I was there." He then continued to carefully spread his bread. Del looked at Harry and shrugged.

"He's right, you know. I know I'm here, surprised you don't!"

Del mouthed, 'Fuck off,' to Harry and turned his attention back to Ben.

"Okay, as you know you were there about that time did you see anything suspicious at all?" Ben stopped again and thought.

"Yes, I think a man was dressed as a woman. That looked suspicious but nobody else cared." Del decided to change approach; he took out the picture of Tony Slugget from his pocket.

"Do you remember seeing this man at all?" Ben stopped making his sandwich again. He looked at the picture for a second and turned back to his bread.

"Yes, he was talking on his phone and walked past me." Del was about to ask if he was sure but he didn't want another lecture about knowing he was him and knowing who the other person was so instead he asked something else.

"Could you tell us what he was saying?" Ben stopped again as if with endless patience.

"Yes, as he passed me he said, 'I'm looking forward to it and I'll be with you in about three minutes.'" Del was very excited now, he had found a bloody gold mine.

"Just one last question for you at the moment, do you know where he went as he passed you?" Ben stopped once more and thought.

"Yes, he walked about fifty metres further up the road and then turned right into Duke Street."

Del thanked him and said, "We'll show ourselves

to the door." Ben looked around in further confusion.

"The door will not know who you are."

Del walked away. Just before he reached the front Harry pushed past him.

"Ermm, door, this is Inspector Martin and I'm Sergeant Gorham, pleased to—"

Del dragged him out of the way.

"Come on, funny guts, stop talking to your intellectual superior and just open it." They both left the house and climbed back into the vehicle.

"What do you think? Reliable or not?" Del looked at Harry and waited for a response. Harry sat and wondered.

"Well, he is obviously a bit odd but he seems certain enough. After all, he knows he was there and finds it odd that you don't know where you have been." Harry grinned at Del. "Look, I know he seems a bit odd but without anything else I think we have to assume he is accurate." Del nodded and agreed.

*

The car was started and they headed back to the station. As he drove Del was chatting about what to do when they got back to the nick.

"If we can get a map and plan out the distance a man can walk in three minutes we'll have a radius from Duke Street where he could have met his possible murderer."

Harry asked him why he thought 'possible' murderer.

"Well, it is only possible. I mean it's likely as far as I can tell but it still may be that the person he met was not the murderer."

"Do you think Ben would have seen anything else on his travels?" Del had already thought about that and it was quite likely that he had come across something but he didn't want to ask too many questions in one go.

"I think the best way to go with Ben is slowly. If he is genuine and I believe he could be, he is going to be a fantastic help for us in the future."

As usual they went direct to the conference room and Del turned on the computer and printed off a map with Duke Street at the centre. They placed it on the table and worked out how far a man could walk in three minutes.

"Okay, if he walked at six kilometres an hour for the three minutes, that would mean he could walk about three or four hundred metres." The map he had printed was too small so Del printed it off again, zoomed in. Harry had the pen and circled a rough line of the required distance and they looked to see what there was in the circle. There wasn't a lot in the direction from Duke Street.

"Most of this is just back streets with houses." Harry was looking and just at the end of the circle, or just past it, was an area that looked clear. It was a car park.

"What do you think? Do you reckon they could have met in the car park?" Del looked at his watch.

"Yes, quite possibly, there is sod all else about there. I'll check that out tomorrow and you can carry on with the Bos enquiries." Del stood up. "I'm going home, I'll see you at the end of the day tomorrow."

CHAPTER 17

Wired

Del had a good evening and a good night; he had a nice quiet meal with Janice, an early night and a decent night's sleep. He woke up fresh and ready to go. He was up and ready early and sat in the chair in the living room sipping a nice strong cup of coffee. The feeling of optimism was high for the investigation now, after yesterday's favourable discovery. The favourable discovery he was thinking of was not the car park that he had pinpointed, it was the discovery of Ben, the young man with an apparent astounding memory. He was looking forward to testing his abilities. Del finished his drink and placed it in the dishwasher, he walked upstairs and into the bedroom. Janice was still asleep in the bed. Del stood and looked at her for a minute. A few tentative steps forward and Del bent down and kissed his wife on the head. She didn't wake or even move.

"See you later, babe," said Del, whispering. He noticed that her foot was sticking out the bottom of the quilt so he moved it carefully to cover her up and crept slowly out of the room and clicked the door shut. The stairs creaked slightly as he walked down and then made his way out and into his car.

*

He was in a good mood and enjoyed the radio on his way to work and was positive he was on the verge of a huge breakthrough in the Graffiti Killer case. He arrived at the station whistling and made his way straight up to the conference room. Harry wasn't in but Del wasn't expecting to see him as he was looking into Bos's past. Del fetched himself a cup of coffee and sat looking at the white boards. He was concentrating on looking to see if they had missed anything. Was there a link between the victims? That fact was more difficult to believe as the last victim was a female, and the only female to have been killed by either the Butcher or the Graffiti Killer. The locations were completely different too – one outside, one in a garage and one in an office. Del stopped and looked again. There was a link. Why hadn't he seen that before? All three bodies had been attached to some kind of mechanism. The first was a mechanical door that could have lifted the body up. The second was a car lift that could have lifted the body. The third was not a lifting mechanism but could have been used to spin the body upside down. This was a possible link. It was a tenuous one, but it was one. The only thing Del was wondering now was why? These thoughts made him wonder about Natalia, the third victim, he couldn't remember the drawings on her body. Was she graphitised upside down or drawn on and then turned upside down? He shrugged and said out loud to no one in particular, "Does that even matter?"

By the time he had finished pondering these questions and a few more besides, it was 09:36. He picked up his keys and headed out of the door. Del decided to go directly to the car park and have a look about. He drove to The Globe and parked nearby. Del had decided to walk the direction they thought Tony had gone if he had headed for the car park on their map. He walked down the street and turned into Duke Street as Ben said Tony had done. Del took out the map and followed the most direct path towards his goal. All the way there he was looking around for anything out of place that may suggest a struggle of some kind had taken place. He was also looking for any CCTV. That was a long shot considering there was sod all about, just accommodation. No security conscious businesses.

It took Del eleven minutes to walk to the car park. He looked at his watch. He knew he was walking slowly so he could keep an eye out for anything relevant but could that be walked in three minutes? He wasn't sure. Del looked into the car park from the end of the road he had walked down; the surface changed from tarmac to gravel. There was not a pay and display box, it seemed it relied on a sign saying that it was for residents and unlawful parkers would be clamped. He walked into the car park itself and there was room for around fifteen cars, and there was another exit or entry on the left-hand corner of the square open space too. The entrance Del had walked through was an open road into it but the other end, the exit or entrance, was in underneath a property. Again, as with his entry there was no barrier, just a change of surface material. He looked around the bricked wall surrounding the car park; if he had met here in secret it had been a bloody good choice, but there were two cameras covering the place. One at each end. Hopefully if Tony Slugget had met someone here they would both be on camera. However, looking around here, who the hell would he check with?

"Sod this." Del walked up to the house nearest the entrance. He walked through and knocked on the door. A middle-aged woman answered dressed in a dressing gown. It was half open at the top but the woman was not an attractive sight.

"Sorry love, just got up, what can I do for you?"

Del pointed to the car park. "If I was to want to see the footage from the cameras from the car park, do you know who I would have to speak to please?"

She asked him why he wanted them.

"I'm Inspector Martin and I'm investigating a serious crime, and those may hold information key to the investigation, can you help?" The unattractive woman pursed her lips in a way she possibly thought was provocative but Del thought the only thing it would be likely to provoke would be the reappearance of his breakfast.

"Well, as you are so lovely I can help. See the house over there?" She pointed to the property that straddled the car park's other entrance, but as she pointed the dressing gown gave an unfortunate glimpse to Del of her unholstered breasts. They really were a hell of a sight; not a pretty one – they really did look like hell. Del was thinking that they needed controlling with some scaffolding rather than a bra of some kind when she said, "Ooh, sorry about that love. I don't suppose you want to come and help me put these to bed, do you? I love a man in uniform." Del looked as she never even attempted to put the monsters away.

"I'm sorry but I'm busy looking into a serious crime, and as you can see I'm lucky enough not to be in uniform. Thank you for your help though." He walked away towards the building that hopefully held the key to the cameras. The front door to the property in question was on the other side of the arched entrance. It was obvious to Del as he looked, that it was the rear of the property that overlooked the car park. He went and knocked at the front and waited. It was not long before a man answered. He was in his fifties, Del guessed. He was walking with a stick and a pronounced limp.

"Hello."

Del introduced himself. "Hello, I'm Inspector Martin and I'm looking into a number of serious crimes." He showed the male his warrant card. "I have been told that you may be the man to speak to regarding the possible footage on the cameras in the car park." The man nodded at him.

"Well you were told right, I have the recording equipment in my place. Do you need to look at some of it?"

"Yes please, that would be fantastic."

The man limped back into his home and told Del to follow him. "The equipment is upstairs so follow me, but sorry, it does take me a little while to get up there with this leg."

Del said it was fine. "How come you have the

cameras and stuff linked here? Do you own the car park?" The man laughed.

"Hell no, I was just bloody stupid enough to agree to it when the place was turned into a car park for all the residents." He eventually got to the top of the stairs and turned right to the room that was over the top of the car park entry. The man lived on his own and this room was a large office for him so it didn't really make a huge difference to have one corner used to house the recording equipment.

"Do you know when you are after seeing?"

Del told him the date and time and then just hoped.

"Okay, right, here we go then." He slumped down in the small office swivel chair. "I'm Frank by the way, grab a seat." He pointed to a chair on the other side of the room that was near another desk. Del grabbed it and took it next to Frank and sat down.

"What am I looking for anyway?" asked Frank.

"I'm hoping at around 20:10 or a little later we'll see this man enter your car park from the other entrance." Del had taken the picture of Tony out of his pocket and placed it on the desk next to the control panel that Frank was using. Frank pressed a few buttons and brought up a split-screen view of the car park; it was the view that was coming in at the moment. He punched in some details and waited for things to happen. It wasn't long before the screen went black for a second and then flickered back to life. The clock in the corner now said 19:50.

"I've played it from 19:50 so we can view it going forward."

"Thank you, that's great, can you view it forward in double speed?"

Frank pressed a button and the view flickered forward with a couple of white lines running horizontally across it. There were a couple of cars parked in the car park and Del could read the number plates.

"Frank, do you know whose cars they are?" Del was quite disappointed to hear that he knew exactly, and he told him where the owners lived. Nothing happened until 20:09 – a car pulled up just the opposite side of the archway under the house they were in. It pulled up and stopped with the front of the car showing through the entrance. It was black but that was about all he could pick out. It stayed there.

"Frank, am I right in thinking there is not a parking space that side of your house?"

"You're right, no bugger should be stopping there, it's right on the corner."

At 20:14 an image that Del had been hoping for popped up.

"Wait, play it." As he watched a male entered the car park at high speed and made his way directly across it. By the time Frank had pressed 'play' he had reached the other end.

"Can you rewind it please and play just as he enters?"

Frank said, "Sure thing," and did exactly what was asked of him. The footage started to play again and Del leant in to see. It wasn't fabulous but he could tell it was Mr Slugget; he was on his phone and walking at a hell of a pace. He walked directly across the car park, straight under the arch, and bent down slightly when he reached the black vehicle. It was a moment after he bent down when he opened the car door and got in. The very second the door was shut the car pulled away.

"Oh hell yes, that could well be the killer's car."

Frank shot his head around. "Killer!"

Del looked to his right at Frank. "Yes, I'm sorry to say it but the man you just saw walking across your car park was found murdered the next morning."

"Holy shit."

Del nodded grimly. "Indeed. Right, I need you to burn that footage off for me please. Can you do that?" Frank nodded back slowly.

"Yes, yes I can do that. Do you want it now?"

Del didn't speak, he just nodded again. Frank became busy for a few minutes sorting things out and after a while handed a disc to Del.

"Here you are."

Del looked at it. "Can you write your name, your address, the date and time on it please? I will then get you to sign my note book. I need to keep a correct paper trail of this evidence."

Once that was complete Del took the case with the disc in and the photograph that was on the table and put them in his pocket.

"Thank you very much for your help on this, Frank." He reached out and shook him by the hand.

Frank said it was no problem and he was glad the

cameras had done a bit more than catching people screwing in the car park. Del followed Frank downstairs, a little quicker than the ascent, and left in very high spirits. He wanted to get back to the station now and see if he could identify what looked like a black car.

*

He headed back directly to the station and went to the conference room. Unfortunately, just as his backside touched the seat his phone rang. He shuffled around on the seat and dragged it from his pocket.

"Hello?" It was silent for a second and then a computer-generated voice kicked in.

"Del, this is the real Butcher. Nice to see you interested in Bos and his past, may help you understand but to really understand him you need to feel a little of what he felt. It is said that you can't judge a man until you walk a mile in his shoes. I can help you there. You do know that Bos went through tragedy with the early death of his wife. To truly understand this you need to feel that loss!"

Del froze for a second as the phone went dead.

"Janice." Del was in a complete and total panic. He shot off his chair, sending it hurtling backward. As he turned he knocked some papers off the desk. He didn't register that at all; even the disc he had just collected went across the floor. It was all a mere blur as he shot towards the exit. He shoved the door so hard it smacked back with a crash – it was a heavy-set door but moved with ease under Del's onslaught. He ran full pelt through the corridors, not even noticing the people he was flying past. He misjudged a corner and smacked his shoulder. This sent him spinning out of control and banging into a notice board. The notices went flying around the corridor as Del continued his relentless speed towards the station exit. He burst through the exit doors and ran to his car. His panic was pure and filled every particle of his body. His face felt like it was boiling but his spine was cold. His stomach was burning and he felt sick; he also felt like his heart was beating in his throat. He fumbled his keys from his pocket and in his haste dropped them trying to get his car key ready. He didn't realise it but tears were rolling down his face. Be that anger, fright, frustration or something else, he wouldn't have known. He bleeped the car open once he had them back in his hand, slammed the door open and in his eagerness to get in smashed his head on the frame. Stars twinkled in front of his eyes and blood now joined the tears in a race to the bottom of his face. The key was rammed into the ignition and reverse was crunched into place. The car roared out of the police car park with officers and members of the public looking on.

He pounded the car down the road as if the speed limit was non-existent, pulled up at his house and seemed to jump out while it was still moving. He looked an absolute mess; he was white as a sheet now and with tears and blood cascading down his face, he looked like a badly drawn clown in the rain. But this clown was in a hurry and certainly in no mood to laugh. He sprinted to his front door and tried hopelessly to open it with speed.

"Come on, come on, you fucking bastard!" he shouted. It did eventually open and he left his keys hanging in the lock as he ran through the house shouting for his wife.

"Janice, Janice!" he bellowed as he ran from room to room. The longer her silence the more panicked he became. She was not downstairs. He sprinted up the stairs three at a time still continuing to shout. If he found her now, he wouldn't know whether to hug her in relief or smack her across the head for not answering him. Unfortunately, he had searched the entire house and she was not there. The last room he ran into was the bathroom and he slumped down on the toilet seat in despair.

"Janice!" he shouted. He sat there for a few seconds, his breathing heavy and deep. The cut on his head was still oozing blood but not to the extent it had been. He still had tears rolling down his face and they were mixing with the snot that was also escaping from him. He didn't know what to do, stood up and felt very unsteady on his legs. His legs had turned to jelly along with his face. As he stood he caught a glance of himself in the mirror; he had been completely unaware that he had cut his head so severely. He blew his nose and that was about the extent of his tidy up, and left the bathroom. He was not running now as he was quite sure Janice was not there. He didn't know what the hell to do now. He walked downstairs on a kind of autopilot as he wasn't thinking about what he was doing, he was at a loss. It was as if his brain had been filled with cotton wool or had somehow rusted instantly. He looked at the front door and dimly registered that it was wide open and his keys were still in the lock. He walked over and removed them and closed the door. This moment stunned him again as taped to the back of the front door was a note.

Oh dear couldn't find her, tick tock, tick tock need to hurry. Remember we can't be All Saints, Janice may be though.

It was signed, 'The Real Butcher'. Del was not one to show anger much but he did vent a little at this point.

"Fucking bastard! You wait till I fucking find you, you cunt." This sentence was shouted and got louder towards the end until the last word could have rattled the windows. He kicked the door and screamed in rage. It didn't really help and his breathing was as fast as it had ever been, his head felt about four times its usual size and his legs still felt like jelly holding up a brick. He stood in front of the door panting and staring at the piece of paper. Slowly, very slowly, he started to think. *I need to concentrate on the note. What the fuck do I do? I need to read and take in this message.* He read it again and again. Gently the fog in his mind started to drift away and he could concentrate a little better minute by minute. Pretty soon his breathing less resembled a dog in the sun after a long run and was more like a human after a jog.

"Right, you fucker, what are you trying to tell me?" He looked again. "That doesn't even make sense. The 'tick tock' bit is obvious – he wants me to hurry." He stared. "But 'we can't be All Saints'… Surely that should be 'we can't all be saints' and why the capital letter?"

He leant against a wall.

"Christ's sake, that's all I need, a dyslexic fucking killer writing me notes."

He suddenly stood upright off the wall.

"Hang on, what if it's meant to be like that? All Saints could be a name, a place!"

He ran out of the door and didn't even close it. He ran and skidded to a stop at his car and hurried to open it. He had thought about names while in the hall and realised it was a church, it happened to be the name of the church he and Janice had got married in. He fumbled around and shot off at high speed towards the church – it was the longest fifteen minutes of his life. Although, if he was driving within the realms of the law it should have taken considerably longer. His car was screeching and squealing around the corners and he was lucky that there were no marked vehicles on his route because they would have undoubtedly pursued him. He was slowed down considerably at one point where he turned the air blue with road rage fuelled profanities. But he did, after what felt like hours, pull up at All Saints Church. He didn't care about parking appropriately, he just jumped out and abandoned his car at the side of the road at some horrendous angle that was sure to have another vehicle ram him up the rear. This was not at the forefront of his mind, he didn't care. The only thing on his mind was Janice.

He ran to the huge wooden door of the church and pushed as hard as he could. The large wooden door swung slowly at first and then gathered pace. As Del pushed at the door something clicked behind it. Del ignored the noise and ran into the church. Straight ahead of him was a font, to the right were rows and rows of church pews each side of a central walkway and at the end was a pulpit, candles and stands. That end also had a large stained-glass window; it looked beautiful and a blast of memory came back to him of when he and Janice were married here. Nothing was out of the ordinary as far as he could tell. Perhaps he had got the message wrong; that thought knotted his stomach. He needed to find Janice.

He turned left and looked down that end of the church, there was the same centre gap a few more rows of pews. It was then sectioned off by a large black metal gated area. This was where the expensive items that belonged to the church were kept. The main church was always open to the public but this part was locked when the vicar was not around. It was locked now but it was easy to see beyond it. Del looked through the bars and could see a large cross on the wall at the far end. He couldn't quite make it out but it looked strange. He walked towards the metal bars with an inquisitive look on his face. This look slowly turned to shock as he realised that there was a body attached to the cross and it was not the body of Christ. Shock turned to horror as he realised that the body was a woman, a naked woman. He couldn't see properly from where he was but it looked like she was nailed on to the cross and she had been drawn on. She had been sectioned off like the Graffiti Killer's victims. He knew it was a female as she had breasts. She had hair the same colour, length and style as Janice. In fact, she did look remarkably like his wife. Panic swelled in his stomach and hit his brain at speed. He couldn't make out if it was definitely her because she had a pig mask over her face. He ran to the metal door and pulled on it to try and open it. It was shut and locked; there was a hefty padlock on it as well as the normal lock and key. He looked again at the female and this time he squinted closer and he could see her moving her head – she was alive! His heart gave a leap of hope.

"Janice, Janice it's me, Del. I'm going to get you out!"

He then noticed something else. Over the top of the metal barrier were six or so fine cables. Not even cables, they looked too thin for that; wires possibly. He followed the line of sight behind him and they led to the top of the stairs. He then followed them in the other direction; they led directly to Janice. Del pushed his face against the bars to see if he could make out what was going on. He couldn't see exactly but it looked like the wires were going behind her.

"What the fuck?" Del looked back again and noticed for the first time that there was a statue behind the door that had fallen over as he opened it. He walked towards it and looked; it was attached to a small rope. Del followed the rope across the church and up the stairs. It led to a landing with a large plastic water tank on it. The tank was full of water but the rope had pulled out about seven plugs that were holding the water in.

"What the fucking hell is going on?" The water was pissing out all over the floor. The tank was right on the edge of the landing overlooking the church interior. It was also attached to a cable that went to the top of the church, the same place as the wires that were around Janice. Del was getting worried now, it was all looking like a very dangerous game of mouse trap. He tried to look up to where the cable went but couldn't see anything. He went around the corner towards the next set of stairs and through the gap, to his absolute terror he could see what was happening. The tank was attached to a large statue at the very top of the church. The only thing stopping the statue falling was the weight of the water tank. Also attached to the statue were the wires from Janice. As soon as the statue tipped it was going to fall and when it fell it would pull tight the wires that were attached to Janice. Del ran back to the tank to try and stem the fall of the water; he could plug a couple of them but it was no good, he couldn't do them all. He looked around for something heavy he could put in the tank but there was nothing around. The tank was already only half full and Del could see it starting to shift. There was no way he would be able to hold it when empty. He ran down the stairs to try and get into the cage again but as he hit the bottom of the steps he heard the tank shift. He looked up and saw the statue tilt further and then drop.

"Nooo!" He ran to the metal gating and pulled with all his might as the statue plunged downwards. Suddenly it hit the point where the wires pulled taught. Del looked on in abject horror.

"Janice!" he shouted with tears flowing. The wires pulled with the force of the statue's fall and the full horror of the Graffiti Killer's design hit home. The wires were wrapped around sections of the woman's limbs – her arms, legs and her neck were wired. They pulled tight and cut through the limbs instantly with ease. The poor woman had been decapitated and had her legs and arms removed in one awful moment. Blood went everywhere as the body parts flew metres away from the body. Del hadn't even registered that the statue itself had missed him by fractions. He couldn't move. He was looking at the mutilated body of his beloved wife and couldn't do anything about it; she was breathing just seconds ago and now he would never talk to her again.

He collapsed in a heap on the floor and broke down. Del couldn't cope. He couldn't move and wanted to disappear from the world of pain. He hadn't got a clue how long he was there but all of a sudden a voice said, "Sir, sir, what happened here?" It was a PC, someone had called the police due to the disturbance in the church. PC Jarvis had arrived, seen the mess and then saw Inspector Martin in a heap on the floor. Del looked up and registered PC Jarvis.

"Sir, what happened here?"

Del shook his head and pointed to the body on the other side of the metal barrier.

"My wife, killed, graffiti bastard."

Jarvis radioed for backup immediately and also requested for senior officers, CSI and an ambulance attendance. Del was collected by senior staff and placed in an ambulance. The entire church was cordoned off and treated as one large crime scene. Del didn't want to leave Janice but was in no state of mind to argue with anyone. He walked numbly to the ambulance and they treated him for shock. He also had his injured head looked at on the journey to the hospital.

*

He was being looked after well and he was put in a separate single room. Once in, he was sedated a little to try and help him sleep a while. He had concussion from the bang on his head as well as cuts to his hands, presumably from trying to pull the metal gates open. Even while sedated he was talking, saying his wife's name or sometimes even shouting it.

Harry was called and headed back from his enquiries. It took him a while but he went directly to the hospital when he got back.

CHAPTER 18

Oakwood Manor

Harry didn't go to the station, he decided to head straight out to Oakwood Manor, the place of Bos's dramatic life change. It was a long drive through congested roads and drizzle rain. It was not a pleasant drive and the case was going through his mind all the way there. He wanted to try and put the case at the back of his mind and concentrate on his task in hand, which was to gather as much information on the early life of Jeff Boston as possible. The clouds became darker the further he travelled and by the time he was a couple of miles from his destination the sky was grey and dark. The rain was coming down steadily now.

He was off the main roads and travelling through small country roads and his satnav said he was only five minutes away from his destination. The road he was on was a little narrow and had large hedgerows occasionally intruding over onto the vehicle's territory. He continued along the road and passed a gate in a field and in the distance he could see a large manor house type building.

"Fuck me, that can't be your house, can it?" It was an impressive sight, even in the rain. He drove on following his satnav's instructions and soon heard, "You have reached your destination," and right enough on his left was the entrance with a sign saying: 'Oakwood Manor'.

He turned in and headed down the large drive; he did notice the trees lining the drive. They were twisted and awful. The manor house was at the end and looked out of place when framed between the trees. The way the trees looked, there should have some spooky gothic castle at the end. Harry drove down between the trees, over the gravel towards the house. As he pulled up he could take in the splendour of the building, it looked fantastic. Was this really where Bos grew up!

He stopped the vehicle near the main door and climbed out. He didn't go straight to the front door, he just stood in the rain and looked around. The grounds were huge, the house was majestic, but the trees were bloody awful. Why the hell would anyone keep those monstrosities! He did then walk to the door and lifted the large bronze knocker. It made a loud echoing sound and Harry waited for some large strange butler to answer, but that didn't happen. The door opened without the expected comical creak and looking out was a middle-aged woman.

"Hello, can I help?" The woman was attractive and dressed smart in a long beige-coloured skirt and cream blouse.

"Hello, I'm Sergeant Gorham and I wonder if I can come in and have a chat with the residents of the property please?" He passed her his warrant card. She looked it over and looked up at him, then opened the door wider.

"Well, at least come in out of the rain first".

Harry stepped through the door and was stunned by the impressive hall and stunning staircase. He lost himself for a second. "Wow."

"I know. I'm Sabrina by the way." She put out her arm and shook Harry by the hand. It was a delicate hand, small with long fingers and perfectly manicured. Harry did think that there had not been a huge amount of labour seen by those, but didn't comment.

"It is impressive, isn't it?" she said. "It's not ours unfortunately, we're just living here."

Harry looked around again. "How are you living here if it's not yours then, if you don't mind me asking?"

She gestured for Harry to follow her, and as she drifted elegantly into the living room she answered him. "My husband works for a bank and they pay for us to stay here; we have a helper included in the package but she has been unwell and has been away for a month staying with relatives." She sat in a very expensive-looking floral chair that Harry didn't think looked very comfortable. She waved her hand as if to say that Harry could sit.

"That is interesting, your husband must be quite well appreciated in his role." Sabrina smiled at Harry.

"Well yes but he does make them a lot of money. The bank looks after its staff and the people who help them. As you probably saw when you entered there is quite a sophisticated CCTV system around the place.

I got them to deactivate most of it as it makes me uncomfortable, but the main camera and mic are still working above the main door. Do you want a drink, Sergeant?" Harry was actually quite thirsty after his drive and could kill for a coffee.

"I would love a cup of coffee if it would not be a problem please." Sabrina stood up and walked out.

"Make yourself comfortable. I will fetch us a drink and be back in a moment."

A moment was not what Harry called it, she had been gone for a good while before gliding back in. She was carrying a silver tray and on the tray were two expensive-looking cups on saucers, a glass bowl with lumps of sugar and two small jugs in the same design as the cups. One contained milk, the other cream. She sat down and placed the tray on the small table next to the chair. Harry could smell the strength of the coffee from a distance.

"Help yourself to sugar, milk or cream." Harry thanked her and tentatively picked up one of the cups and a saucer. They felt very light and thin, as if you held them too tight they would shatter.

"Okay Sergeant, how can I help?" she said, pouring a drop of cream into her cup. Harry had been thinking about the best way to bring this up on the journey in and he had as yet not come up with a suitable way.

"Erm, well, it is a little delicate. Have you heard of anyone called Jeff or Jeffrey Boston?"

Sabrina thought for a moment.

"No, no, I don't believe I have. Should I?" Harry

sat back in the chair, which on reflection was surprisingly comfortable.

"No, it's not a case of should know more than you may have. Jeff Boston was a detective inspector and a very good one." Harry sipped his coffee. "Unfortunately he also turned out to be a serial killer." Sabrina raised her eyebrows.

"Now that is unfortunate," and she emphasised the word 'is'.

"Yes, quite. The reason I asked if you knew or had heard of him is, as a young boy he lived here."

Sabrina didn't say anything in reply to that, she just waited.

"He lived here until he was around eight or nine years old, when he was involved in an awful car accident in which his parents died." Harry took out of his pocket a newspaper cutting with the picture of the twisted wreck with the tree spearing it. He handed this to her. Sabrina put her cup down and leant forward to take the clipping.

"Oh heavens, that's the plac tree."

Harry was immediately interested. "What do you mean by that?"

"Do you mind a walk in the rain?" she said, standing up, as if she knew the answer would be yes. They walked out the front and up the drive; luckily the rain had slowed to a slight drizzle. They reached the end of the drive near the corner and Sabrina went off the gravel and onto the grass verge towards one of the ugly trees. She pointed to the trunk of the tree. Harry looked and it was a little worn but you could see the word PLAC etched into the wood. He looked closer and he could just make out a further two letters. The word was visible enough at the P but as it progressed it became less apparent. He made out PLACAR.

"What on earth does PLACAR mean?"

Sabrina looked. "I don't know, Sergeant, but this is the tree in your snippet."

They walked back to the living room to finish their drinks. When he sat Harry continued, "So you had not heard anything about Jeff Boston or the accident?"

Sabrina explained that she knew and knows nothing about the history of the place. "The only thing I do know is it belongs to a Lady Belina Wellingborough and she allows the bank to let it to key workers and has done for a long while, I presume for some kind of payment."

Harry asked if she had ever seen lady Wellingborough.

"No, not at all. We were told that for our entire employment with the bank we should class this as our home." She smiled. "And it is a stunning place, more than we could ever have dreamed of."

Harry thought for a moment. "Could you tell me what bank your husband works for please?"

Sabrina told him and he made a note of it.

"Can I ask you a question, Sergeant?"

Harry said, "Of course."

"If you know this Boston man was a serial killer and you use the word 'was' this would suggest he was caught, so why the questions and visit here?" Harry was quite impressed with this.

"That is an excellent question. Jeff Boston was caught and to cut a long story short died in the process. However, now a year later we have more killings by someone saying they knew him. I'm trying to gather as much info on Bos as possible." Sabrina nodded.

"Okay, that's fine. I do not know how long the bank have had this agreement with Lady Wellingborough but if it was running then, they will know who was here."

Harry thanked her for her time and coffee and asked if he was okay to look around the grounds before he left. Sabrina told him he was welcome and he could walk around all he liked. Harry shook her smooth hand once more and left. He walked through the large door and was thankful that it had stopped raining; it was still overcast but at least now he could walk about the grounds without getting soaked. He decided to walk around the rear of the property first.

*

Harry walked around the ground as he noticed that the trees that lined the entrance were prevalent in other areas of the grounds too. As he continued he saw one that stood out amongst the others, the grass around it seemed to be compacted down as if this area saw more footfall than others. He bent down and looked at the soil between the grass – it was a brown red rather than the pale brown like other parts. He looked at the tree and then around the grounds.

"Why are you so different then?" he said out loud.

He did notice a rather prominent branch sticking out horizontally. He didn't know exactly why it caught his attention but he looked at it and noticed it looked different to the other branches, the bark was different somehow, smoother. This area was odd, it was well away from the main building but obviously used regularly. He continued to walk around for a little while and then decided that he would head off back to the car and phone the bank that rented this place out. He walked back, admiring the house and knowing that he would never be able to afford to live in a place like this. He climbed into the car at just about the right time as it spat with rain and then quickly became faster until his windscreen was being heavily rattled.

"Bloody hell, this place should make up its mind!"

Harry picked up his phone and dialled the control room; he asked for a contact number for the bank and waited, thankful that he hadn't got caught in what was hammering down now. He was given the number and he called it right away. The next forty minutes were not fun for Harry, in fact he would describe them as torturous. His call went from 'press this button for this', to 'another button for that' and 'a different one for another'. Once he had got through this he went to another set of questions, then another. He was eventually put through to a person who put him on hold, then through to someone else. They put him on hold and transferred him elsewhere. Each and every time he was transferred he had to describe who he was and what he was phoning for. This went on for a mind numbing forty minutes, when finally he had someone that actually knew what he was talking about.

"Hello sir, I understand you have some questions about the Oakwood Manor property." At that point Harry was ready for his brains to seep out of his ears.

"Oh thank God for that, now you're not going to put me on hold are you?"

The male said that no, he wouldn't be doing that. "My colleague said you are a police Sergeant looking into a crime." Harry breathed a little easier.

"Yes, that is right, I'm looking into a serial killer who I believe lived at Oakwood Manor when he was young."

The man asked who it was.

"Okay, when he lived there he was called Ben and he and his parents were involved in a car accident where his parents died." The phone went quiet for a little bit.

"I know who you are talking about, Sergeant, that was Mr and Mrs Oscar and young Ben Oscar. It was awful. I wasn't here at the time but everyone here knows about it. Poor little boy."

Harry was relieved that he was speaking to a human that actually understood what he was talking about and may have some useful information.

"I'm very pleased that you know what I'm talking about. That young boy Ben grew up to murder people and I need to find as much information as I can about his life at the manor."

The man hummed down the phone. "Okay, have you a police email address I can send the information to? I will get some things down in print and send them to you."

"That would be absolutely fantastic. Yes, I do have a police email address." Harry went through his email and gave the man his contact number too. "If I need to speak to you again is there a number I can get to you on please? I do not want to have to go through the mess I did today again."

The man said, "Yes of course, I'm Charlie and my number is—"

Harry asked him to wait a second to get a pen and then jotted it all down. Harry thanked Charlie profusely, hung up and sat back rubbing his temples. He started his car and headed back in the horrendous rain. It was thirty minutes later when his phone rang. He pulled over and answered it.

"Hello, Sergeant Gorham."

"Hello Sergeant, this is PC Terry Jarvis, please come back as soon as you possibly can. Inspector Martin is in hospital, under sedation." Harry was stunned.

"Why? What the fuck has happened?"

"I'm sorry Sergeant but I believe he has had a shock and has seen his wife killed by the murderer you are trying to catch."

Harry just said, "What hospital?" He was told and then said, "On my way," solemnly and threw his phone down.

CHAPTER 19

Hospital

The journey to the hospital for Harry was not a nice one; he was deeply concerned about his colleague who he classed as a friend. He didn't like the word 'sedated' either. What the hell had Del witnessed? How had Janice been killed? These and hundreds of other questions were running through his head as he drove the fastest he could get away with to get back to his friend. It was an hour and a half later when he pulled up in the hospital car park. He slammed into a space and bundled out of it, rushed into the building and went straight to the nearest reception desk he could find.

"Hello, I'm Sergeant Gorham, I'm looking for Inspector Martin. He was admitted a few hours ago and has been sedated due to being in or seeing a traumatic event. Could you tell me where he is please?" This was rattled out within a second and the poor lady behind the desk hadn't got a clue what he had just said.

"Sorry?" she said.

"Yes, so am I!" He leant forward and spoke again. He knew it wasn't her fault but at the moment he did not care.

"I'm Sergeant Gorham." He paused.

"I'm looking for Inspector Martin." Another pause.

"He was admitted to your hospital a couple of hours ago. He was traumatised by something. Could I find out where he is please?" His patience was quite thin at the moment. The woman looked down and tapped about on her computer. After about twenty seconds she looked up.

"He is in room seven in ward B, blue section in the Coronation Wing."

Harry looked again and said, "Pardon?" She leant forward.

"Room seven," she said slowly.

"Ward B." She waited.

"Blue section." Another gap.

"Coronation Wing."

Harry understood her sarcasm. "Can you tell me how to get there please?" She smiled.

"Yes, follow the yellow line until you reach the Coronation Wing, then just follow the blue line and look for room seven." He said thank you and headed off. The line system led him straight to where he needed to go. He stood in front of room seven and took a deep breath. Harry opened the door and went in, he could see Del laying in the hospital bed. He was asleep and there was a PC standing in the corner of the room.

"Hello Sergeant, I'm Terry Jarvis, I called you." Harry stepped towards him and shook his hand.

"Thanks for calling me. What happened?" Terry shook his head.

"I'm sorry to say it really was not a nice place to be. It happened in All Saints Church." He went on to describe the church as it looked when he arrived. He told Harry that Del was on the floor next to the metal sectioned off area; behind was the torso of a woman. "I say torso because her arms, legs and head had been removed."

Harry butted in then. "How?"

Terry said he didn't know. "But Del had obviously seen something and he said when I turned up that it was his wife that had been killed." He went on to then describe that there was a large statue on the floor next to Del in the church, it was smashed and had wires attached to it coming off in different directions.

"I could also hear water running, it was a confusing scene and I wanted to get the Inspector out of there, he was in a real state."

Harry looked over to the bed again and saw that Del was bruised on the top of his head and at the centre of the purplish mark was a large cut. His hands were bandaged but he was sleeping. Harry went to the side of the bed and sat in the chair next to it.

"Thank you for calling and waiting with him, Terry, but you can go and get a drink or something now if you want, I'll keep an eye on him." Terry didn't say anything, he just nodded, smiled a sympathetic smile and walked out. Harry wanted to wake Del up and ask him what the hell had happened but he knew he had to be patient and wait. He sat there for a while, twitching every time Del moved and moaned. It was around forty minutes later and Harry nodded off to sleep too.

It was 17:47 when Harry woke up abruptly. He was woken by Del screaming out, "Janice!" He was still sedated but obviously had full control of his vocal cords. Harry sat bolt upright, he felt like shit and looked pretty close to it as well. He rubbed his eyes and smacked his lips as if needing a drink. Del had a cup and a jug on a small table next to him so Harry poured a little and drank it. Del opened his eyes; he was groggy and still very spaced out.

"Hello Del, I've been waiting for you to wake, are you able to talk?"

Del focused for the first time for real, and then tried to sit up quickly. This didn't end well. Harry told him to stay lying down as he was in no state to try and get up.

"Janice, Harry, my poor Janice, she, she, she's gone." Harry leant in.

"The PC told me you said that. What happened Del?" Harry felt like a real shit trying to ask about it but he needed to know what had gone on.

"I was at the station and got spoken to, he said he was going to kill Janice." Del lifted his arm and scratched his head; he was still feeling the effects of the sedation but he flinched with the pain as he scraped across his head wound. "I went home and he said she was at the church." Del lay back and seemed to drift off a little.

"Del, then what?" Harry touched Del's arm to try

and cause a response. It worked.

"Woman on the cross, water leaked, statue and she flew to pieces."

None of this made any sense to Harry whatsoever. He was not going to get any clarity from Del until the sedative had worn off more. He let him go back to sleep and Harry sat down again and decided to try and do the same; this was going to be a long night. It was 19:46 when Harry was awoken again, this time it was a bell ringing. He woke and muttered, "Ah, for fuck's sake," mostly to himself. He looked around to track down the cause of the noise. On the side table was a mobile phone, it was flashing and ringing. Harry walked over and read the screen, it had a red and a green phone on it asking whether to answer or not and it had the name 'Babe' written on the screen. It was obviously Del's phone and he was in no fit state to answer it. Harry picked it up and pressed the green button.

"Hello, this is Del's phone, Sergeant Gorham speaking."

"Hello Harry, is Del there please?"

Harry was taken aback for a moment.

"He's asleep at the moment. Who is this please?" He spoke slowly, as if suspicious of something.

"Come on Harry, don't piss about, I just want to know what time my husband will be back tonight." Harry froze and didn't say anything. "Look, I just want to know if I should wait up or not, he usually lets me know by now. Harry, Harry!" Harry snapped out of his unwanted muteness.

"Janice, are you able to meet me at Saint Marie's hospital?"

Janice spoke slowly. "Why? Is everything alright? Is Del okay?"

Harry's voice picked up. "I can one hundred percent say he definitely will be when you turn up."

Janice said that she would be there in around fifteen minutes. Harry said that he would meet her at the A & E entrance. Harry put the phone down and stood still, staring at Del lying in mental pieces on the bed. *What the fuck happened to you today?* Harry waited five minutes and then left to walk to the A & E entrance. Sure enough, ten minutes later Janice walked in. Harry had never been more pleased to see anyone in his entire life. He walked towards her and as she smiled at him he grabbed her and hugged her.

"What's going on, Harry?"

Harry led her by the hand and sat her down in one of the A & E seats. "Look, I don't want you to panic at what I'm about to say because believe it or not everything that I'm about to say is excellent news, okay?" Janice slowly nodded her head.

"Yes, alright."

"Okay, Del is in a private room and has been heavily sedated to keep him calm after an awful shock he had today. He has also had his head stitched up after cutting it quite badly." Janice frowned at him.

"I thought you said this was good news." Harry laughed and Janice on the other hand did not move a muscle.

"Alright, how can I put this with a better spin on

it?" He thought for a second. "Del is in the state he is because the shock was that he thought he had seen his wife brutally killed in front of him, so can you see why I'm more than just a little happy to see you here. And to know that when he sees you everything is going to be better." Janice stood up.

"You mean he thinks I'm dead?"

Harry nodded. "At the moment, yes."

"Well where is he then? I suggest we go and fucking enlighten him!"

This shocked Harry, he had never heard Janice swear but it did make him laugh, and laugh physically out loud.

"Come on then." They walked together to room seven in the blue section.

"Janice, do you think I can go in before you, just to see if he's awake first?"

Janice pushed out of the way. "Screw that," she said, walking past him and directly into the room. Del was actually still asleep so Janice walked over to him and kissed him on the lips. Nothing happened. Janice took her shoes off and climbed on the bed. Del was under the covers but Janice lay on top of the sheets right alongside her husband. At that particular point Harry felt a bit of a gooseberry.

"Janice, I'm going to get myself a drink and a packet of crisps, okay?" and before he even had an answer he walked out of the room, not that she did answer him. Janice at that point was stroking her husband's head and whispering in his ear. Harry met PC Jarvis at the hospital shop.

"Terry, did you see the body in the church?" He finished the mouthful of chocolate he was chewing.

"Yes, well no, I saw the body but not all of it. The body didn't have a head, legs or arms." The shop had a few customers in and they turned around and looked when that sentence was uttered.

"Come here." Harry walked out of the shop with Terry. "Are you saying you couldn't tell if the victim was Del's wife?" Terry nodded.

"To be fair she could have had all her body parts and I still couldn't say if it was Del's wife."

"Why?" asked Harry.

"I've never bloody seen his wife, how the fuck am I going to know who she is?"

Harry smiled. "Yes, okay, that would be a challenge."

"I just went on what Del said because, well, I was presuming he knew what his wife looked like! Why anyway?" Harry looked at him.

"Because as we speak here, Janice, his wife, is laying on his bed next to him."

Terry smiled. "And I suppose she has all her arms and legs, does she?" Harry snorted his drink.

"Yes, funny enough she does, and even better, a head too."

Terry asked the question Harry wanted an answer to. "So why did he think the woman in the church was his wife?"

"That, my friend, I don't know. Can you get on to Control and tell them that the body in the church is not that of Janice Martin, it is an unknown at the moment?"

Terry said he would do that right away. Harry walked back to room seven and hoped that Del woke up soon. As it happened it was around twenty minutes after he re-joined them in the room.

Janice was still whispering to him when he shouted. "Janice, no!" and woke up. He sat bolt upright but his eyes were still all over the place.

"It's okay babe, lay back down."

Del did lie back down and shut his eyes again, but not for long. He opened them again and turned to his left; he was looking straight into the eyes of his wife. She smiled at him and kissed him. Del looked around the room to check if he was still alive or dreaming.

"But, how? I mean, erm, you're here, how? You died."

She kissed him again. "I never died, babe, I'm here with you." Del slung his arm over her and hugged her. He held her so tight.

"I thought I had lost you, it was awful. I didn't know what to do." He was light headed but he wasn't sure now if it was the drugs or the feeling of being with his Janice again.

"Why did you think it was me?"

At last, thought Harry, who was in the corner quietly trying to merge into the paintwork. *At last a question I want to hear the answer to.*

"I had a call at work from the killer, he said he was going to kill you. I rushed home and searched our house and you were not in."

Janice interrupted him.

"But I was out with Sue, you knew that, I told you." Del shook his head.

"I didn't remember that but then there was a note on the door saying you were at the church we got married in." Janice looked sideways.

"Babe, how the hell would the killer know where we got married?"

Del cleared his throat. "I know it's odd but I have been through all this before, the Butcher knew everything and that case was a fucking nightmare."

Harry piped up then. "I think this killer is playing on your hang-ups about the first killings."

Del looked over and saw Harry. "I don't know but there was a woman nailed to a cross in the church; she was naked and looked your build, honey. She also had a pig's mask attached to her." Del then explained about the elaborate trap to make sure he witnessed the death.

Harry spoke again.

"That was a fucking nasty way to go!"

"Yes and at the time I thought it was Janice up there and I went to pieces, I was trying to stop it all but couldn't, I was helpless." He started to breathe heavily and panic rose in his voice. Janice calmed him down by stroking his arm. Harry stood up.

"Look, lover birds, I'm going home to bed. I suggest if you are able you do the same. Night night." Harry left the room and went home.

CHAPTER 20

Back To Work

It took a remarkably short time for Del to recover enough to come back to work. It was in fact the next morning. He turned up a little later than usual with his head still the colour of a rainbow and the cut still looking menacingly raw.

"Fuck me Del, are you sure you should be here?"

"Yes I should, unless of course I do have to fuck you and if that is the case I'm going home!"

Harry stood up and shook Del's hand.

"It's good to see you up and about mate, any plan for today?"

Del sat down with a thud and the wheeled chair skidded backwards about a foot. "Yes, my first action of the day is to get you to make me a fucking drink." Del grinned and Harry stood up.

"Okay I will, but you need to tell me first how you did that to your head, your explanation yesterday never mentioned anything about getting a whack on the noggin."

Del put his hand up to his multi-coloured bruised head; he snorted with suppressed laughter and was treated to a sharp pain in his head.

"Well this was a diabolical part of the Graffiti Killer's plan. He knew I was going to be in a hurry and bash my head on my own bloody car's roof!"

Harry laughed. "What a devious bastard." He continued to laugh as he walked out of the conference room to fetch a couple of drinks. Del felt his head again and winced as he came into contact with a raised stitch that sent a wave of pain through his skull. Truth be told he was still feeling a little bit woozy and a little sick too, but he was not going to take time off to recuperate. Using the words he said to Janice when she suggested it, "No fucking way, I'm going to catch this bastard. After all, that could have been you up there on that cross," and he was determined to track him down and stop this barbarism. His mind kept flashing back every so often with the image of the poor woman's limbs being sliced through with that wire. They flew off so quickly as the weight of the statue crashed down. He thought for a second as to what it reminded him of, it was like a cheesemaker cutting his product with his wire cutter.

"I think our Butcher seems to be getting his careers mixed up," he said out loud and chuckled to himself, then instantly regretted it. His head did not like the idea of laughter at the moment. Harry came back into the room carrying two mugs of coffee.

"Here you go, Your Majesty." He put Del's drink next to him and then sat down too.

"Okay, before you fill me in on what you were doing do you want to hear what I found out about Bos yesterday?" Del was obviously very keen to hear anything and everything he could. "Well to start with, Bos, well, Ben I should say, was a very lucky boy. The house he lived in was out of this world, it was a true country manor house." Harry went on to describe the drive and the trees and then the house itself.

"So how come it wasn't left to Bos when his parents died in the accident?" asked Del.

Harry told him about the arrangement with Ben's parents' employers.

"Jesus, they paid for them to live there? Must have been worth it for the bank, real high flyers then."

"I have contacted the bank and they are going to send me details about the arrangement back then to my email address."

Del nodded appreciatively. "Anything else?"

Harry took out his note book and looked at it. "Yes, actually, the lady that is staying there at the moment showed me the tree that the Oscars' car crashed into. It had letters carved into it!"

Del asked Harry to write them on the Bos white board. Harry walked over and wrote 'PLACAR'.

"This was written but the further right, the more faded the letter. I could only just make out the A and R and the lady originally thought it just said PLAC."

Del looked and pondered at that for a second or two.

"Another thing, I walked around the grounds after I had spoken to Sabrina and I couldn't put my finger on it but the trees were odd, particularly one of them in the back of the grounds."

Del asked him to try to explain.

"It was just a strange-looking tree like the others but the area was in the middle of nowhere and was worn away as if it was used for something regularly. The soil was a different colour to the rest too. Oh and one branch was smooth when none of the others were. As I said, it just seemed strange when I was there." Del was intrigued; his head hurt but he could feel more than pain niggling him at the moment. He had a feeling he was missing something with what Harry had just told him.

"Have you an email from this bank yet?"

Harry said he had checked first thing and nothing had come through yet. Del sat staring at the board.

"PLACAR." It didn't make sense! He gave up thinking of that for a bit.

"While you were touring some posh and fancy house I was trying to track down the movements of our second victim."

"And?" said Harry.

"I visited the car park we pinpointed on the map and after an encounter with the indigenous wildlife I tracked down some CCTV footage of our man."

"What did you see then? Did you see the killer?" Harry was sat forward in his chair waiting for the critical piece of information.

"No, I didn't see the killer but I did see him walk across the car park still on the phone. He walked across and got into a car that was waiting for him. As soon as he entered the car it sped off." It wasn't the news Harry was hoping for.

"What was the index of the car?" This answer was a little disappointing too.

"I don't know but it was a black car."

Harry sat back in his seat and said, "Oh."

Del was a little disappointed himself on hearing the information said out loud, he was pleased with yesterday, but hearing it again in the cold light of a new day, it seemed a bit meagre. Del looked around. "Did you tidy up when you came in?"

Harry acknowledged the fact and said, "I had to, it was a right mess, papers and shit everywhere."

"Where did you put everything?"

Harry opened a drawer and held the disc up in the air. "Oh, thank you very much for picking up my fucking mess, Harry! No, don't mention it Del, that's fine." Harry was smiling and waving the disc about.

"Yes, okay funny guts, I happen to have been in a hurry to try and save my wife, I realise now I should have said fuck her and tidied my desk first." He grabbed the disc from Harry. "Twat," he said and put it in the computer. Del found the right program to use and started to play the footage. He turned the computer monitor so Harry could see it too. It was a split-screen view of both of the cameras from the car park. It was blank to start with, just a couple of cars parked.

"Those cars belong to some of the residents," said Del, waiting for Mr Slugget to appear. Before his arrival the black car pulled up under the arch. Del pointed to it "There, that is the car he will get into."

Harry looked closer. "Can we zoom in on it as it pulls in, just to try and see if we can pick up a partial index?"

Del pressed a couple of buttons on the control panel from the on-screen menu. The image rewound slowly and he paused it just as the car came into view. He tried to zoom the image in; it went in but the further in it went the less helpful it became. The best view was only slightly closer than the original view. They couldn't make out the index at all, however Del looked in and he noticed something.

"This is one of those number plates that are in two rows, not in one line." He then pressed play again and they watched. A minute later in real time Tony came into view on his phone. He walked across the car park as Del said and got into the car. Just as Del said, as soon as his arse must have hit the fabric the car sped off.

"So what have we learnt from that?" said Harry. Del looked at him.

"Not a fucking lot it seems, the possible killer has a black car with a square-set number plate. It is also a case that the Graffiti Killer is very aware of his surroundings and surprisingly doesn't want to be caught!"

Both men sat and thought about the facts they had picked up separately. Del stood and walked over to the boards and started to update them. As he was doing this a thought slapped him across the face; he turned to Harry.

"Explain to me again the tree you saw in Oakwood manor."

"It was a very strange-looking tree, the ground around it was compacted as if people were around it a lot and the soil around it was a different colour to the other soil."

Del asked him what colour and Harry told him it was a reddish brown.

"And what else did you say about it?"

Harry thought. "Yes, it had a branch sticking out that was smooth, why?"

Del couldn't believe it. "Hang on," he said, and went into his drawer and looked around the files he had put in there. He riffled through them until he found the one he was after. He then looked through that and picked out a picture.

"Look at this, does this look a little bit like the branch you saw?" Del passed the picture to Harry who looked closely.

"It is possible, yes, but the tree I saw was a lot more smooth than this."

Del took the picture and froze again. He turned and looked back at the white board, at where Harry had written 'PLACAR' in blue pen. Del walked over and picked up a red pen and wrote an 'I' after 'PLACAR'.

"What does that say then?" asked Harry.

"This is mad but the tree branch I have just shown you was one that was used by the original Butcher. Bos strung someone up by that, it was smoothed by the friction of the rope being pulled and hoisting up a body on it." Del then pointed to the word he had completed. "I was told a while ago that 'placari' was

Latin for 'appease'. Bos told me that and it was used by the Butcher in a phrase 'placari arbares', which he told me meant 'appease the trees'." Harry sat stunned by what had just fallen into place.

"Are you saying Bos was a killer at a very young age and was using the tree in Oakwood Manor to practice his, for want of a better word, craft?" Del was shocked at the connection too.

"I don't know what I'm saying yet but there is no way this can just be coincidence, we now have a link between the Butcher killings and Bos's past, now we just need the link to the Graffiti Killer and we can nab him."

Del went and sat down to try and make more sense of the information he had just connected.

"Have you got that email from the bank yet?"

Harry started tapping on the computer to check. As he did, Del's phone rang.

"Hello, Inspector Martin." Del went white as he heard the voice on the other end, it was the mechanical voice again.

"Hello Del, nice to visit church occasionally." Del was shocked but thought quickly enough to put the phone on loud speaker so Harry could hear too.

"We should all go to church to repent our sins. I now think you understand a little of the pain Bos suffered, only a little though because Janice as you know now is still with us. Bos was not so lucky. You failed my star, you killed him. His career and life ended with the Butcher investigation, so will yours. Catch me before I get you." Then the phone went dead. Del looked at Harry.

"That was the voice that phoned and hinted to me that Janice was in trouble." Harry was stunned, it was direct contact from the Graffiti Killer and very personal too.

"Del, that is a specific threat, you need to pass that to the Chief."

"No fucking way, he will pull me from it and that ain't happening, not after what this fucker did to Janice." Harry looked on sympathetically.

"But Del, he didn't actually do anything to Janice!"

Del's head was throbbing and he didn't know if it was due to the injury from yesterday or the adrenalin from the call. "Yes, but he could quite easily have, he was in my fucking house." Harry could at least understand Del's approach. At least if he was on the case he felt like he was doing something; if it was with someone else he would be kicking his heels just waiting.

"Okay, what do you think that was about?"

Del thought for a while. "Not sure, but they are obviously motivated by the death of Bos, he called him his 'star'." Harry nodded.

"Okay then, what's next?"

Del answered short and swift. "For a start tell me if that fucking bank email is in!" Harry remembered and tapped a few more keys on the computer.

"Del, is it in?"

Del hit the table. "Yes! Print the bugger."

The attachment was opened and sent to the printer.

"I have sent it to the printer, perhaps you'll want to get it as it comes out."

Del said, "Hell yes," and headed straight out of the door. As Del went to collect it Harry looked at the attachment on the screen. It was just one A4 sheet and it was headlined notes on Oakwood Manor renting. The email said:

Dear Sgt Gorham,

Here is as much information about Oakwood Manor as I can find. I hope you find it useful.

Kindest regards

Charlie Edwards.

Del was not gone for long and came rushing back in after a minute or so.

"Right, let's have a look at this shall we?"

It said that the owner of the property was a Lady Belina Wellingborough and by all accounts she was a well-known eccentric. She wanted the bank to pay moneys every month for the upkeep and for that she would let them put a high-flying employee in the house. This was not all; she insisted on being in the house at the same time, but would be there as the maid or nanny or cook or some kind of service personnel. This arrangement had gone on for around fifty years and still continues to this day. The estate belongs to Lady Wellingborough and it is quite an estate. The sheet went through the size and contents of the estate. The manor house was not the only property, others were rented out privately. The land owned by her was huge too, it was not only the manor and its grounds. Lady Wellingborough's land consisted of many other sizable plots too. It said that Lady Belina was a widower; her husband was found hung in the garden after a few years of marriage. She has one heir to the title and that is her daughter Suzie-Anne Wellingborough.

"Del, when I was at the manor the resident there said she has a worker that is off at the moment visiting a sick relative, that must have been this Belina visiting her daughter or Suzie visiting her mum."

Del shook his head. "Why the hell would you rent your huge home out and then work there for the people living in it!" It was something that neither Del nor Harry could quite understand. Del stood up. "We're going to church."

"Need to repent, do you?" Del was quite quick with the reply to this.

"No I fucking don't but I do want to have a look at the place with a clear head rather than a panicked one."

CHAPTER 21

Back To Church

They parked up near the church and walked towards it – it was a very busy site. There was barrier tape around the entire grounds and a PC guarding the entry at the front and one at the rear. A CSI van was near the front and unfortunately there were a few reporters hanging around trying to get information. As Del came closer he went direct to the PC at the front.

"Hi Marvin, I need a bit of a change here. Can you get the cordon extended? I don't want the press nosing in and getting wind of anything we don't want them to know in there." The PC agreed.

"Definitely boss, they have been getting right on my tits anyway." It always made Del cringe when anyone called him boss, it brought back sharp and painful memories of the times he had with Bos. It was, however, something that he knew he could not remove, he was an inspector so automatically in some cases would be called it.

"Excellent. If you can set that up ASAP it would be good. Who have we got inside at the moment?"

PC Marvin Dumont said he would do it right away and that there were three CSI staff and the Chief Inspector walking about at the moment.

"Oh shit, I didn't know he was here." Del signed the scene log and ducked under the tape. The Chief was standing in the middle of the church, not moving, just looking around. He saw Del and instantly headed directly towards him. Chief Inspector Charleston was an excellent boss. He would back his men to the hilt but was brutal with his approach at times.

"Del, what the fuck went on here? I have been told you broke down in pieces here. Are you burnt out and fucked, or not?" Del laughed on the inside and thought that it was typical Charleston.

"No, gov, I'm fine."

Charleston looked at his head. "You don't fucking look fine, fine people don't have a bloody rainbow on their head, fine people don't get carted away in an ambulance, fine people don't have to be sedated because of a crime scene. I was told you went cuckoo because you thought these body parts belonged to your wife. Is that the case? And do you want to enlighten me as to why you fucking thought that? I need to know I have someone I can trust investigating this, I'm not going to go through another fucking Bos fiasco!" The chief stood there in front of Del, stationary, waiting for a response to his onslaught. Del took a deep breath.

"First things first, the rainbow on my head is purely because I banged my bloody head getting into my car, so clumsy doesn't represent cuckoo." He breathed again. "I was brought here as part of the investigation and thought it was my wife because of the simple fact that she fucking looked like her. Lastly, I didn't go cuckoo, I was taken away in an ambulance and sedated because I had spent a lot of energy trying to free this woman." He pointed to the torso that was limbless. "Well, what was a woman! And having lost a lot of blood due to my injury." And he then pointed to his head. "So I can categorically ease your concerns that I'm fit for duty and that I'm not a serial killer myself and will catch this fucker."

The chief hadn't moved a muscle while Del had spoken but once finished he leant towards him. "That better be the case, Del." He then turned to Harry. "Watch him and watch yourself, your career is entwined in this too!" He said nothing else, he just walked out of the church with huge meaningful strides. Del watched him go.

"Now that is classic Charleston. Don't you just love him?" He looked at Harry's face which looked rather shocked. "Don't worry, he's always like that. If you need help he is there for you but he calls a spade a spade." Del grinned and then added, "But obviously if you fuck him about he will bring that spade down hard across your head and bury you with it!"

Harry said that he hadn't really had many dealings with him and that after the verbal blast he had just heard he was sure he didn't want any.

"He is actually a good bloke and an excellent governor." Once that little bit of Del bullshitting was done he looked around the church with a fresh pair of eyes.

He could see the statue that had been demolished in the fall. He hadn't really taken in the size of it before but looking at it now it was no surprise that the poor woman was ripped apart by it. He could see the body parts that were scattered in various places behind the metal section that was actually open now. He followed the line of cable that ran in the other direction and then walked along it. Eventually he found it attached to the large water tank with the holes in that let out the water. He looked across the edge of the building and he could then see the corks that were originally keeping the water in the tank. He walked to the victim; she was the build of Janice as far as he could tell, although it was difficult to tell with the state she was in now. The torso had been strapped to the cross and her arms and legs had been nailed to it but the pressure of the pull of the wire had stripped them from the wood. He explained to Harry the process that the trap, for a want of a better word, had taken.

"That is hugely technical!"

Del nodded. "Yes, and the weight of that statue would be huge. I know it was already in situ but it would have still taken quite some effort to move to the brink of falling like it was." He looked seriously at Harry. "I think we're after more than one person, you know!" Del walked over to Buddy who was taking pictures of one of the arms. "Bud, do we know who she is?"

Buddy put his camera back around his neck.

"Unfortunately for her, yes we do. We also know who the other victim is!"

Del was stunned. "What do you mean other victim?"

Bud tilted his head slightly. "The male. Didn't you know about the male in the back room?" Bud pointed to a door at the other end of the church, the end that the water tank had been.

"I hadn't gone in there. Who are they then?"

Bud said for them to follow him and he walked to the front door. There was a notice board and on it there were pictures of people. They were all of people who were important to the church. Bud pointed to the male at the top. "That is Reverend Henry Bernard, he is the vicar and he is the body in the back room. The lady strewn across the place is Deborah Jinks, the warden."

"Fuck, how can you tell?"

Bud looked back to the horror show. "Well it's sick but I could tell by looking at her head, it had a pig mask on at the start but when that was removed you could tell it was Ms Jinks."

Del asked Bud to show them into the back room.

"Okay, but it ain't pretty." Bud walked over to the back door and lifted the old black latch. He pushed the door which creaked open. The room was very wet as the tank had leaked down through the ceiling all over the place. There was blood everywhere and it looked like an absolute massacre, but the water had mixed with the blood to make the place look a lot bloodier than it was. There was a table in the room and it had a head on a plate – it was the vicar's and it was not surprising to see but he didn't look happy. The expression on the decapitated head's face looked horrified. On the floor to the left was the body and it looked a mess, it had most of its limbs but his insides were hanging out. There were other plates on the table and none of them were empty. As Del looked he could see a heart on one, on another was a slab of meat rolled and tied into a joint.

"What the fuck is that?" Del pointed to the plate with the joint on.

"I believe that is from the reverend." Bud rolled him slightly and showed Del the absence of his backside. It was a nightmare of a table, on another plate was the vicar's liver and then Del saw the last one. He looked sideways with suspicion.

"And what the fuck is that!?"

Buddy nodded. "Unfortunately your suspicions are correct; they are sweetbreads." Del shuddered in disgust. That is not all, Del, look." Bud stepped over the poor vicar's shell of a body towards the table. He placed his gloved hand on top of the head on the plate. He took hold of the hair and lifted him up a few inches. He opened his jaw and showed Del the piece of paper inside the mouth.

"Are you ready to take that out yet?" Del was desperate to see what was written on this note.

"I will go and ask Steve if he has done all the initial in situ photos." Bud disappeared out of the room. Harry was looking around.

"This is a bit of a step up in gruesome, isn't it?"

"Yes and I notice there is no writing on this body but there was on the one I witnessed in the main church." Del was looking at the vicar's body on the floor and was wondering how he was actually killed. He didn't know why any of the Graffiti Killer's victims were picked. The only reason he could think of with this one was they were in the church that was important to him. Bud came back in.

"Right, I'm told by Steve that he's taken all the initial pics, so if you are urgently wanting to see what is in that note I will do it now, but you will need a little patience because I need to do this right."

Del held his hands up. "You do exactly what you need to do and we'll wait in the main part of the church." Del and Harry walked back out into the main building. It took a little while and Del had been walking about outside the cordon area as Bud came out to him.

"I have bagged and tagged the note. Have a look at the message." Bud clicked about with his camera. He then turned it in his direction and showed him the screen. The three heads were close together trying to read the writing.

I told you I'm the Real Butcher, you doubted me but how did it taste? Being wrong. Sit down for tea with the vicar. Enjoy. The warden was so cut up she missed it.

*

Del stood up straight.

"Thanks Bud, as soon as you get the report can you send it on please?"

Bud said he would and also told him that the report on the travel agents had been sent to him. They walked back to the car and Del was deep in thought. He didn't say a word until halfway back to the station.

"I'm definitely of the mind that we have more than one person now. The amount of work it took to do that and the complete contrast to the two deaths says to me two minds and a joint effort." Harry agreed but didn't like to, as it made it much more dangerous with at least two killers.

*

They arrived at the station and Del rushed up to get to the report on the third victim. He went direct to the conference room and sat down. He saw the A4 envelope on his desk and ripped it open to find out what Bud and the CSI department had found. He waited for Harry to sit and then pulled out the papers. At the top of the page it had the victim's name, Natalia HORINSKI. Del pulled out the photographs and looked over them, it wasn't a pleasant sight and the worst part of all the photos was the mutilation to the leg. She was a nice-looking girl by all accounts but she definitely didn't look her best at these angles. It was disturbing to look at but a thought flickered into his mind.

"Harry, what does a butcher do?"

Harry shrugged and said, "Kill animals don't they?"

Del shook his head. "Well no, not usually, that is usually done at the abattoir. What does the butcher do?"

Harry sat for a few seconds and thought.

"They cut the carcasses up and sell them."

"Yes, right, but why? What are they selling them for?"

Harry was a bit confused. "They sell the meat to make money, what are you going on about?"

Del put the photo on the desk in front of Harry.

"Look at the flesh that has been removed; the second victim had his rump removed, and the vicar we have just seen had parts of his body put on plates, so why does a butcher sell meat?"

Harry then looked up, stunned. "For people to eat!" he said slowly.

"I have a feeling that to prove he, or they, are the real Butcher they are killing people and eating them." Del paused and picked up the picture to look again. "I think we could have a fucking cannibal around."

Del continued to look through the report. Just as the others Natalia had been drinking heavily too. It said she had been killed by the cut to the neck with loss of blood. It was noted that it was likely that the leg flesh had started to be removed before death had occurred. Death was timed as approximately 02:00-03:00. There was no sign of recent sexual activity. No CCTV in the premises but there was a set of fingerprints found on the white board and they matched the ones that were found on the tank. These prints did not receive a hit on the police national computer. It confirmed Del's theory that she had been cut while upside down but significant bleeding from the leg suggested the possible amputation started while blood was still pumping (at least briefly). Del picked up the photo he was after, it was of the note that was wedged in this victim's mouth.

Bos had a pattern I do not, the Real Butcher will take anyone. This one was so sweet she had to go on the board.

"I hate these double fucking meanings," said Del as he passed the photo to Harry. "Does he mean sweet as in a nice girl or sweet as in nice to eat?"

There were now five victims and each one was getting more violent and the messages more bold. The first victim was killed and drawn on and the last one was totally dismantled and placed out ready for some Godawful banquet. Both men stood up and started adding as much detail as they could think of to the boards. All of the boards were getting full now, including the one that had the info on Bos and Ben. Once the new information had been added there was string, pictures and notes everywhere. Some parts had been underlined in red as key facts or suppositions. It had been a gruelling day and quite a bloody one.

CHAPTER 22

Home Cooked Meal

Del entered his home and it smelt gorgeous. The smells from the kitchen flowed through the entire house.

"Evening babe!" shouted Del from the front door. Janice came running up to him and flung her arms around him.

"I'm so glad you're home, I have a surprise for you." She told him to shut his eyes and when he did she removed his shoes for him and led him into the dining room. She guided him gently into a dining room chair and then said, "Surprise!" He opened his eyes and his stomach churned with nerves but his groin stirred in anticipation. The table was set for a posh meal including a large white table cloth, and Sue was standing on the other side of the table. She was leaning over and already showing off her breasts in a very low-cut top. She walked around the table towards Del and this was enough for movement in his underwear. *Oh fuck*, were the words that entered his head; in fact, as she slowly walked towards him those words were repeated again and again. Sue reached him and bent down towards him, as she did she smiled and then kissed him full on the lips as usual.

"Hi Del, I hear you had an awful time of it recently so Janice and I are treating you." She looked down at his manhood and smiled. "Ooh, for me?" she whispered and walked away, brushing her hand across his shoulders as she walked to the kitchen. He seemed to be holding his breath but eventually breathed out. Janice then came back over, she kissed him too.

"Sue has been so great, she's doing another meal for us." She stood up and went to the cupboard and poured some drinks for the three of them. Once he had his drink he downed most of it in one.

"Could I have a top up please babe?" He really didn't know how much of Sue's teasing he could take. He really did fancy her but he loved his wife so much and didn't want to do anything to hurt or upset her.

"You okay babe?" said Janice.

"Yes, yes I'm fine, just a bad day with work." She poured him a very large glass.

"Don't worry now babe, you're home and I'm with the two most important people in my life, I love you both." This did not make Del feel any better but he thought somehow it was meant to! Janice sat down opposite Del like last time.

"Is Sue cooking on her own in our kitchen then?"

"Yes babe, we have both been in there but now you are home I'm with you and she'll be out in a minute." She was too, she came out looking absolutely stunning. The skirt she had on was not short but it had an enormous split up one side. The split looked so long that Del was sure that one tug and it would come away, this thought did not do much for his blood supply either!

"Here you are, for starters we have a pâté with garlic bread." They all sat down, Sue rather close to Del again. Each plate looked lovely, there was a perfectly damped lettuce leaf with a one-hundred-or-so-gram portion of heart-shaped pâté in the centre. Around the edge were two pieces of crispy garlic bread, lightly toasted. It looked and smelt perfect.

"So you say you've had a bad day at work babe, what happened?" Janice said this and put a piece of garlic bread covered in pâté in her mouth. "Oooh, wow. Sue, this is gorgeous." Sue leant forward to Del, she put her hand on his.

"Oh honey, have you had a bad day? We shall have to try and relax you, won't we?" Del felt her foot rub up the side of his leg.

"Just work stuff, the Graffiti Killer has upped his game a bit, that's all."

As the conversation progressed Sue's foot travelled slowly further up Del's leg. All three polished off the starter. Sue leant into the middle of the table and with perfect sleight of hand placed her left hand on top of Del's crotch which had, to the relief of Del, reduced in swelling. However, a couple of strokes and squeezes from Sue it was soon brought to life again. "You two hang on in here and I will arrange the main course for us." She looked into Del's eye and pouted as she patted his now erect manhood.

"Did you enjoy your pâté, Del?" Del was again frozen in her charismatic headlights.

"Erm, yes, it was lovely thank you." She winked at him.

"Yes, nothing like a nice piece of meat in your mouth," and she gripped hard around his penis as she said it. Sue then stood up fast, collected the three plates and walked back into the kitchen. Janice could obviously see the panic in his face but took it as another meaning all together.

"Was it really that bad in the church then?"

Del, strangely happy to get the conversation back to dead bodies rather than thinking of other stiffs, said, "Yes, it was quite nasty actually," and repeated the setup in the back room. When Sue arrived back in the room she had another three plates in her hands and on her arm. She placed these on the table and again sidled up to Del. He was amazed that his wife was okay with the behaviour but she was smiling on intently. It was a roast dinner with all the trimmings and looked amazing.

"Tuck in," she said. "Dessert is quite light tonight, it's a bed of chocolate sauce with melon balls." Was it just Del or did she emphasise the words 'bed' and 'balls'? The food was actually delicious.

"Del was just telling me more about the killer he's been looking for, he thinks there is more than one of them now."

Sue looked at him. "That's awful. That means you really do have your hands full." Her hand was under the table again, cupping him. His manhood was up and down so often it was like being in a gym, one moment fit to burst the next curled wanting a rest. Whatever state it was in now it was extremely uncomfortable in there. He waded through the roast dinner and sat back.

"That was lovely, Sue." She smiled and leant forward again. Through the whole course she had been running her foot up and down his leg but now she leant in again.

"I'm glad you liked it, it was especially for you." Again the hand on him under the table. She collected the plates.

"I will be back right away as the desserts are ready." She was right as well; she was gone less than a minute and re-entered with another three plates. These looked professionally done too, there was a covering of chocolate sauce and on this was scattered chocolate shavings. In the middle was a pyramid of melon balls. It seemed a bit of an odd match but it was very good. All three plates were polished off quickly. And Sue took the plates away again. As she had gone Janice stood up and came over to Del.

"I'm just going to the little girls' room, babe." She then walked away. She looked lovely again tonight and he watched her walk off. Sue then came back in with three large glasses of alcohol – it looked like brandy. She sat down and placed the glasses on the table.

"Where's Janice, big boy?" Del felt hot again.

"She's just gone to the toilet." He then added quickly, "She won't be long." She smiled at that.

"I see my melon balls went down well."

Del was very flustered. It was odd because he had

never been affected like this before; she had such a pull on him. Del could hear Janice coming out of the toilet. As her footsteps hit the top of the stairs Sue took a napkin from the table and dropped it. She immediately went to ground to pick it up. It happened very quickly and as she disappeared her chair was pulled in. Del froze as he felt her hand on the inside of his thighs. He slammed his hands on the table and Janice walked in. She walked to her seat and sat down as the hand under the table travelled from his thighs up to his groin and unzipped his trousers. He was in a total state of panic but couldn't move. Sue under the table released him from his underwear and went to work with her hands.

"Where's Sue, babe?" Janice asked.

Sue grabbed hold of his testicles with her nails. Del tried to keep his voice normal.

"She popped out for a minute." This seemed to calm her and she picked up the glass from the table. Del was in the middle of hugely contrasting emotions, he was scared to death that his wife would find out what was going on and blame him. He was frightened of the threat to his testicles by the sharp nails, but was also feeling huge pleasure at the hands and mouth of Sue. He was trying to converse with Janice but he was finding it extremely difficult. Fortunately for him because Sue was very good at what she was doing and with the fact he had been sexually on edge all night, it didn't take long before he reached his climax. Sue tucked him back away and patted him again. Then nothing, she didn't come out but then again how could she? Del coughed to clear his throat.

"Babe, are going to look in the back to see if Sue is

okay?" Janice stood up.

"Yes, that's a good idea, she has been gone a little while now."

As Janice left the room Sue re-emerged. She rose above the table smiling and wiping her mouth. She winked and walked to the front door. She opened it quietly and then shut it loudly. As she re-entered the dining room so did Janice.

"Are you okay Sue? I went in the back to find you as you had been gone a while." Sue nodded at Janice.

"I'm fine now thanks, honey, I just felt a bit dickey for a while there." She looked directly at Del, she then said, "Are you okay Del? You look a bit flushed, perhaps you should have come outside!"

Del was just jelly on the seat now, he was totally under her control. All he was thinking was, *She could shop me at any moment to Janice and that would be it.* The rest of the night dragged past eternally for Del, wincing at the comments from Sue with things like, 'things must have been hard for you recently Del', 'in his job oral communication is the key', 'you just have to suck it up', comments about alcohol and 'drinking him under the table', and a myriad of other sentences passed that Sue winked at but Janice was blissfully unaware of and treated as normal conversation. It did eventually draw to a close and Sue was at the door ready to leave. She leant in, grabbed him by the crotch and kissed him again full on the lips, right in front of Janice this time.

"We must do this again sometime," she said. Del umphed a reply and Janice laughed, actually laughed! Sue went to Janice and kissed her full on the lips too, in fact Del was sure he saw her grab Janice by the arse too.

"See you later gorgeous." And she left. The door shut and Del was speechless, Janice was smiling.

"What the hell just happened?"

Janice looked at him in complete confusion. "What?"

Del's eyebrows couldn't have got any closer to the top of his head without disappearing amongst his hairline.

"She grabbed me by the, well, you saw, and then grabbed your arse too."

Janice chuckled. "Oh, come on babe, she's just like that. She is very flirtatious and very tactile too."

Del just 'but, but, butted' for a second and then gave up.

"It's nothing, she's stroked my breast before." Del couldn't believe what he was hearing.

"What?"

"Yes, it was quite nice actually, a very feminine gentle touch." Del stared at his wife, not knowing what to say or do. "I don't know, she's just very good at making you feel comfortable with whatever she does."

He sat down in the living room with his head spinning, not only from the alcohol he had consumed and not only from the oral sex he had just been treated to but due to the revelation that his wife was being groped by another woman and was quite happy about it. Janice came over and sat on his lap. She kissed him and then she grabbed him too.

"Is that better babe?" She kissed him hard and leant him back in the chair. It wasn't long before they were upstairs and Del was climaxing again. He went to sleep that night thinking about a very odd day.

CHAPTER 23

Penny

The next morning the situation was still no clearer in his head. But he did get up and ready for work with a smile on his face. He did have a plan of action today. He headed off for the station in good spirits. Harry was in already as Del turned up.

"Morning Del."

Del said good morning and sat down at the desk in the conference room. He looked over at the board in the fresh cold light of day.

"We need to speak to Natalia's partner, see if she knows anything. I'm going to do that, I want you to look at the crime records for the area of Oakwood Manor, I think that is a central point for this situation."

Harry agreed.

"I don't only mean known murders either, I'm talking about anything suspicious." Harry said he would give it a go. Del added, "I think it's very fucking odd that someone of that stature, breeding and money would rent out their house and then work in it as domestic staff." Thinking of it like that Harry could see the strangeness of the situation, it had seemed okay when the bank spoke about it, as if it was a totally ordinary thing to do. But this Lady Belina was either a bit tapped, on the make somehow, broke or some kind of workaholic eccentric. But could she be a murderer! Harry wasn't sure about that one. Del looked through the paperwork and found the address of Natalia and her partner. Her partner was called Penny and they had lived together at 15 Lancaster Gardens.

"Okay then, I'll catch up with you later." And he walked out. It was early and Del hadn't got it in his mind to go straight to Natalia and Penny's house. He was going to go to the café for a hearty breakfast.

"On your own today, Del? What's the matter, Harry pissed off with you?" Brian was behind the counter as usual with seemingly the same dirty apron on.

"Ha, no, I left him working at the nick, I just wanted to grab some food before I got started." Brian asked if he wanted the same as usual and Del said yes. Five minutes later Brian shoved a plate full of food in front of him.

"You any closer to catching this killer then, Del? People are starting to get worried. It's not you, is it? I would hate to lose another customer because they went around killing people."

Del picked up his fork. "Listen to me, Brian, some may say that if I wanted to kill people I could just as easy bring them in here with me rather than string them up! But you know me, I would never be so rude!" Brian chuckled away as he walked back to his station behind the counter. Del was quite hungry this morning, which was surprising considering the meal he had last night. He waded through the breakfast in front of him and at last sat back and exhaled and put his hand on his belly.

"You outdid yourself this morning, Brian, that was perfect." He then sank the rest of his coffee and slammed the cup on the table. Del stood up and went to the counter.

"Go on then Brian, how much was it?"

"Well the full breakfast is usually £5.50 but as it's you, that will be £5.50 please." Del smiled and put the money on the counter.

"What, £5.50, no tip!"

Del walked away towards the door. "I'll give you a tip – food goes on the plates, not on your apron. See you later." Del opened the door to the usual ping of the bell and made his way to the car.

The time was now 09:47 so he headed off to Lancaster Gardens. He pulled up to the house and walked up to the door. It was a tidy place but nothing wonderful; it did have a plain white door which he stepped towards and rang the bell. A minute later a female answered the door, she didn't look how Del was expecting. She looked perfectly fine.

"Hello, how can I help you?"

Del was thrown for a second.

"I'm Inspector Martin. Can I come in and talk to you for a couple of minutes please?" Penny opened the door for him.

"I take it this is about Natalia?"

Del told her that it was.

"I'm surprised it's taken you this long to come and see me, I was questioned for a brief time in hospital but did expect more." They walked into the living room and sat down. It was a contemporary place that was decorated in black and white and very crisp lines.

"Okay, first off I'm sorry for your loss but do you know anyone that would have wanted to hurt Natalia?"

Penny snorted. "What, apart from me you mean!" This shocked Del more than anything else.

"Pardon? What do you mean by that?"

Penny explained that they had been together for about six years and Natalia had gone and had about three affairs. "I knew and I had forgiven her for them but I also suspected she was about to do it again."

"Why? What made you think that?"

Penny sat back and crossed her legs.

"I heard her talking and arranging to meet someone; the speech was very sexual so I let her go. She didn't know I knew but I was going to leave her because of it." Del was feeling a little suspicious.

"Okay, I can see that would upset you enough to break up and want to go your separate ways, however you were distraught and had to go to hospital when she was discovered." Penny frowned at Del.

"Are you serious? I was with her for six years and had just found her sliced up for fuck's sake. I was fed up with her infidelity, not psychotic. Of course I was upset, imagine you had just found your partner cut up. How would you feel?" Penny had gone red in the face and was quite obviously angry. Del could see why and was thinking about his emotions while seeing what he thought was Janice being killed.

"I'm sorry, that was particularly insensitive of me." Penny calmed a little and Del asked her something else.

"Do you know who she was meeting?"

She shook her head. "No, unfortunately I don't, I just heard her talking about meeting, I didn't even confront her with it. Not even when she called up that evening and said she was staying at the shop because she had drunk too much to drive."

Del thought carefully about how to ask the next question but it was a difficult one and no other way but straight out with it would do.

"I'm sorry but I have another very personal question to ask but it is important."

Penny said that it was fine.

"I know you were in a gay relationship but was Natalia gay or bisexual?" Penny smiled at this, thank goodness.

"The only way I can answer that is this: she told me she had boyfriends when younger and did have straight sex with them but once she turned a certain age she realised those were not right and from then on all her future partners, sexual or otherwise, were female. So with that in mind I can only assume that the person she was meeting was a woman, however, she lied to me about the affairs so why not about other things?"

Del thanked her for her candid honesty. "Can you think of anything from your overheard conversation that may be of use to us, anything?"

Penny sat thinking, trying to relive the overheard phone call.

"I'm sorry Inspector, I don't think there was anything. Oh, she called the person 'honey' but that was about it really, sorry."

Del told her that it was fine and any information was a help. "Did you hang out in a usual bar or restaurant? Natalia had been drinking quite heavily the night she was killed."

Penny had welled up now but wiped her eyes and said that sometimes they went to the Pink Pussycat on West Street, it was a busy and vibrant gay nightclub. He handed her his card.

"If you can think of anything else that may be of use please call me and let me know, thank you for your time." He stood up and Penny showed him to the door.

"I will let you know if I think of anything."

Del left the place a little knotted; he had the feeling that Penny had not been through all her emotions with this situation yet. He got in the car and sat still for a little while. *Perhaps we do have a female killer and perhaps we have a couple.* He thought a little more. The victims were all naked but there had been no sexual activity at all. *What if the reason is they are having sex together and find the killing a turn-on? There would not be any sexual activity with the victims then.*

Del started the car and headed back to the station.

*

Del pulled up at the station and headed with purpose to the conference room. He wasn't surprised to see that Harry was not in. He sat and picked up the phone. It wasn't a full number that was dialled, it was internal. A few rings in and it was answered.

"Hello, this is Inspector Martin, is it possible to have a word with Buddy please?"

He was told that Bud was not in at the moment but the male on the other end asked if he could help.

"I hope so, I'm calling about all the sites relating to the Graffiti Killer."

He said he knew a lot about them as he had attended some of them too.

"Excellent, I'm after a question answering. Was there any trace of any sexual activity at the scene and was it searched for?"

He was told that the report should have said there was no sexual activity found with any of the victims. Del was expecting that answer.

"No, I don't mean relating to the victims. I'm hoping the scenes themselves were searched and swabbed."

The man stuttered at that one. "I, erm, I don't actually know about that, sir. I'll contact Bud and ask him though."

Del quickly jumped on that. "No, don't you do that, I'll call him on his mobile. Thank you for your assistance." If he knew Bud at all, and he thought he did, he would have done a very thorough job and the entire scene would have been searched high and low for any evidence no matter how small. He flicked through his little book that was in his pocket and pinpointed the number he was after. He laid it out on the desk and kept it open with his left hand; he held the phone in his right and punched in the number with the same hand.

"Ah, hello Bud, it's Del, can you talk for a moment?"

Bud said yes, he was still at the church but could step out for a bit. Del waited for a moment or two and then Bud spoke again.

"Okay Del, I'm out of the church, shoot." Del liked Bud; he was an amiable fellow and also bloody good at his job.

"Okay Bud, I think I already know the answer to this but need to check. I have just called your office and the bloke there didn't know if this was done or not."

"Okay, spit it out then."

"This is with regards to all of the crime scenes relating to the Graffiti Killer. Were they all checked for any sexual activity?" There was no gap or hesitation at all.

"Yes, and they are all clear."

Del paused.

"I don't only mean the victims, Bud."

Buddy actually laughed and then responded with a couple of muffled grunts.

"What the fuck was that, Bud?" He laughed again.

"Oh, sorry Del, I couldn't speak properly for a

moment there, I seemed to be sucking on eggs for a bit, but I've taken them out now." Del sat back in his chair in the conference room and grinned. He really did like Buddy.

"Yes, okay funny guts, thank you for that. I just needed to check out a theory, a shit theory now but still."

"No problem Del, there was no trace of any type of sexual activity in or around the victims or the properties in which they were found."

Del thanked him for his time and hung up. He swung his legs away from the desk and looked at the boards again.

"Alright, so there was no sexual activity taking place, so that was not a part of the killer's overall plan." He stroked his chin and then immediately stopped; it was a habit that he had picked up from Bos and he was trying to stop it.

"That doesn't mean it was not at the forefront of the victim's minds." He stood up and left the station again.

CHAPTER 24

Police Records

Harry decided that he would visit the police around Oakwood Manor in person. He could then get hands-on with any record systems they may have. He left for the journey as soon as Del left for his enquiries. At least it was a better day. The sun was out instead of the horrible drizzle from his previous trip, he just hoped that his return this time would not be so dramatic. It was a largely uneventful drive but he did occasionally miss driving a marked car; people were not so quick to drive like idiots when there was a marked unit about.

He had set his satnav to take him to the regional headquarters building and as he stood outside it looked quite impressive. It was fairly new and was a pristine white, and the public entrance was in the centre of the building. The entrance was a large glass dome effect with revolving doors into a decent-sized reception area. It was not packed which was always a good sign, there were no people shouting or looking frustrated. That was not only good but a rarity as far as Harry's experience went. He walked up to the counter that was a sign of the times, behind Perspex with a microphone and speaker attached.

"Hello, how can I help you sir?"

Harry pulled out his warrant card and showed her. "I'm Sergeant Gorham, could I have a word with a duty Sergeant please?"

She smiled pleasantly at him and asked him to take a seat and she would try. She had only been gone a minute at the most before she returned. "Sergeant Gorham."

Harry walked over. "Hi. Just call me Harry." She smiled again.

"Thank you Harry, Sergeant Deex will be with you as soon as he can."

Harry thanked her and sat back down. It was actually ten minutes later before the door to the left opened and a uniformed Sergeant popped his head through the door.

"Sergeant Gorham?"

Harry stood up and walked over to the Sergeant.

"Hello, are you Sergeant Deex? I'm Sergeant Gorham, Harry." They shook hands.

"Nice to meet you Harry, I'm Gary. Come through."

Harry followed Gary through and around the loop of a corridor, then eventually into a quite sizable office with two desks with computers, phones, files and other stationary placed in various states of tidiness.

"Take a seat. Please excuse my colleague's mess but he has, in his defence, just run out to help with something. How can we help?" Harry did take a seat and the seat was surprisingly comfortable.

"Okay, firstly thanks for seeing me, I know how busy things get, so I will be as brief as I can and hope you can assist me."

Gary nodded. "Go for it."

"Right, last year we had a case that was titled 'The Butcher'. It was a case involving a serial killer."

Gary leant forward. "That was the inspector, wasn't it?" Harry was shocked but very impressed.

"Yes, I see you have a good memory and are aware of the news."

Gary grimaced. "Hard to be unaware of that story, may not have been here but hit us all, did that one." Harry knew exactly what he meant, it damaged the police's reputation hugely.

"Yes, I know what you mean. Okay, our inspector turned out to be the killer but we now have a similar case building up."

Gary asked about Bos. "But didn't he commit suicide?"

"Yes, and we have reasons to believe that the new killer is connected to Bos's past. Believe it or not he was an adopted boy and he spent part of his early life here at Oakwood Manor." Gary sat back and digested the info.

"Right at the eccentric Lady Bella's."

Harry asked immediately, "Bella? I thought she

was Belina."

"Yes, her title is that. Lady Belina Wellingborough, I believe, but she gets everyone to call her Bella and she works at her own house! Odd but as I said, eccentric."

Harry said that his parents died at the manor in a car crash. He was trying to find as many details about Bos as possible because they suspected he started his killing there. "To help with that I'm wanting to have access to your crime files and missing reports and well, basically anything and everything I can search so I can try and find something."

Gary furrowed his head for a while. "Wait here a minute." And he marched straight out. He was gone for around three minutes while the phones were ringing and PCs poked their heads around the corner after him. He walked back in.

"Okay Harry, I've just spoken with our inspector and he's fine with it. He said anything we can do to put more about that case in the open, the better for all the police services in the country." He walked out and gestured for Harry to follow. They walked back the same way they came and Gary collected a visitor badge and lanyard. "This will gain you access to a lot but not everywhere in here, certainly everywhere that you may need. As you will be aware please wear it at all times while in here, you can leave the building but please return it to Mandy here at the end of the day." Harry was stunned but extremely pleased with the welcome he was getting.

"Thank you so much, this is going to be an enormous help."

Gary walked away and again waved for him to follow. He walked a little way past the office he was in and then entered another room. It was empty apart from a desk and a computer.

"If you wait in here I'll get someone to help; as you know our systems require passwords that you won't have and will not be privy to but I have a PC on restricted duties who I'll put with you for the day."

Harry shook him by the hand and thanked him again.

"No problem, Harry. I hope you find something."

Harry sat down while Sergeant Deex walked away. It was about five minutes before another person walked through the door. It was a female PC with a plaster cast on her left leg. She was around five foot ten and average build; she walked directly over to Harry and shook his hand.

"Hi, I'm PC Latchford, I have been told to assist you with any enquiries and searches you want to make on our systems." She sat down at the computer and winced as she tried to move her leg under the table.

"Thank you, I'm Sergeant Gorham but please call me Harry."

She typed on the computer for a few seconds.

"I'm Esme. So what is it you want me to look for?"

That took Harry by surprise a little, he was here for help but hadn't made a list of what he was going to ask for. To be honest he wasn't expecting such a welcome. He asked her to track the missing person register for basic numbers over the last fifty years, then what percentage of those were found or still missing.

Esme looked at him. "Wow, nice and easy to start with then!"

It was a big task and Harry knew it, but it was one list that he knew he wanted and needed. It was all very well having a list of murders but if this had been where Bos had started it was obviously not detected otherwise he would not have made it to inspector. He sat and watched Esme tap away, correlating the information he had asked for. It took about an hour before she sat back and the printer whirred into action.

"While you have a look through that I'm going to get a drink, do you want one?" Harry most definitely did want one.

"Yes please, that would be wonderful, could I have a white coffee please?"

"Sugar?" Harry was so tempted to say 'yes honey' back but thought better of it. It seemed an accommodating nick but sexual harassment could be mentioned by anyone wanting to gain some brownie points.

"No thanks, not for me." *Chicken shit,* he thought to himself as she walked out of the door.

He took the paper that had been printed and had a quick look. Harry knew that on average a single police service area will collect about twenty missing person reports per day. This force reports an average of about twenty-two, that is not a stand-out 'punch you in the face' figure but if you look closer at it, the district that Oakwood Manor falls into is in the top twenty-five districts for missing persons, but more alarming was the fact that it had a high disappearance rate along with it. The numbers were not extreme which is why it had not sent alarm bells ringing, however, Harry would not have expected these numbers for such a rural area. Esme came back in with two mugs of coffee.

"Anything interesting in that for you, Harry?" Harry was very open with his response.

"Yes actually, you do seem to have a lot of missing person reports in and around the Oakwood Manor area, a lot more than I would have expected." He then asked her to search for the murder rate for the area too.

"Okay, but what is it you're trying to find out?"

Harry explained the situation to her. Esme thought for a while.

"Would you mind if I put in a comment?"

Harry shook his head. "No, of course not, any assistance would be welcome." She spun her chair to face him.

"I've been a PC for a good few years now and there is one form I hate, but a part of it does seem relevant here." Harry was interested. "Domestic violence. What is the question you ask when you have an out-of-control young person and need to check they are not on the way to, well, being dangerous!"

Shit, Harry thought. Why hadn't he thought of that?

"Fuck me, you're right. Oh, sorry, didn't mean to swear like that."

Esme smiled and turned back to her computer. "I can't at the moment, my leg hurts." She then typed in and looked for reports on missing, mutilated or wounded animals. This was a major sign to look for in a young person – cruelty to animals is linked as a sign of possible things to come. This information took a while too, but ten minutes later Esme printed off another sheet. She leant back and pulled it from the printer and handed it to Harry. After a quick look he commented again.

"Sorry Esme but this is truly shocking, have you looked at this?" She took the sheet and had a quick scan.

"Shitting hell!" There were a huge amount of missing animals; both domestic and farm animals had been going missing for years at a much higher rate than expected.

"Either your pet owners and farms are particularly careless or you have an underlying problem on your hands." Harry stood up. "Thank you so much for your help, especially that last tip. I'm going to Oakwood Manor and will be back later."

She smiled and said it was no problem, as he rushed out. Harry had a feeling that he was close to something but he didn't know what. This place had a high rate of missing persons who stay missing, and it also had a very poor record of looking after its animals.

He climbed into his car and set the satnav for Oakwood Manor.

That many bodies disappearing? Something is wrong around here.

The display said it would take him thirty-six minutes to reach his destination. He was thinking all the way there that those people or bodies had to be going somewhere, and if Bos had started his murderous spree at the manor then that is where he should start. But fifty years of bodies? That is a lot of carcasses. Did the manor have a big enough and ongoing patio project? He was sure that if they were buried in the cellar then each new resident would smell it. Plus, after fifty years surely there would be no cellar left.

He entered the grounds again and this time during a better spell of weather. The trees still looked bloody terrible and he immediately saw the one that the Oscars had crashed into. He didn't call at the house, he just walked directly to the tree he had picked out as a bit of a focal point. He stood still, just looking about to see if anything stood out, like an enormous mound of dead bodies. At least that would be easy to solve but not, he feared, Bos's style. Then again, this is where Ben started, not Bos!

There was a large outbuilding a couple of hundred yards away so he took a stroll towards it. It was unlocked when he reached it and so he took a deep breath and walked in. It was empty.

"Oh well, worth a try." Harry walked out and continued to walk around seemingly aimlessly. However, as he walked he could feel a slight difference underfoot. He walked back again. He stamped his foot on the ground; this really didn't seem right, and oddly enough there was a metal pole just sticking up out of the ground a little way to his left. He bent down and took a pen from his pocket.

He stuck it in the soil. It didn't go down very far before it hit metal. Harry stood up dramatically and dug his heel into the ground; some of the soil came away and he scraped it back. Harry slammed his foot down onto the bare metal and it sounded like there was a vast void underneath. He looked around to see if there was anything around that might help him. There was a hut in the distance so he went over to investigate it. Again, this wasn't locked either, so he opened it and grinned a very lucky grin. He had found a tool shed. Harry looked around to try and find a spade but saw something even more perfect, a shovel.

He made his way hastily back to the metal and started work to clear the top. After ten or so minutes scraping away he had cleared the large metal lid. He wanted to lift it; he tried to get the shovel under the corner. Again and again he tried with no luck, but then suddenly it caught and he lifted the great sheet. It was heavy but he got his hands under it and lifted it up. The stench hit him in the face like a furnace blast – it stank. Harry dropped it and wretched.

"Urrrggh, urrgggh! Holy shit."

"Well, close, Sergeant. What you have there is the old cesspit, so not exactly holy shit but it did at least contain something similar in the past." It was Sabrina, the lady who lived there with her husband now.

"Sorry I didn't knock but I just wanted to walk about and have another nose about."

She laughed. "Yes, and I'm quite sure your nose regrets that decision now, doesn't it?"

Harry stood up, looking a little sweaty and a little dirty. "I would shake your hand but I don't think that would be good."

She said, "No, you're probably right there."

"I'm sorry about this but I'm at the cusp of a discovery. I can feel it!"

Sabrina was having fun now. "Believe me, Sergeant, go anywhere near that water and you will feel very little in the future." Harry started to try and put the soil back.

"Leave that, Sergeant, and tell me what you mean about being on the cusp of something."

Harry explained that he thought a lot of people and animals had disappeared over the years and they may be around here.

"Well, I don't know about that, I'm afraid. I've been here for a little while and have not come up against a lot of bodies."

Harry asked if it was okay to continue to walk about.

"Yes, that's fine with me, just be careful not to land yourself in anymore shit." She laughed, waved and walked away.

Harry was quite disappointed with what had just happened. He was confident he had found something then. But he was not giving up, there was something wrong with this place. He continued to walk around; he seemed to go around in a bit of a circle but did hit on a lovely lake and it truly was beautiful. The trees in the distance hanging over onto the surface, the calmness of the water. There was a quaint-looking wooden pier jutting out around ten metres out. There was a newer one just a little way up along the bank too. Harry looked at it and his first thoughts were about how picturesque it was, but then as he took in the view he started to think again. Why would you build another pier just a little way away? It's not as if they are inundated with moored boats. But that wasn't all, something else was niggling at him but for the life of him he couldn't find out what. However, a couple more minutes standing watching and it suddenly clicked.

The water was lovely, the trees were lovely, the grass and flowers were lovely, but where is the wildlife? There were literally no animals about, it was silent. Not a bird in the sky, insect in the grass or any duck or fish in or on the water. Harry walked slowly out onto the first pier. He just stood still for a while. It was an eerie atmosphere; it was definitely quiet and peaceful. "Too bloody peaceful!"

Ten minutes he must have stood there, in that silence it seemed like an hour, nothing, not even a bird flying past overhead. He looked about and then looked down at the wooden deck. It had markings along the boards; they were odd and looked like something heavy had been pushed off the pier.

"What the fuck have they been pushing off here?" It looked to him like they had been dragging anchors off the pier but there was not even a small row boat let alone anything that would require an anchor! He bent down and felt the marks. They started in the centre of the pier and went out to the edge of the water. They were like this each side into the water. Harry peered into the water to see if he could see anything but it was far too cloudy. He wondered what could be under there, if anything? He stood up and looked about; he wanted to find out what was under there. He walked away and went to the large barn to see if there was anything that could help him. He was filthy and sweaty but he could feel something coming close. The barn was still empty; he was becoming frustrated. He kicked the door open and left to go to the shed. The shed was a help uncovering the shit hole so why not now!

The door pushed open and rattled on its rotten door and rust hinge. It was a bit of an Aladdin's cave with cupboards and drawers all over the place. The walls had rusted tools hanging in crooked lines. They were covered in cobwebs and had obviously been abandoned for a good while. He searched in the drawers and cupboards but nothing was going to help him. However, when he looked up, on a rack in the ceiling were a number of dowel rods and metal bars. There was also a drainpipe through the rack. Harry reached up and pulled it from its cobweb prison. The dust and rubbish that fell was immense but he was already in such a state he didn't care now. It was in good condition and was about eight feet long. Harry put it on the floor outside and continued to rummage around; he did remember seeing some duct tape in one of the drawers so went back to find it. He had an idea forming in his brain. He did find the tape and then carried on looking for his last item. He had been through the entire shed and hadn't found what he was after.

"Fuck, fuck, so close." He threw the tape across the shed and it bounced off the boarded up window, however, it didn't thump exactly, more rustled. Harry looked closer and grinned an enormous grin. He clambered over to the window and touched it.

"Yes." He pulled at the covering that was over the space and it came off in one go. It was a three-foot square piece of plastic sheeting. Harry then had to search around the floor to find the tape he had just thrown. It was found and he climbed back out and went towards the drainpipe. Harry put the sheet over the end of the pipe and wrapped it around. He then picked the tape end free and went round and round taping the sheet to the pipe. After a couple of minutes he picked it up and inspected his results. He now had a tube with a semi-transparent cap on the end. The plastic was covered in tape for around six to ten inches so went seamlessly from plastic to pipe.

"Right, let's test you out, shall we?" Harry marched over to the pier in the lake with the drainpipe held in his hand and balanced on his shoulder. He looked like a toy soldier with a ridiculously large rifle. He reached the pier and did one last check that the tape was pressed down as much as it could be. He then found a part of the wood that had the most scratches and gouges. He picked it up and placed it plastic side down on the wood close to the edge near the water. Harry took a deep, expectant breath, stood with his toes hanging over and then placed the pipe in the water. He peered into the pipe and could see the bottom – it was not letting in water yet. He lowered it deeper and deeper and was stooping down. The pipe was now only out of the water by about a foot and he could see a trickle of water coming in and flowing over the plastic. It was small rivulets at first but then more. Then beneath the water he could see something on the bottom of the lake. He lowered it a little more and just before the water restricted his view he caught a glimpse of what he could swear to be sacking in the shape of a body. Harry took the pipe out of the water and his heart was racing. He put it on the floor and sat down.

"What to do now?" he said out loud to himself. He knew it was a cliché but he could feel something wrong; it was all around the place. It seeped out from its very existence. Harry stood up and brushed himself off the best he could and walked away, just leaving the drainpipe where it lay. He walked slowly but deliberately to his car and headed directly back to see Sergeant Deex.

CHAPTER 25

The Pink Pussycat

Del left the station and headed downtown and parked along the high street. He couldn't park where he wanted to go, there wasn't room. He exited his car and blipped the key fob and the car locked. This part of the high street was in disguise, it thought it looked like Las Vegas – unfortunately it fell hopelessly short of that. It made Del sick whenever he came to this part of town; it was not nice, it was not pretty. Del thought of it as tacky and shit. The gulf between Las Vegas and Blackpool was huge. Well, this place had the same kind of gap but below Blackpool. However, some people liked it. He walked along the street and shop after shop had lightbulbs flashing with some kind of crass design. He walked on until he reached his destination, The Pink Pussycat Club. The lightshow on this building was a pink cat playing with a ball of string. Even at this time of the day it had a string of people waiting outside. Del looked at his watch and it was 14:17. He walked up and ducked under the rope that was keeping the line in order.

There were a chatter of complaints and the doorman stepped forward. He was waiting for that anyway, he would have been stopped even if he had waited in line. Del didn't have the right equipment to get into The Pink Pussycat without his warrant card. It was a female only gay nightclub. 'Nightclub' is a very broad term for it, as it ran permanently.

"What do you think you are doing, SIR?" The 'sir' was meant to emphasise the point that it was not a place for men. Del showed the bouncer his warrant card.

"Look, I'm not here to party, I need a chat with the boss." The doorman took Del's ID and held it in his sausage fingers, it reminded Del of an adult playing with a child and their mini cooker set. He looked ridiculous holding it in his thumb and forefinger like a bloody postage stamp.

"Wait 'ere." He turned and stuck his head in the door and spoke to someone.

Another member of staff came out and waved Del in to the building. The place was dark but lit with lots of small bulbs so gave out a very weird impression. It was dark but you could see exactly what everyone else was doing. However, if you went out and described the inside you would undoubtedly use the term 'dark'. He followed the member of staff that had called him in, this one was a female and presumably waited on tables as she had a little pinny on. She went upstairs and he continued to follow until she came to a large black door.

"Wait there." And she went in and left Del standing.

It was around two minutes later when the door

opened. "He will see you now." It was the woman he had followed, and then she just walked back downstairs. Del shrugged and walked in.

"Holy crap," said Del out loud automatically without thinking. It looked like the room that taste forgot. It had mirrors on walls, a bloody disco ball as a light, a very large white fluffy rug that you would lose small children in, a black leather sofa and a black desk too. It really did make Del feel a little queasy.

"Come in."

Del couldn't believe it, he was sure he had been zapped back to the seventies into an office of a fucking pimp! He walked towards the voice that had beckoned him.

"Sit down, Inspector, I know what you are thinking!"

Does he? Del thought. *I very much doubt it!*

"You are thinking, 'Who the fucking hell decorated this place?' You are right. Extremely vulgar, isn't it?"

Del sat down. "Yes, it makes me feel sick just looking around." The person laughed.

"I've had this place for a few months and I'm doing it up but with me it's a case of the public areas come first. I only really come in here when I have to make calls or to meet people. I always find people's reactions fun." Del could see he had a real character in front of him.

"I can see how that would be enjoyable but is there somewhere a little quieter we could go? Quieter as far as senses go!" Del couldn't see the man but he laughed.

"Follow me."

Del followed the silhouette of him. They walked out of a door at the side and then went down some stairs and entered a smallish kitchen.

"This is the staff kitchen, it doesn't really get used a lot." Del was more than just a little shocked and relieved that he had not said anything earlier because it was not a man he was talking to, it was a female with a very gruff voice.

"Thank you for seeing me, I just have a couple of questions about a lady who visited here a few nights ago?"

"Oh, well in that case you don't need to talk to me, I have little to do with the shop floor and more to do with the managing and running of the place." Del was not happy with that answer but she continued. "You need to speak to Veronique, she is fantastic, she knows everyone." That was more music to his ears.

"That would be great. Could you tell me where to find her please?"

"No, I can do better than that, I'll take you to her." She walked out past Del and went back into the main area. There was a bar at the far end of the room which they headed to.

"Veronique, can you leave here for a moment and talk to this inspector? Tell him anything he wants to know, okay?" She turned to Del and shook his hand; he was expecting a bone crunching shake but was relieved when it turned out to be very feminine and gentle.

"Good to meet you, Inspector."

"Thank you for your help." Del turned to Veronique. She was Latino in appearance and very attractive. There were a lot of people milling about. "Could we go somewhere a little quieter?"

She smiled sweetly. "Oh, if only I had a penny for every time I've heard that." She walked out from behind the bar and Del followed her. They only walked a little way before she opened a door. It was a room around four metres square, and was kitted out with comfy chairs and a TV on the wall.

"What is this room?"

Veronique sat on one of the comfy chairs. "It's our staff room."

Del was a little confused. "But I thought there wasn't a staff room. I was just speaking to the boss in the kitchen."

"That is just Harriet's way. She is a lovely person and doesn't like to intrude on the staff room. Sweet, really." Del sat down too.

"I need some info on a woman that comes in occasionally, her name is Natalia." He took the picture out of his pocket and handed it to her. She looked at it quickly.

"Yes, that's Nat, she does come in sometimes." She stuttered and then added, "She had a skin full a few days ago actually." Del leant forward.

"Do you know who she was with?"

She thought for a few seconds. "She was on her own for a while, and getting a little sloshed too, she was hitting on everyone." Del was getting somewhere at last.

"Okay, can you tell me exactly what she did that night?"

"Well, I'll try. She was hitting on lots of people but everyone could tell she was emotional and more than a little tipsy. But a woman that I had never seen before started speaking to her and they got on REALLY well."

Del butted in. "What do you mean?"

"I mean they were getting close and physical, let's just say there was kissing and touching going on, but the other woman was not drinking – she was sober but Nat was plastered by the time they left attached to each other."

"Have you CCTV in here?"

She told Del that there was no point, you couldn't see anything in here, plus the customers dropped when they did have it. "And we have the man mountain at the front door."

Shit. Del was pissed off. *So close.*

"I could describe her though." Del nodded in hope. "She was white, had long blonde hair and plain makeup with lipstick on her full lips. Well, until that disappeared onto Nat's face! She was around five foot six, slim build with large breasts that she wanted people to see. Blue dress and black heels."

Del frantically wrote all that down. He was pleased. Without CCTV that was a great description.

"Just a couple more questions. Did you see which way they went?"

She told Del that they had gone left out of the building but she didn't know after that.

"Wonderful. And lastly, did you see her wife that night?" Veronique looked genuinely shocked about this revelation.

"I didn't know she was with anyone, she always acted single in here."

Del thanked her and stood up to leave.

"Is she okay, Inspector?"

Del hated this question. "No, I'm afraid not, she was murdered that night. I'm sorry."

She gasped in shock. "But how? That is awful."

Del told her he should not go into details but he was doing his very best to find the killer and the information she had given him may be a real help.

Del left the club and headed back to the station. He had built up a bit of a picture about what was happening. He wasn't one hundred percent clear on it but he had the idea that a couple were luring their victims away with the promise of a sexual encounter after getting them drunk. He needed to find the blonde that Veronique had described. These and other thoughts were still swimming around in his head as he pulled up, parked and exited his vehicle at the station.

He glanced at his watch as he made his way through the entrance towards the conference room. It was 16:23 and he wondered if Harry was back; he was wanting to run his theory past him. The conference room was, however, void of any personnel, it was still just full of white boards and the white boards full of scraps of information and details on the numerous victims, crime scenes, witnesses, and suspects.

However, this last section was visibly lacking in cast-iron detail. In fact, to be totally honest he thought it looked emptier than a bulimic's stomach.

He examined all the points on the board. His supposition would fit, it would hold water that the victims were being snared by way of sexual enticement. The one who went off with Natalia was a female who was gay and the two men that had gone had been straight and drunk. The church victims were an anomaly but Del thought they were merely a way of provoking emotion in him.

"Bloody worked as well," he said out loud. He looked at a corner on one of the boards and smiled. He was looking at the name of the informant who told them where Tony went. Ben. Del knew where he was going next.

"Fuck." He looked at his watch again – 16:49. Tonight was too late, Del remembered that Ben ate at four and after that would be walking God knows where until God knows when. That was a meeting he would have to do tomorrow. Del was hoping that he was as good at recalling a person from a description as well as by photo. He picked up a dry-wipe pen and wrote up the description of the woman who went off with Natalia the night she was killed. He didn't know who she was but she definitely sounded stunning. Thinking of stunning women, he was hoping that Janice had not arranged another night with Sue, he was not sure he could cope with that again so soon. She seemed to have an extraordinary pull on him, in more ways than one after their last encounter! Although the experience was not without a certain pleasure it was not something he wished to go through again any day soon. Del tried to put her and her body out of his mind as he turned on his computer. He groaned as his email account kicked in.

"Why? Why the fucking hell do I get all this shit? I will spend an hour wading through all this crap and delete ninety-six percent of it as either useless, pathetic, bullshit or all three."

One percent he could deal with here and now, one percent he would have to deal with soon and the other two percent he would file, until such time he could give a shit. He eventually finished up and drifted off home, where he breathed an audible sigh of relief when he realised that he was not going to have the strain on his nerves or his underwear of putting up with Sue tonight. Instead he spent a relaxing evening in the company of his wife, although the conversation did contain a lot about her friend.

CHAPTER 26

Frog Man

The car pulled up at the front of the pristine white police station again and this time Harry knew exactly where he was going. He marched into the glass dome and directly to the door on the left. He took out the lanyard from his pocket and hung it around his neck. He pressed the pass to the black security unit to the right and it bleeped open. He walked straight through and headed for the Sergeant's office he was in earlier.

"Ah, hello Sergeant. Jesus! What happened to you? Esme has a broken arm but she sure seems to have put you through the ringer."

"Your PC Latchford was an absolute diamond and was more help than I could have ever expected. Could I have another quick chat with you?"

Sergeant Gary Deex showed him the empty seat. "Come in."

Harry did and sat down with the enthusiasm of a body not used to manual labour.

"I gathered a lot of info from PC Latchford and to

be honest I found that your district is missing a lot of people and animals. I think the key to those disappearances is linked to Oakwood Manor."

Sergeant Deex nodded but said the word Harry didn't want to hear. "Why?" This was not an easy one to answer.

"It's a mix of a lot of things and they all point to that place."

Sergeant Gary Deex leant back. "Okay, I'll go with you on it at the moment. What are you not saying yet?" Harry sat forward in the chair.

"I made a makeshift underwater viewer and I believe I saw a body wrapped in hessian."

Sergeant Deex puffed out his cheeks and stroked his chin. Harry instantly thought, *I wish he wouldn't do that.* It always made him shiver as it was a trait of his old Inspector Bos. The room was silent for a moment.

"How certain are you? Give it to me in percentages."

Harry thought about things, everything he knew and suspected. "Ninety-five percent."

Sergeant Deex picked up his phone and then dialled. Harry didn't know what was going on but found out soon enough.

"Yes, hello boss, it's me, Deexy. I need you to pull in a favour."

Harry couldn't hear what was being said on the other end.

"I need a search diver as soon as possible." Silence fell again. "Could you let me know how soon?" Then the phone was replaced on its cradle. Harry looked expectantly.

"The boss will let me know how soon we can have a diver here, let's hope the five percent doesn't pop up, shall we!" That made Harry nervous.

"Are you hungry, Harry? There's a canteen on the third floor, go get yourself something and come back in an hour. I may have some news then. Oh, tell them Deexy said it's to come out of the neighbourhood watch budget, and if he gets shirty say code 447."

Harry was shocked. "Wow, thanks."

Gary smiled. "Well let's face it, if you are right we're going to have a hell of a find."

Harry went and found the canteen. It was a very long hour for Harry; the food was nice but the time waiting was excruciating. Bang on an hour after he had come up Harry stood and made his way back down to Sergeant Deex. As he stepped foot in the office he was directed to the chair opposite.

"Any news?"

Sergeant Garry Deex nodded. "They will be here in," he glanced up at the circular clock on the wall, "about ten minutes now." He told Harry that they were coming to the station to have a bit of a briefing and then they would all head out together.

"Are you coming then?" asked Harry.

"Ha! You bet your fucking arse I'm, if there is nothing there I want to be the first to call you a twat and to say it was all your mistake."

Harry laughed. "I think I will be first with that, but what if we do find something?"

"Well in that case I will say how marvellous we all are."

Harry laughed again. "Yes, that sounds about right but I really don't care as long as it sheds some light on Bos and his past and then obviously onto our current killer."

It didn't take long before Deex got a call and they took off to a briefing room. As Deex and Harry walked in there were four men already sat waiting.

"Hello everyone, I'm Sergeant Deex and this is Sergeant Gorham." Deex stood to one side and put his hand out to Harry. "Sergeant, could you fill our divers in as to what is going on and what you expect to find please?"

Harry wasn't perturbed by this surprise, he just took it in his stride. "Sure, thank you Sergeant Deex." He stepped forward. "How much are you aware of Oakwood Manor?"

Three of them shook their heads but the other one spoke.

"Not a huge amount, Sergeant. I know there is quite a sizable lake on the grounds and I believe some batty aristocrat owns it but that is about all I know."

Harry nodded. "Well it does have a huge lake and obviously that is the area I'm interested in otherwise you wouldn't be here. The aristocrat you mentioned is Lady Belina Wellingborough and yes, she does seem to be a little eccentric. However, she is not on site, a lady by the name of Sabrina is living there at the moment and she is welcoming and accommodating." Harry went on to explain briefly about the old Butcher case and then the new one. "I believe that something sinister has been going on about that place for quite a while and I think we're going to find out what, today." Harry stepped back and looked at Sergeant Deex. "Sergeant."

Deex stood up.

"Thank you for that update. Let's go, gentlemen."

*

The cavalcade of vehicles travelled along the twisting side roads, making its way slowly towards their destination. Oakwood Manor eventually loomed into view and the five vehicles drove gently down the drive between the parallel lines of awful trees. There was Harry's car, the two diver vehicles, a marked police unit which contained Sergeant Deex and two other officers and a plain white van containing CSI personnel. They all pulled to a stop near the front of the house and spilled out their police contents across the gravel. Once all were out Harry addressed them.

"I'm going to knock and speak to the resident. I'm positive she will be fine with our little adventure and I will be back shortly." He walked away and made his way towards the front door. He knocked and it wasn't long before Sabrina answered.

"Oh, hello again Sergeant Gorham, have you come to dig through more crap?" She smiled and opened the door for him to enter but then noticed the rest of the people waiting on the drive. "Wow, you brought some friends today."

Harry looked over to the small crowed of people. "Yes, these are all police staff and are here to help me with a theory."

She asked, "What theory?"

"I believe over the years something has been going on here and I have been looking to find out what."

"Yes, I know, and up to now have uncovered a load of shit, yes?"

Harry laughed. "You are not going to let me forget that, are you?"

Sabrina asked him why on earth she would want to remind him of the fact that he crept onto the property and tried to sneak into the old cesspit?

"I'm thinking I'm going to find something in the lake, which is why I've brought some colleagues from the diving unit. Are you okay with us taking a bit of a dip in the lake?"

She thought for a moment. "Only on one condition?"

Harry was not expecting that response but rallied. "What is that condition?"

"I want to watch, it sounds wonderful." Harry raised his eyebrows.

"Okay, it is your property at the moment so that is okay. However, if anything is found it will turn into a crime scene and that may change the situation somewhat, also it may be a bit grim to watch!" She ran off and shouted behind her that he should wait as she wanted to get her shoes and a coat. It wasn't ideal as far as Harry was concerned but at least she was willing to let them go ahead; he had a feeling a warrant to search the place would have been difficult to achieve on the basis of the evidence he had. Sabrina soon came hurtling out of the door with her long black coat flapping behind her like some kind of aristocratic batman or woman! Harry followed her towards the rest of the search party.

"Sabrina, this is Sergeant Deex and his colleagues. Sergeant, Sabrina has kindly agreed for us to poke around in the lake but is insistent that she comes and watches what is going on. I have obviously warned her that it is possible that the area has the potential to turn into a crime scene and that it could be potentially disturbing." Sergeant Deex shook her hand.

"Nice to meet you. Thank you for the permission and Sergeant Gorham is quite right, it may be a bit nasty out there."

The introductions were completed and they walked to where Harry knew the piers were. Harry pointed out the marks in the wood and showed them his makeshift underwater viewer. He told the divers where he saw the hessian-type material that looked like a body and suggested that was where to start. The divers took in the information and then started to chat about the job in hand. Harry was eager to see what was there, however, he was in for a long wait. The divers didn't come back in their diving gear, they came back with clipboards and forms. *I might have known it,* thought Harry. *Of course we can't do anything without a raft of bloody forms first!* They walked around taking notes on different things; one of them even took a note of the temperature of the water. Harry watched in fascinated irritation as there were talks of depth, current and indigenous wildlife. He looked about and to his astonishment Sabrina had a grin from ear to ear – she seemed to be enjoying this nonsense.

"How long is it going to be before we get someone in the water?" he asked as politely as his sinking mood would allow.

The person that seemed to be in charge shouted back, "Not long now, we have to go through all the preliminary checks first."

Harry sighed. "And then you can get in?"

The man shook his head. "No, not right away, we have to do the equipment checks then."

The words, "For fuck's sake," exited from Harry's lips into the cool air, thankfully without actually hitting anyone's ears. He continued to watch with ever-sinking patience as the four of them strolled away from the lake and over to their vehicle. They then started emptying their van and lining equipment up out on the grass. There was loads of it.

"Surely you don't need all of that, do you!"

They didn't answer him, they could sense his mood and just tried to ignore him and get on with their checks. It didn't seem important but the checks were vital and all the equipment had to be ready to go in case of any possible emergency. They were not in a job that was easy on shortcuts! Eventually all four men were kitted out but Harry was shocked to see that only one was getting ready to go in.

"Why are you the only one going in?"

The leader of the four had had enough then.

"Look, I appreciate you are heavily invested in this venture, Sergeant, but with all due respect can you just let us do our fucking jobs? We know what we're doing."

Sabrina found this hysterical. "Ha! Harry you really do know how to make friends, don't you?"

Harry actually lightened up at that point and smiled at her. "Yes, drawn to crap situations as you know."

Sergeant Deex walked over then. "Well now we find out. I hope you're right about this, Harry."

Harry was thinking the same thing. What if he was wrong? His palms started to sweat and itch now and he was getting nervous. The one diver had got himself ready and was sitting on the edge of the pier. He had a rope around him and was being held by one of his colleagues. Slowly he sank into the water. Harry knew the water was not overly deep as he had seen the bottom using the eight-foot-long drainpipe. The diver had disappeared underneath the murky water. Harry noticed that there was still an odd atmosphere around and it continued to show no sign of any wildlife. Suddenly after a very short while under the water the diver came back up. He spoke to another colleague who left and went to their vehicle. He came out with what looked like a large basket on a rope. The basket was taken to the pier where the diver was and lowered slowly into the water. The diver disappeared under the surface again. The rope that held the basket was slowly eased out too. It seemed like a lifetime to Harry before he saw the man holding the rope being tugged gently. He started to pull on the rope and wind the basket in. Harry stared at the water waiting for the surface to be broken, then suddenly it was. He gasped but then swore.

"Fuck's sake." He was extremely uptight at the moment and was frustrated to see that it was the diver that had come to the surface. However, his frustration was short lived because a second later the basket rose from the depths and hit the fresh air. Harry smiled. It was what he had seen. Inside the basket sling was a hessian-type cloth tied together with what looked like a nylon cord. It looked about three to four feet in length.

"It's a body, it has to be a body," said Harry.

"How exciting," was Sabrina's response.

Harry walked towards the divers as they hauled the basket onto the pier.

"Wait." It was Sergeant Deex who had said that. "We're not doing anything with whatever that is until it is recorded how it looks first."

The CSI guys had not done anything; they had been standing near their van really quite uninterested. They didn't think anything was going to come of their little paddle in the lake. They did move quite quickly when they realised they were actually going to be needed. The quickest one grabbed his camera and headed for the water's edge; he was setting his camera up for the best quality shots his equipment would get and Harry relaxed a little, watching the action take place. He was feeling a huge wave of relief wash over him. He hadn't noticed how tense he was until the pressure lifted. The CSI man took a few shots from different angles and included a foot rule for size comparison. He then looked at Sergeant Deex. "Do you want us to open this, Sergeant?"

Deexy nodded. "Yes, but wait until Harry here is in sight. I think he is eager to get a look."

Harry grinned. "How could you tell?" And he rushed over.

The CSI man cut the nylon and slowly unwrapped the hessian while the other one snapped the pictures. The hessian was unfurled and a sudden stench drifted up and instantly hit everyone's noses. Those who had the experience knew that smell, it was a smell that once you came into contact with it, you would recognise it anywhere – it was the smell of death. The smell of rotting flesh drifted around and hung in the air, however, it was not what Harry had expected or wanted. It was not a person that had been wrapped and sunk, it was a dog. The word 'was' was very accurate because it must have been a while ago that this creature was wagging its tail and chasing a ball.

"Fuck!" Harry shut his eyes. "Fuck, a dog, a fucking dog."

The diver from the water was standing next to him. "Sorry to butt into your expletives but that language may, just may be a little premature."

Harry looked over to him. "What?"

"I mean that you may be a little too quick on the old 'what a waste of time' scenario."

Harry quietened down. "Why? What do you mean?"

The diver pointed to the area of the lake he had just come from. "I mean there's more than that parcel down there."

Harry's eyes widened. "Are you saying there's another one?"

The diver shook his head. "No, I'm saying it looks like there are more than that. From what I could tell in the murk it looked like a fucking Christmas tree on

Christmas morning under there." The diver explained that from the hessian wrap that he picked up there seemed to be another underneath it, one on each side of it and it looked like one each side too. He looked over to Sergeant Deex, "Deexy, I think you're going to need to call for more men. We four can handle the dive but you're going to need a lot more for removal, I.D. and storage. Like our friend here said, there is something seriously wrong in this place." He looked at Harry and winked.

"Looks like you've found a real mess here." Sabrina had covered her nose due to the stink. "I think I'll go in now," she said and turned and walked away. Harry could hear her clearing her throat on her way back, it really was a smell that grabbed you!

"Okay, first things first, if you believe there are man parcels down there we need to get some plastic sheeting laid out on the grass to move them to so you can continue to bring them out. Do that and I'm going to call the boss." Although Sergeant Deex was relieved to find out Harry was right about this place, he was not exactly over the moon about having so many bodies, even if they were all canines.

He walked away from the main site and pulled out his phone to dial his inspector. He took a deep breath and dialled. "Hello boss, it's Deexy, I'm at the manor."

There was a pause where the inspector had asked if they had come up with anything.

"That is exactly what I'm calling for. Sergeant Gorham was right, there is a big problem here and I'm giving you the heads up."

His inspector asked what kind of big problem.

"The diver has been in the water just the once and come up with a body of a dog wrapped in hessian and sunk." A pause as the inspector spoke. "Yes you are right, sir, that is not, however he has said he has seen a considerable amount of hessian-wrapped objects under there." Another pause. "Yes, I know, but if Harry is right and let's face it, it is quite probable at this moment in time, one or some of those wraps are going to contain people!"

The inspector agreed and quickly said that he was making his way to the scene too. It was very soon an extremely busy and well-trodden area. Within the next hour the number of men had quadrupled and included the inspector. They were just about to bring up the next hessian package; it had taken a while to get ready for the second but everything was in place for things to go quicker now. The next package was hauled out and it was bigger than the first one. Unfortunately as far as Harry was concerned it was not a person, it was another animal. This one was, however, from underneath the dog and so was in a further state of decay. So much so they wouldn't know what animal it was until they could get an expert on it. This was speedily taken to the plastic-sheeted lawn area and the diver sent down again. When the next one came up Harry instinctively knew it was different.

"Shit, this is it."

Sure enough, as the hessian sheet was undone it was a decomposing human body. It was in a very poor state but they could tell it had been naked when sunk. Harry did not jump up and down in celebration as that would have been in very poor taste, but he did feel vindicated, relieved and very happy because he had just uncovered a huge clue as to the link between the old Butcher and the new Butcher.

As the hours passed more corpses were removed from the lake and two sets of divers deployed. The second diver was going from the other pier and it seemed like the entire length of each pier was lined with different animal and human remains. The last one was a male who had not been in the water for a huge amount of time. He was decaying but you could tell he had had his throat cut and his stomach split. This was the evidence Harry was after – it was similar enough to the Butcher to draw the link. He was thinking that due to the amount of bodies here and the differing decay (some mere skeletons) the killings had been going on for a long time. Harry walked over to find Sergeant Deex.

"Sergeant Deex, thank you for your trust and kindness, but I have found the link I was looking for so am going to head back home as it is now getting late."

Sergeant Deex shook Harry by the hand. "You are very welcome and the trust was obviously well placed. You have landed us with a huge task but we have uncovered something that we should have realised a long while ago."

Harry continued to shake Gary Deex by the hand.

"Could you do me one last thing please?" asked Harry.

"Sure, what?"

"Could you send me an email with the details of

what you do eventually drag out of there please?" He stopped shaking and took a card from his pocket. "They are my details."

The card was taken and he was told that would be the least they could do. Harry took one last look at the plastic sheeting that now stretched across a large area of the grass and all of the bodies that covered it. It reminded him of a disaster scene when the recovered bodies are lined up for identification. The divers had not finished either, not by a long way. Harry turned away from the corpse fishing and headed for his car. He stopped just before and turned back to the manor. He knocked on the door and waited for Sabrina to answer.

"Oh, hello Sergeant, how can I help you?" Harry smiled at her.

"I just wanted to thank you for your help, we could not have found what we have so soon without your co-operation."

Sabrina told him that he was welcome and it was an interesting encounter.

"Thank you again and I hope the intrusion into your life does not take too long." Harry walked away back to his car. He headed back home and arrived very late.

CHAPTER 27

All In A Row

Del did turn up bright eyed and bushy tailed the next morning. He had a restful evening and an early night and was ready for an update from Harry to see what he had got up to yesterday. He arrived on time and grabbed his usual cup of coffee and got one for Harry too. As he sat drinking his drink and waiting for Harry, he was deep in thought. It was not the thought that you would have expected, it was not about work and serial killers. It was about his wife Janice and her relationship with her friend Sue! He knew she was extremely attractive and quite frankly a sexual predator, however, he was starting to be concerned that his wife was becoming infatuated with her. He was thinking that Sue may 'swing both ways'. Would Janice be so infatuated that she would dip her toe around the waters of Lesbos? All these thoughts and more were swirling around his head. It was 09:42 when the phone knocked him out of his thoughts. He was wondering where the hell Harry was as he picked up the phone.

"Hello, Inspector Martin." Del shut his eyes. This was not good news. "Fuck." It was at that precise moment that Harry walked in.

"Well good morning to you too."

Del slammed the phone down. "Come on, don't get comfy." He stood up and stormed out of the room. Harry jogged to catch up.

"What's going on?"

"We have more murders." Harry picked up on the plural.

"What do you mean 'murders'? How many?"

Del stopped and looked at him. "Six. Six all in the one place. I'm not looking forward to seeing what we find." There was a very distinct reason he was not looking forward to this. The address of the massacre was one he had been to recently; it was the butcher he had spoken to a while ago. The rest of the journey to the car was silent but as they sat down Harry spoke.

"I do have a lot to tell you from my travels yesterday, but I will go over it when we finish where we're going, which is where by the way?"

"That is the reason I'm so concerned about what we're about to find. Remember the butcher I spoke to and got advice from?"

Harry was nervous about this now. "Yeees," he said slowly.

"Well our victims are at that address!"

"Oh shit."

Del hummed and said, "Exactly."

The car pulled up at the shop and at the door was a PC on scene guard as usual.

"Morning sir."

"Morning Tim," said Del as he ducked under the tape. The entrance to the shop was as normal as ever, clean and tidy. He stepped into the office and that was the same. He went back to the PC.

"Tim, how did we find out about this?"

The PC explained that he was the one that found it; he was called purely because of an insecure premises. "However, when I looked in to check all was okay, well… it wasn't."

Del listened and it seemed very credible. "Where are the bodies? You haven't eaten them, have you?"

They were always joking about Tim's eating habits because he was one of those people that ate and ate but never gained any weight. However, as soon as Del said it he knew it was a little crass considering what they suspected of the killer.

"They're in the freezer room, Del, and I left some of them, I couldn't manage them all."

Del uttered his thanks and turned away, regretting the direction the conversation had headed. Their humour was usually quite close to the edge but there was a line to be drawn and Del as an inspector knew this more than anyone. Okay, that line was normally quite a distance away from most other people's but still a line nonetheless!

They walked towards the freezer room and opened the large metal door. The sight that met their eyes was a shock for even them, and that was amazing considering Harry had just spent a day fishing rotting bodies out of a lake. The freezer was an absolute massacre. Del didn't think he had seen so much blood anywhere and hoped never to see it again – the floor was swimming in it. The freezer was not as you would be expecting, cold. It had obviously been turned off, either so he or they could kill in the warmth or so the bodies would not freeze. Whatever the reason, the blood was still very much in liquid form.

On entering the room the eye automatically went to the shimmering red carpet of blood but Del then raised his sight up to the bodies. It was a horrendous scene, five bodies hanging on meat hooks and the worst part was that Del knew every single one of them. He knew this but only because each body had had their heads removed and stuck on a separate hook next to their lifeless body, with the exception of the last one. That had a head but no body. Del left the room and sat down on the chair in the office he had sat in with Vince, the owner. He was breathing in deliberately, slow and deep.

"What's up, Del?"

The inspector looked up at him. "What's up is the killer is fucking us about and doing it like a fucking pro. I'm telling you, we're seriously fucked here." Del's language was raw, he was seriously worried. Harry leant against the doorway.

"Why? What are you getting at?" Del had closed his eyes but he opened them to answer.

"Remember me saying about the barman at the Pocket and Shilling helping me?"

"Yes, called Desmond wasn't he?" Del nodded,

they both had superb memories.

"Yes, but unfortunately, 'was' called Desmond is about right, he is the body hanging upside down on the far fucking left! You know, the one with his throat cut open."

Harry looked on in shock but had a feeling where this was going. "Where do you know the others, Del?"

"The second one is Vince, the owner of this bloody butcher's shop; the third is Ryan, the manager from The Globe; the fourth is Dawn from the travel agents next to where Natalia was killed; the fifth is Ben Garrick, the special walker who told us where Tony Slugget had walked; and lastly the poor cow on the end is Veronique, the helpful member of staff at the Pink Pussycat."

Harry was stunned. He didn't know what to say, he just stood there with his mouth open.

"Yes, exactly, every one of those poor fucking bastards in there has helped us with this case."

Both men felt sick, it was a nasty job at times but this really did take some getting over. All the people they had spoken to and got a decent response from, were decapitated and to vastly different degrees mutilated. It was a long while before either one of them wanted to speak, let alone actually trying to. After what seemed like eternity it was Harry who moved first.

"I'm going to see what went on in there." He dragged himself up off the floor and headed very slowly back into the freezer room. It was odd; it was the same room but seemed a whole lot darker now.

He looked over to the first body. He was naked and hanging by his feet but apart from his head being on a hook next to him he was as he should be. There was still the odd drop of blood occasionally dripping from the open neck of his body. Harry had never seen such a grim sight, it was the way it kind of doubled in the reflection of the surface of the blood lake. The surface rippled at sporadic moments due to the dripping but it didn't look like water. Harry looked in grotesque fascination as the surface moved like a mix of water and jelly. As the drips hit the bottom they rose in slow motion and then when at the top gravity took hold again, kind of dragged the drip in and under. Harry found it quite hypnotic for a moment and then realised what he was looking at.

He looked at the second body in the row and remembered that Del said he was the owner of the butchers they were in. He was also stripped naked and his head was off and perched grimly on the hook beside him. He was mutilated a little more than the first and in fact, as he looked along the line each in turn got worse until the grizzly end hook. Del came in then.

"Did you notice the way each victim along was more defaced than the previous?"

Del said that he hadn't really, the only thing he noticed was the identities.

Harry continued, "Desmond had just his head removed. Yes, I know that sounds odd!" and he looked at Del. "But Vince next to him has his head taken off and his belly sliced down the middle and his insides scraped." Del nodded and looked on at the third; he had only spoken to these people days ago and most of them were extremely likable and very helpful too. Is that what got them hanging in this freezer!

"Who did you say was the third one across?"

"He was the manager of The Globe, his name was Ryan."

Harry looked on in disgust at the state of him now, he too was missing his head which was now seemingly watching his own right foot. He had been gutted like Vince but his arms had been removed and placed on the floor, but not before they had their hands removed and put with the pile of offal that was lying under the body. The rest of the arm had been sliced into a couple of portions: one contained the forearms and the other the biceps, which were quite big as he was a large built man. Harry then glanced at the body next to him. "Fuck's sake, who was she?"

Del shook his head in sad reflection. "That, I'm afraid, was Dawn from the travel agent next to where Natalia was found." She was the fourth along and possibly looked the worst. That fact seemed odd but she was the last one that you could really recognise as a proper human being! The other two were a complete mess. She had had her head removed. Her organs and insides were in a tangled mess on the floor under her body like Ryan's. Her arms had been removed like his too but they hadn't stopped there. She had been cut in half so only half of her body was left hanging. The other half had been cut into neat-sized joints of meat and laid next to the arm pieces. It was truly disgusting to see and God knows what it would have looked like to be here.

At that very moment he shivered with a cold wave rushing through his body. All the hair on his body stood up and he shivered. It had absolutely nothing to do with standing in a butcher's freezer, but everything to do with the thought that had just flicked through his mind. Had they been alive while the others were being killed! He looked at Del who was just standing staring too.

"Del, do you think some of these were alive and watching what was going on?"

Del nodded sombrely. "That is what has been going through my head. I don't actually know but I can only go on what I know already. When I was caught by Bos I was wrapped and witnessed his other kill." Harry was appalled. He had never been told that aspect of Del's part in the Butcher case.

"Fuck, that just doesn't bear thinking about," said Harry as another shiver blasted through him.

The fifth one along, Del said was Ben, the man with the special talent for remembering people but who walked permanently around the town. He only knew this because of the head on the hook as the so-called body next to it was, well, in pieces. He had quite obviously gone through the same disturbing procedure as the previous four but again, his treatment had progressed even further. Like Dawn, one side of his body had been separated into joints and lined up with his arms. However, Ben had his other half removed too and that carved up alongside the first. The result was perfectly revolting; the only thing hanging on this hook was a pair of legs attached to some hips and a backbone. It reminded Harry of one of those cartoons when a fish is hung in front of a hungry cat and it is stripped clean in one go, to just leave a fish skeleton hanging free.

Del was not a queasy man but he did feel quite sick standing there looking at the local citizens who had been good enough to try and help him. He walked out for some air. Harry noticed but looked at the last hooks – the empty one, and the one with the hook and head next to it. This victim, he recalled Del saying was Veronique who worked at The Pink Pussycat. She looked attractive, well, as attractive as you can get being a head on a hook! As far as the rest of her was concerned he hadn't a clue, there was nothing left of her. She was just a collection of cuts of meat. The most awful piece was that the killer had gone to the time of mincing the offal and waste parts. So for Veronique there were no feet, no hands, just a head, a load of meat cuts and a large heap of minced meat. It was then that Harry noticed a few white containers at the side of the room on a metal shelf unit. He looked into them and they were all stained red with blood. Harry stood looking at them and then turned and looked at the macabre scene around him. He needed to look at this with the thoughts he would usually, to try and remove the link to their investigation. If this was a fresh case, what would he be thinking? He took another look around the red blood-covered room. A thought hit him.

"How?" He stooped low and looked across the smooth sheen of silken blood. He stood and looked at the containers and there were ripples of blood down the side of each one.

"You fucking sick, cocky bastards." Harry had wondered how they had not made any prints anywhere. If anyone was to walk across that or even be standing amongst it when the atrocities were committed there would be prints everywhere. Blood is that kind of substance, it clings and transfers like a bitch. After looking at the containers he knew what they had done. They had drained the victim's blood and kept it all until their grizzly tasks were complete and then they had gone over and poured the contents of the buckets across the floor. Whether that was aesthetically pleasing to them or by deliberate act of sabotage Harry couldn't say, but what he could say was it would have wiped any trace of footprints! Harry walked out to join Del. He was sitting in the office again. Harry walked in and sat in the other office chair which was at the other end of the small room. He slumped down and its wheels skidded along the floor a little way.

"You feeling alright Del?" Del shook his head. The truth was that he most definitely was not alright. The sight of those victims in a line had sent him reeling back to the experience he thought up until about a month ago he was over. He was obviously not over his capture at the hands of the Butcher; he had witnessed an awful murder and had tried to sweep it under the carpet. Unfortunately, it wasn't like a little dust being swept under the carpet, unobtrusive and unnoticeable! This was more like a log that had been placed under it and today the unavoidable had happened. He had gone tits up straight over it and surprisingly to him it had come as a bit of a shock.

"No, not really. As I said, that has sent me back to when I was helplessly bound up by Bos and watched as he killed and mutilated a victim. Looking in there made me think, and I really do hope they never witnessed what was happening to the others." He took a deep breath. "Whoever the bastard or bastards are that did this are somehow watching us and keeping track of what we're doing."

Harry nodded. "Because they've got to all the people that have been a help!"

Del said he was right. "But there is even more to it than that; unless it is a ridiculously lucky coincidence, those victims in there are lined up in the precise order I met them in!" The room was silent for a while.

"So what are you thinking now then?"

Del answered in a worryingly quiet voice, "I don't know, the last time these coincidences took place it was the person I was working with that was doing it!" The air was silent and now a little colder as both men thought about the possibility the other one could be the killer. Then suddenly the silence was broken.

"Look, this is fucking stupid, neither of us are capable of this type of atrocity, it's daft!" It was at that moment the atmosphere lifted as Buddy came in through the door.

"Hello you two, what joys do you have for me today?" Both stood up.

"Well Bud, I hope you have a strong stomach 'cause this ain't pretty." Del said this and walked past Bud to the door of the freezer. Bud frowned.

"I have seen a lot of weird shit in my time, I can tell you, not much gets under my skin."

"Okay, but someone got under these people's." Del walked back into the freezer and Buddy followed.

"Holy shit, I think I'm going to need my wellies for this one. Jesus, it looks like some warped evolution of man model!"

Del nodded. "Yes. I don't know what message they are trying to send with this…" And he halted mid-flow. He had totally forgotten about any messages. He glanced over to the row of hooks and looked at each victim in turn to see if there was any message visible in their mouths. There was none that he could see but some had their mouths closed, not all. It looked like a couple were mid horrified scream. Del asked Buddy if he could let him know if he found any messages this time.

"Yep, course I will, but I'm going to get my camera and take some initial shots of the scene first. Anything I need to know before I start?"

Del looked at him. "Only that the freezer has been turned off by the perpetrator, it seems, and each of these victims are already known to this investigation. They have all been of use with information pertaining to the attempted tracking of our killer or killers."

Buddy looked over to him. "Shit."

Del said nothing more, he just nodded and 'mmmed' back. Buddy left the freezer and went to his van to collect his equipment. Harry moved towards Del.

"Look, we need to go back to the station, I have to update you with what happened yesterday."

CHAPTER 28

Manor Update

The journey back to the station was a sombre affair and not filled with the usual smiles and humour. It was only when the car had pulled up at the station and they both climbed out that either one of them spoke.

"Did you get on okay yesterday then?" asked Del as they walked towards the station doors. Harry glanced over.

"It was an interesting day and one that I need to catch up with you about, when we're in the conference room." Del read between those lines and asked no more questions until the conference door shut behind them.

"Okay then, Mr Secret Squirrel, shoot."

Harry sat down at his normal place and got comfortable.

"I started yesterday deciding to travel back to the manor area and visited the local police headquarters." As he was talking he noticed something different about the place, but couldn't quite see what. Harry told Del that he went in to their station asking for as much info as possible on the manor and crimes around that area as he suspected something was going on.

"Ha! Fuck me, you have some balls, man. I bet that went down like a fucking lead balloon."

"Well you would think, wouldn't you? But they were absolutely fucking superb. The Sergeant set me up in a room with a restricted PC and gave her the instructions to look up the information I was after for me."

Del sat, amazed at that. "I could imagine what would be said here if someone tried to pull that!"

Harry was about to speak again and noticed what was different. There was a picture frame on the desk; he picked it up and looked at it.

"What the fuck is this? Personalising the place? Unlike you, isn't it?"

Del agreed. "Yes, I know. Janice gave it to me and insisted I bring it into work with me."

Harry took another look.

"Jesus, who is that with her tits nearly hanging out, short skirt and if I'm not much mistaken," he looked closer, "holding on to one of your wife's tits, who by the way looks fine with it." It was explained that it was Sue her best and very sexually precocious friend.

"She really is as fucking hot as she looks, in fact a damn sight hotter in the flesh!"

He was going to mention his concerns about his wife and her possible dip in the waters of the dark side but thought better of it. Harry looked again at the picture and nodded in approval. He then put it down and told him about the information he had asked for at the station.

"Well, what was the result?"

When Harry told him the percentage of missing persons Del's reaction was unexpected as far as Harry was concerned.

"That is about the same as ours so yes, what else?"

"Hang on, don't you find that odd?"

Del sat and thought for a second. "No, should I?" Del had not actually been to the area himself so was not familiar with the geography of the place, but being that Harry new it was fields and farmland covering a great area of the district he had a slight advantage with his thought processes.

"Del, most of their policing area consists of farmland. They do have town but not to the extent of ours."

Del's forehead furrowed. "Right, okay, so why have they had so many missing persons?"

"Precisely, and the amount that stay missing is higher than average too."

Del was leaning forward in his chair now. Harry said that the PC that was searching for the numbers for him had an idea and asked if it was okay to add her thoughts.

"Was it useful?"

"Fuck yes, was it ever." Harry explained about her idea on the animal cruelty aspect. Del smiled and nodded impressively.

"I like her."

"Yes, and when the numbers came back it was more evidence to suggest something wrong with that area."

Del asked him what he did with the info.

"I went and had a private nose about the manor grounds; honestly just walking around the place I could feel something, I don't know, wrong with the place!" Harry smiled with a recollection. I have to admit my first look about didn't go well." The tale about the cesspit was told and the laughs that came from Del were deafening. The humour of the story was possibly enough to cause this response, but it was more than likely an escape valve letting off a bit of built-up tension from the morning.

"That is classic, you are searching some mansion for some Scooby Doo type mystery and find a shit hole." He continued to laugh and Harry thought he was going to explode and piss himself when he told him about Sabrina's reaction. When Del had calmed down slightly he spoke again.

"Sorry, that is priceless, I think I may move to this place when I retire."

Harry then told him about his experience at the lake, with noticing there was no wildlife anywhere. He described the marks on the pier and explained how he made the tube to look under the water.

"I'm a bit thirsty now, I could do with a cup of coffee."

"Yeah, right, fuck off. What did you see?"

It was Harry's turn to laugh now. "Okay, I didn't

see a lot to tell you the truth but before the water leaked into the tube, blocking my view, I thought I saw a hessian bag that looked like a body." Harry then went on to explain that he went straight back to the Sergeant and asked for men to search the lake.

"You really are a cheeky fuck sometimes, but you are not telling me they actually went for it?"

"They did actually." Del was told about the wait while the inspector of the area was spoken to, the hospitality shown and the subsequent arrival of the dive team.

"Okay, cut to the fucking chase now, was that bag a body or not?" Harry didn't mess about with the answer to this.

"Yes it was, but! It wasn't a human body. It was a dog!"

Del stood up in frustration. "You twat, you dragged me back here all cloak and dagger style to tell me you found someone's dead fucking pooch. Jesus Christ, Harry, what the fuck are you on!" Harry shook his head at his inspector's despair.

"Del, wait a bloody minute, give me some fucking credit here will you?" He then told him that when the first diver brought up the dog his reaction was a pit-of-the-stomach lurch too. "But Del, the diver told me the bottom of the lake was covered in hessian-wrapped things. When they started bringing the rest up there were animals of different types and human remains. All in differing stages of decay."

Del sat down and chewed through this info.

"Del, they were still removing bodies as I left to

come back, it's why I was late in this morning, they have a mountain of corpses to get through now." Del was quiet for a little while and just sat in the small office chair swinging slowly back and forth. All of a sudden he leant forward.

"How long do you think this has been going on for?"

Harry didn't know but said he was presuming it started with Bos when he was there as a boy called Ben. Del asked for the contact details of the Sergeant he was with at the other station. He was given them and called him directly on the phone. Del found it a useful conversation as he found out that not only had they pulled out numerous bodies, they still were. The divers were still at the manor and continuing to pull things out of the water. After ten or so minutes talking to the Sergeant he put the phone down.

"You made an impression, Harry. I think I can use you as a torch from now on." Harry hadn't a clue what he was on about, but his confused expression was all Del needed to continue. "They are under the impression that the sun shines out of your arse!"

"Oh yes, very good. I wondered what the fucking hell you were on about. What now then?"

Del picked up his pen and tapped it on the table; he was feeling a little more like himself again now after the depressing experience earlier.

"Well to tell you the truth I was intending to go and see Ben Garrick again, but after seeing him this morning he wasn't very talkative and hasn't got the stomach to help any more."

Harry smiled. "I see you are feeling better!" He

agreed that he had recovered a bit of his composure now.

"But I'm not one hundred present sure I want to go questioning other members of the public yet, I think we need to look at what we have already before we attempt to risk dragging more people into the firing line."

Harry thought he was right, it was sensible after today's find that they tread carefully. Harry leant back on his chair and swung around in thought.

"Look, I know we touched on it earlier but who the hell on earth knew about the people we spoke to in our investigation? I don't believe for a fucking second it is either of us, be it asleep or awake." Del gave that some serious thought and after a while turned to the boards.

"To be honest, any fucker that may have seen them!" And he was right, every piece of information they had collected that was noteworthy was used as the word suggested and noted down. Harry looked around the room but there was no CCTV in the conference rooms.

"So we're looking suspiciously at anyone who has access to this part of the building, because there is no CCTV to hack."

"Yes, but it has to be regular or very recent because the last name was only placed on the board a little while ago."

As their discussion continued it was broken by the sound of the phone. Del picked it up.

"Hello, Inspector Martin." He listened for a

second and then covered the handset and whispered to Harry, "It's Bud," and then uncovered it and continued to listen. "Okay, I'll be there in a little while." He put the phone down and looked up at Harry. "Bud has found a message and wants me to have a look."

Harry stood up but Del put his hand out to stop him.

"No, I'll have a look and make a note of it and come right back, I want you to scan the information we have on the board and write down the top facts we have, and also find out who has had possible access to this room over the last three days."

Harry sat back down a little despondently. "Okay, you're the boss, I will give it a go."

Del turned and left without a word.

"Fuck it," said Harry as he grabbed a piece of paper and started looking at the boards.

CHAPTER 29

Bloody Message

Del arrived at the butcher's and greeted the PC on scene guard again; he then ducked under the tape and feeling a lot better prepared than earlier walked directly over to the freezer area. Bud was just outside the door so Del didn't actually need to go in.

"Hi Bud, what have you got for me then? Go on, what bloody head did they hide it in? The last one I presume?"

Buddy shook his head. "No, no note in the heads at all I'm afraid."

Del frowned. "Okay, but you did find something."

Buddy held his arm out to the freezer room.

"I think you better come and have a look." He walked in to the freezer and stopped just inside the door. Del didn't know what was going on but followed. The initial thing that the CSI unit did was photograph everything in situ; once they had gone over all they could from a distance they moved in for sampling of parts of the blood. These samples were taken from different areas of the floor area. Bud explained this to Del as he stood at the door looking in with his mouth open.

"Once we started to take the samples we noticed markings under the blood." He needlessly pointed to the floor at this point as Del could see what was going on. "When I had done all I could before it, I did a clean-up of the blood on the floor to uncover what was under it. As you can see the result was, erm, striking!"

Del continued to look but then asked Bud if it was okay to walk in.

"Yes, it's okay to step in, just don't touch anything else."

Del walked forwards into the room, the room that had a message written on the floor. The message was written in what looked like marker pen and was obviously permanent marker otherwise it would have disappeared when the blood was removed. The writing was huge and covered the whole part of the floor that was away from the victims, and was addressed to him directly unlike the other victim notes.

Del, if you haven't got the intelligence to catch me on your own don't use the local plebs. Bos's blood was on your hands and now so are all these. You have tasted the death of my past victims and now before you die you will taste some of these. Don't worry about Janice when you are gone, I will take care of her, she tastes fine. I won't kill her like I did Bos's lovely Helen, she needed to go. No one should have been able to take my place in his life.

And it was signed, 'The Real Butcher'. Bud looked at Del.

"See why you needed to see it? What the hell is all that about?"

Del read through the message again. "I'm not sure but I think after all this time we know who killed Bos's wife, it was this fucking psycho." Del jotted the message down on his pad. "I have had some very odd messages from this bastard and they don't all make sense, but I do get the idea that they blame me for not stopping Bos killing himself."

Buddy started to answer, 'But that's ridiculous,' however, he only managed to get the 'but that' out before Del's phone went off. It sounded horrendous inside the confines of the freezer.

"It's Janice, Bud. I'm taking it out here." And he walked outside the unit to answer it. "Hi babe, what's up?" The voice on the other end was not Janice but it was panicked and crying.

"Please hurry, hurry Del, please," Del could not understand perfectly. "Who is this? What's happening?" The crying person tried to calm down but was finding it difficult.

"Del, it's me, Sue, we're in trouble. Help, please." He hadn't recognised her voice as she was usually so calm, assured and sensual.

"What is going on? Where are you?"

Sue tried to explain through bouts of sobbing. She said that she was with Janice at their home. They had both been attacked and tied up; she said that they had both now been stripped naked. Janice was hanging up by her feet on the pan hooks in the kitchen and she had been strapped to a chair near her.

"What is happening now? How have you managed to call me?"

"Del, he has gone out to get something he forgot. I'm scared, he's going to come back." She started to get hysterical; she was crying, sobbing and trying to talk. Her voice when talking was coming out in sobbing bursts of shouting. "He is going to cut us up, I don't want to die!"

Del didn't wait for any more; he ran full pelt from the butcher's. All that was going through his mind was, *I'm not going through that church hell again, I'm not going to see Janice decapitated.* He sprinted to his car and jumped in, luckily missing cracking his head on the frame of the door this time. He hurriedly but clumsily put the key in the ignition and tried to start the car. He was in such a hurry that he let go of the key before the engine had caught.

"Come on, you stupid fucking twat!" He pounded the steering wheel in frustration and then tried again. This time it started and it was in gear, handbrake off and speeding down the road in a blink of an eye. He was a response driver years ago so knew how to put his foot down but this speed was beyond even that territory. It was not long before he was screeching and skidding to a stop outside his own address. He jumped out of the car and ran as fast as humanly possible to his front door. He pushed it open and ran directly in; he had totally lost any police brain and was running on pure panic for his wife. He ran into the kitchen and sure enough, Janice was naked, unconscious, upside down on one of the hooks they held the saucepans up on. She was swinging helplessly. Sue was sat completely naked on a chair to his left; she had tears rolling down her face.

"Del, please help, he will come back. I don't want to die, please." She was still hysterical and shouting. He wanted her to be quiet so he could surprise the bastard. He walked towards her to try and comfort her and quieten her. He didn't want to get too close because even in this situation she was stunning. He bent down with his finger to his lips.

"Sue, shh, it's going to be fine just calm d—" The word was not finished. Del crashed to the floor from a blow to the head from behind. Stood behind him was a woman smiling. She looked in her seventies or even older, holding a lump of wood. She had knocked him out with one strike; unfortunately she was very good at it and had done it many times before in her life. She dropped the piece of wood on the floor and walked slowly to her left and picked up a large knife that was on the grey marble counter. She held it in her right hand and felt how sharp it was with her left. She then slowly made her way, walking towards Sue who was tied to the chair. Sue was tied by her feet; her hands were bound behind her and she had been fastened by one strap that travelled just under her breasts. The old woman reached Sue and leant down, stretching out her knife-wielding hand towards the defenceless Sue. She put the knife to Sue's skin between her cleavage and sliced sharply downwards. She had cut cleanly through the binding that held Sue in place and then went round and released her from her other ties. Sue stood up in all her naked glory and hugged the woman.

"Thanks Mum." The elderly woman didn't smile or show any type of emotion. As the hug finished the mum looked down at the unconscious Del. She flung out her right foot at surprising speed and kicked him in the thigh.

"Come on then, let's gut this fucker." Sue put her hand out as to stop her mum.

"No, not yet, Mum. I want some fun with this one." She then smiled at her. "You can strip him though, if you want to." The mum looked down at him and then shook her head.

"No, I think I want the bastard awake for that bit. We want him to enjoy that, don't we!"

*

Del had his hands tied together with cable ties; they were extremely tight and you could see them digging into his skin. His shoes and socks were removed and his ankles underwent the same treatment as his hands, but his ankles had quite a few ties on them. Sue looked around the kitchen. She wandered back and forth pulling on different hooks, handles and levers. She went round the place a couple of times and settled on a hook that was on the back of the kitchen door. She was totally unabashed that she was still as naked as the day she was born.

"This one, Mum, this way he'll be able to see Janice and she will be able to see him."

They dragged Del's still-limp body over to the door and in one clean movement Sue grabbed him by the legs and hauled him up. She didn't manage to lift him fully off the ground but the way he was lifted was still very impressive. Her body held a strength that was certainly not visible in its lines and build. Her mum joined in at that point and they both lifted him up and hung him up on the hook at the top of door. Del was now bound by his ankles and hanging on a hook from them. His arms dangled and lay on the floor as outstretched, he was longer than the door.

"How long before she wakes up?" Sue looked at Janice hanging a few metres away.

"Not long now actually, I think she'll probably come round in about forty-five minutes or an hour."

Sue then looked at Del. "What about him?"

The mum shrugged. "The lump of wood method is not an exact science, may be ages, may be minutes." She looked her daughter up and down. "It may give you time to get dressed, my girl." Sue smiled.

"What, Mum, don't you like my birthday suit? I don't want to get dressed anyway, I think it will be more fun with these two like this."

*

It was an hour later when Janice woke and she was in a bit of a groggy state. She came round and was very confused to start with. She couldn't quite focus correctly and couldn't understand what was going on. She was awake but couldn't move or see right. After a minute or so her eyes started to focus; she was still confused as to why everything was upside down. She looked around and there was no one in the room except a person hanging on the door. It was a split second before she realised that it was her husband that was strung up. She wriggled but all that achieved was to make her swing backwards and forwards.

"Del, Del! What's going on? Del?" She was talking at first but pretty soon her words became louder until she was shouting at him to wake up. She was upset and angry that he was not answering her. Was he dead! Why were they both upside down? It was only then that she realised that she had no clothes on, not a stich. What was the last thing she remembered? She was with Sue and they had some lunch at her place. She then wondered how she got home and where her friend was.

"Sue!" she shouted, and then she was shouting for Sue and for Del. Her frustration and fear soon turned to tears. It was ten minutes later when Del came round and his was an altogether more painful experience. He opened his eyes and his head pounded with pain; he felt like his head was in a vice and being tightened then loosened at an awful rate. It also felt like his head was about four times its usual size. He opened his eye and the light hurt; he could see a silhouette shape in the light coming in through the back door but couldn't make out what it was but he did realise he was upside down. Then the pain in his wrists kicked in he moved them so he could see, he was tied up.

"What the fuck is going on?" As he said that he heard a shout from the other side of the room.

"Del, Del! You are alive!" He recognised that voice, it was his wife. He concentrated on the shadow in front of the door and after a while his eyes adjusted and he could tell it was Janice hanging naked upside down. *What the hell is going on? What happened?* Then a memory flicked in front of his eyes. He remembered running through the house looking for his wife and seeing her like this. He then recalled seeing Sue tied to a chair. He looked around and the chair she was in was now empty but there were the ties that were used to bind her, on the floor.

"Janice, listen to me, I came here because I got a call from Sue saying you had both been caught and tied up. When I got here you were there and she was tied up on the chair over there. Do you know what happened?" Janice was still sobbing occasionally.

"No babe, I remember me and Sue having lunch and then waking up here, I don't know what happened."

"I'll tell you what happened." It was the elderly lady who walked in and said that. Del turned to face her.

"Who the fuck are you?"

She walked up to him and used the knife to make a slice across one of his feet. Blood trickled down over the ties that bound him and Janice screamed. He could not feel his hands but lifted them up and crashed them into her left thigh. She squealed a little and stepped back.

"I'm the person that is going to kill you and then cut you up. I, my doomed little shit, am the Real Butcher. Well, one of them."

Del was stinging now; his head still hurt, his ankles hurt, his hands hurt and now his fucking foot hurt. Overall he thought that his day was not going to plan.

"I knew there were more than one of you sick fucks. Where is your girlfriend then? Because I know damn well a fucking old hag like you couldn't lure people to their deaths under the pretext of sex." Del was pissed off and in pain. If this was the Butcher, and let's face it, the evidence suggested it, then he was in all likelihood going to die. However, he was fucked if he wasn't going to go out spitting and kicking, if not physically then definitely verbally.

"You're right on the fact that I was not alone, one of the only things you have deduced correctly, you useless little shit. However, girlfriend? No. Meet my daughter."

Sue walked slowly and provocatively around the corner and into view. Full view being right because as she suggested earlier to her mum, she had not got dressed.

Janice screamed, "Sue, help us!" but Del put two and two together very quickly.

"So your flirting was not an attempt to get into my pants but to keep getting information."

She sidled towards him slowly with her hips swinging from side to side.

"Careful Sue, he gave me a whack in the leg." Sue stopped and went to the kitchen drawer. She picked out a large carving fork and then continued towards him. She stooped down close and quickly grabbed his hands. The fork prongs were placed each side of the cable ties and then slammed down into the floor.

Janice screamed hysterically and started crying. "Sue, what are you doing?"

The mum walked over to her and slapped her hard across the face. "Shut up, bitch."

Del's hands were stuck now, they had been pinned to the floor by the fork. "Well, you have forked me now." He smiled at her.

"Oh yes, and you're not the only one either." She then walked over to Janice. Sue walked a little past her and then turned to face Del with Janice on her left. She lifted her left hand and placed it between Janice's legs. "You are not the only one I forked." She stroked Janice intimately and then slowly ran her hand down her body, eventually caressing one of her breasts. She continued down until she reached her head. She grabbed her hair and forcibly pulled her up towards her. She kissed the sobbing Janice on the lips and then dropped her.

"I told you in one of my notes I had tasted her but you are too stupid to read properly."

Janice was crying even harder now.

"I'm sorry Del. I... don't know why I did it."

Sue explained that they had sex a few times. "It was after I gave you that blowjob under the table." Sue then turned back to Janice. "He didn't tell you that bit, I bet, after our meal at yours. I hadn't gone for some fresh air, I was sucking off your husband under the table, right next to you!"

Janice's cries didn't increase as she was already in a bad way.

"Why? Why do all this?" asked Del.

CHAPTER 30

A Picture Talks

Harry was a little fed up that he was stuck in the office while Del went off to read another message from the killer. He knew he wouldn't be gone long but still! He looked at the job in front of him. He had to look through all the info and try and pinpoint the key pieces of information. He wrote a number one on the piece of paper.

"Okay, that first one is easy." He then wrote 'linked to Bos aka Ben'. He then wrote a number two. After a couple of seconds, he stood up and walked over to the boards. He read through a lot of information. The trouble was, when all was said and done they didn't have a lot of solid info on this. He went back to the sheet and completed number two. Victims were all drunk. The next was a little more difficult so after a while he continued to write the numbers down the side of the page but without any facts. He looked again at all the information and realised an important one.

"Everything we knew, they did too, but how?" It

was then he decided to follow up on the other task Del had left him, to try and find out who had access to this area. He phoned up the admin office and spoke to staff there; he wanted to find out which staff had access on their tags for the conference room level. After what seemed like forever on the phone it turned out that it wasn't good news. It was not a particularly sensitive area so every member of staff in the building could have made their way to the room at any time. Even worse than that, some members of the public that came into meetings in the building, if not watched constantly, could wander past as well. Harry knew there was no CCTV about here so he was beginning to think it was a lost cause to track down any individual that may have seen the information in here. He picked up his pen and started doodling on his pad, wondering where the hell Del was. He seemed to have been gone for ages. He looked at his watch; Del had been gone for an hour and a half now.

"Funny, just reading the bloody message my arse!" Harry's mind drifted off course slightly and thought about the bodies in the manor lake.

"I wonder how many they will find in the end." He leant forward and clicked on the computer. Once it was up and running he highlighted the internet search and typed in 'Lady Belina Wellingborough' and highlighted the image tag. There were not many images of her but there were a few. Nothing particularly out of the ordinary. He then typed in her daughter's name, Suzie-Anne Wellingborough, and tapped on the images tag again. This time there was a multitude of pictures and Harry whistled. Most of them were stunning and most with a lot on show; she was a gorgeous girl and knew it by the looks of things. He scrolled through a few pages and nodded appreciatively at some of the assets on show. He decided eventually to turn it off, at least he knew what the owners of the place looked like now. He wondered if they were tied to the killing. After all, they had owned it for the time the bodies had been filling up the lake.

He tapped his pen on the desk and thought about the case again. *We believe it is more than one person and that the victims were lured in by promises of sex.* Harry wrote all this down too, he was starting to feel like he was getting somewhere now. Some of the messages were directed at and specifically for Del. He decided to have a bit of a break with a coffee. He walked to the kitchen and made himself a drink. PC James Alsop was in there too; they hadn't met for a while and James asked how he was getting on.

"Well, you know how it is, I'm stuck here while Del has fucked off looking at something exciting." James asked where he had gone and Harry told him. "It's only a few minutes away and he's been gone two bloody hours now."

James finished making his drink and on leaving said. "Well, good luck Harry. Del is more than likely at Brian's greasy spoon café eating his way to a coronary."

Harry made his drink and quite frankly was getting a little pissed off with Del's disappearance. He made his mind up. He finished making his drink and sat down in the staff room for a little while just watching the world go by. Well, the station anyway. However, even ten minutes of that wouldn't ease his edginess, so he stood and walked back to the conference room. He tapped away on the computer and found what he was after. Buddy's phone number. He dialled and waited impatiently for him to answer. He did eventually.

"Hello, Buddy speaking, how can I help?"

"Hi Bud, it's Harry here, can I talk to Del please?"

"No, sorry mate, he left ages ago, I thought he would be with you by now."

It was what Harry suspected. He stood and frustratedly started pacing up and around the room.

"Yes, I bloody knew it, Bud. I bet he is poisoning himself at that bloody café. When did he go?"

Buddy thought for a while. "Well, to be honest he wasn't here for long, he looked at the message and then ran out after a call from Janice." Harry calmed down then.

"Oh okay, thanks Bud. Did he say what the call was about?"

Buddy told him no, and that he just ran straight out. Harry put the phone down and wondered what could be wrong. He started to get concerned. The last time Del ran out he thought Janice was being killed by the Butcher. He walked back to his seat and froze. After a second he walked slowly over to where Del sat and picked up the picture he had brought in of his wife Janice and her friend. He looked closer.

"Oh fuck, shit!" He dropped the photo and ran. He didn't seem to give a shit that it fell on the floor and the glass shattered in pieces across the immaculate blue carpet. He just ran straight out of the door as fast as he had ever done. Officers were in the way and he was shouting at them to, "Get out the fucking way! Fucking move!" and when one didn't move quickly enough he pushed him through an open doorway and unflinchingly just continued on his way. It took him a matter of around two minutes to exit the entire building, which considering the conference room was on the third floor was pretty good going. He got in his car, started it and wheel spun it out of the station as if he was some boy racer at a seafront gathering.

CHAPTER 31

Why?

"Why? Why do all this?" asked Del as he hung on the door hook in his kitchen. Sue moved closer to him.

"Because of you, Del." And she stood on his fingers.

Del didn't react but Janice did. She screamed, "No!"

"Ben was a great student, one of our best. He took to it like a duck to water, but then forgot. When I eventually tracked him down I had to put him back on track so killed his lovely Helen. This brought him back to us."

"You're fucking mad, so why all this shit with me?"

She had looked away at that point but with this statement she faced Del again and her face changed in an instant from beautiful woman to something resembling a Disney witch. The transformation was horrendous to witness.

"Because he was back with us and then you took him," she spat out venomously. "You followed him and let him die. You could have stopped him but you let him go." She slapped his face hard and his head jolted right with the force. An instant red print shone on Del's face.

"I didn't kill him, you psycho tart, and why try and say you were the Real Butcher?"

Sue's face had turned back to angelic female again now. "I wasn't trying to say it, I was saying it. I'm the Real Butcher. We created him, you fool."

"Doesn't mean you're better than him. He had an ounce of morality. He only killed unconsciously, you kill deliberately."

She went dark again. "I AM THE BEST." She calmed instantly. "You should know that you tasted my cooking. What did you think you were eating? I proved I'm the Butcher as you enjoyed the meat I prepared." Del thought and then dread filled his mind; he thought the Butcher was eating the victims but now he thought he was wrong. Sue could see the realisation on his face and laughed hysterically. "Yes, Del, that's it. Finally the penny drops. You and Janice were eating Tony and then Natalia." She bent down right up close to him. "Nice, were they?"

"Well to be honest I thought they needed more pepper but what do I know?"

Sue slapped him hard again. She was becoming fed up with his lack of fear and his persistent disrespectful comments.

"I will tell you what, Mr Funny, how about I show you what Janice is made of? That seemed to get you last time!"

She walked over to Janice who was still sobbing. She held the knife out and pushed it towards Janice's belly. She was not watching Janice, she had her eyes fully on Del and watched his face go white, which was certainly some feat considering he had been upside down for a while now. He was horrified and sick to watch the knife get closer and closer to Janice. The blade made contact and Janice started to panic and wriggle. The trouble with that was as she wriggled she moved closer to the knife itself. It was an incredibly sharp knife and was soon shredding at Janice's belly. They were not deep cuts but enough to make Janice scream and Del fill with anger.

"Leave her alone, you fucking crazy bitch! You and granny over there should burn in hell."

Sue never moved the knife. She did, however, laugh again. "That's better, Del, a bit of fire."

The elderly woman walked over and planted a hefty kick right into Del's right ribs which cracked under the force. He yelled with the pain and fire burning in his side.

"I may go to hell if there is such a place, boy, but believe me you are here now." She then went to the kitchen drawer and started rummaging around.

"It still makes no sense to me. Why all the sexual behaviour, you crazy fucker? Why tart about with me and my wife?"

Sue moved the knife, making a wound around three inches in length in Janice. She had turned her emotions again and was looking as evil as ever. "You stupid little shit, why do you think? You were talking to your dipshit wife and with me controlling her sexual emotions she spilled out information to me. How the fuck do you think I knew about the plebs you were speaking to?"

"So why act the harlot around me?"

Sue looked at him with her beautiful face on again now. "Because you were so sweet and innocent, to see the pure panic on your face was priceless. Especially when Janice was in the room too. Little did you know she was getting some too. Oh, she does love to squeal, doesn't she!" She walked back to Janice and took hold of her breast firmly and squeezed, while again concentrating on Del's face. He wriggled in frustration and at that moment the elderly woman threw something at him that she had taken out of the drawer. It was an ordinary kitchen fork but she threw it with venom and it landing with force and imbedded deep into his left thigh.

"Oh, well done Mummy, that deserves a goldfish." They both giggled and Del grimaced with pain.

"I warn you, funny man, wriggle and I will slice your girl into pieces right in front of you."

She picked up a large knife from the drawer and walked towards him. She pulled the fork from his leg which spurted blood and made an instant red bull's eye in his trousers, and that bull's eye grew rapidly in size. She held the knife to Del's throat and then cut up and sliced through his jacket buttons and his shirt. She then moved the grip she had on the knife and in one hugely aggressive and frenzied attack, ripped through his sleeves and he was then topless. She placed the knife on his chest and scraped it up to his trousers. These were cut and removed effortlessly by the sharp knife and her obviously well practiced hand. Del was now naked apart from his boxer shorts.

The elderly woman looked at the black garments with lipstick emblems on them. "Nice, very elegant."

"Fuck off," said Del in a harsh voice. He had now got to the point where he didn't give a shit about himself. She leant forward grabbed the waist of his boxers and sliced right through them. Del was now as naked as the day he was born.

"Oh dear. Never mind, they say it's personality that counts." She turned to Sue. "You mean you had that in your mouth? I bet you needed a tooth pick to get it out." They both laughed at her amusing penis size joke.

"Yes, well, nature can be cruel sometimes but you know that with the state of your fucking face." She immediately raged into the cutlery drawer and threw another fork full force. This one hit him but not prongs first so harmlessly dropped to the floor.

"Oh dear, was the other one beginner's luck!"

With that she continued until one did hit its mark. It took another six goes but Del winced in pain as it sunk in to his right side just above the hip. He was in pain but he wasn't giving in yet.

"Now, now, don't throw your teddy out of the pram."

She was just about to lunge in after him when Sue stopped her. "Mummy, no, we want to enjoy this. Calm down."

"Yes, calm down Mummy, don't be such a bitch."

Del winked at the elderly woman which enraged her further. "Come on then Sue, why all the pissing about with the different notes and codes and traps and shit?"

Sue looked pitifully at him. "You don't get any of it, do you, you stupid little boy. One reason and one reason only. To fuck you about and mess with you until the day came to kill you. Today is that day!"

Del huffed. "You are just as crazy as your bitch of a mother!" There was real venom in this sentence; Del was pissed off with this shit and wanted to piss these two freaks off as much as he could before he died.

She held her mum back and walked towards Del with absolute hatred in her eyes. She bent down towards him, snarling like an enraged pit bull. As she leant down the door flung open. It was Harry and he had been waiting for a little while on the other side of the door for the best opportunity. The door frame caught Sue on the side of the head and she flew backwards, immobile and unconscious. The scream from the elderly woman was primeval and could have cut through steel. She ran straight at Harry with the knife held out in front of her; she had murder in her eyes and a brand new target for it. She crossed the kitchen with astonishing speed.

Harry was quick to move but not quick enough to get completely out of range. The knife sank deep in his left side and blood poured out from the open wound. She removed the knife and thrust again but this time he did get out of the way and lunged forward himself. He caught her full on the right cheek with a punch and he assumed as an elderly lady she would have been out for the count but she was not a regular old lady – she shook her head and growled. The knife which had blood spatter flying from it with each pass, came hurtling back towards him and caught him on the left arm. It cut clean through his suit and made a four-inch gash across him. This made her cackle with pleasure. Harry grabbed his left arm with his right in pain and stumbled to his right. He was feeling dizzy now and could see her running for him again. He stumbled to his right and used his right arm for support, however, more than just support, his hand came across a handle – it was a saucepan. As she ran and thrust towards him he moved to his right as quickly and as far as his ailing body would allow and threw out an arcing swing with his right hand which now had the stainless steel saucepan in its grip. It made a sickening ringing sound as it made firm contact with her head and she was sent careering towards Del. Harry's centrifugal force sent him whirling round like a spinning top and collapsing on the floor underneath Janice, who was still crying. The hapless helpless old woman landed with a crunch in front of Dell. She twitched for a second and stopped, motionless.

"Harry, you alright?"

Harry took a second to answer. "Bit woozy, mate."

Del chuckled an insane type of laugh. "Not surprised, you have just forked a rather old lady, you dirty bastard." The woman had been smashed on the head and landed directly on top of the carving fork that had secured Del's hands to the floor. The fork handle had gone straight through her left eye and had imbedded itself up to Del's hands. It was by Del's fascinated guestimate that it was sticking out of the back of her skull by about an inch. It had to be a guess due to the bone and gunge that had come out with it.

"Well if you feel up to it can you remove this old lady? Her brains are dribbling out onto my hands, and I would seriously like to get down from this fucking hook now." Harry did stand up and he was a mess; he was grey in the face and had lost a lot of blood.

"Change of plan, Harry, phone an ambulance and tie that bitch up." He looked at Sue who was curled up naked on the floor with a rather large egg lump on her head. Harry did call for the ambulance and tie Sue up but unfortunately that was all. He then collapsed, unconscious.

CHAPTER 32

Hospital

Harry lay in the hospital bed asleep after his ordeal. He had lost a hell of a lot of blood but he had pulled through. Del sat in the chair on the opposite side of the room waiting for Harry to wake. Del had recovered quite quickly after his ordeal. He had some wounds from the forks that were nasty and a couple of broken ribs. His hands and feet hurt from the bindings but he was in a hell of a lot better shape than Harry considering he was the one that was upside down at the two maniacs' mercy. Janice was on a chair next to Del too; she had some superficial wounds to her stomach and some sore hands and feet, but was fine. The thing that hurt her the most was her stupidity to get so carried away and infatuated with her friend Sue.

"I'm sorry, Del."

He smiled at her. "I know, babe, it's fine. I don't blame you, she was smoking hot."

Janice laughed and stroked his arm lovingly. What

Del was waiting for was Harry to wake up, he wanted some answers. It seemed a long wait but eventually Harry stirred, he opened his eyes and groaned. He felt like shit, his mouth was as dry as a camel's foot and probably tasted similar too. His side was as sore as hell with stabbing pains compelling him to hold his breath every few seconds until they subsided. His arm stung like a bitch too. He turned his head and tried to make a grab for a drink but his stomach had other ideas and quickly told him to fuck off and think again!

To Harry's eternal relief Janice came into view and picked the drink up and put it to his lips. After a quick drink he smiled.

"Hi Harry, our hero." Janice bent down and kissed him on the cheek.

"Okay babe, leave him alone, you don't know where he's been."

Into Harry's peripheral vision popped Del. "Hello Harry, are you able to talk yet?"

Janice scorned her husband's insensitivity and impatience. But Harry did whisper something through his still-parched mouth. "Help me up a little," he said.

Janice went round to the other side and Del stayed where he was, and they both grabbed Harry under an armpit and lifted him slowly up into a type of sitting position. He signalled for another drink and gulped it down and then held it out for a refill.

"Alright, alright, I ain't going to be feeding you bloody grapes as well you know."

After the second drink Harry tried to speak again and found it a lot easier. "Oh, that feels better." His

PAUL DAVIDS

side still stabbed him but he did feel a lot more human now.

"Okay then, smart arse, not that I'm not grateful and all that but how the fuck did you know where we were?"

Harry smiled. "That was easy, I asked Bud where you had gone." Del sat on the bed and made Harry wince with pain from his side.

"So it wasn't a bloody rescue mission, it was just you wondering where I bloody was."

Janice smacked him lightly across the head. Harry shook his head.

"Not exactly, it was most definitely a rescue attempt."

Del asked again, "So how did you know we were in trouble?"

Harry pointed to the drink again and downed another. "Look, you had taken ages so I called Bud to see where you were. He said you had only been there minutes and ran off because of a call from Janice. I assumed you had gone for a bite at Brian's but when I sat down I saw the picture you put on the desk." Harry looked expectantly but Del shook his head. "It was of Janice and Sue."

"Yes, but we didn't know Sue was the killer then," said Del, frowning.

Harry nodded. "No, but I had just looked up who Lady Belina Wellingborough and Suzie-Anne Wellingborough were and fuck me if the Sue in your picture was Suzie-Anne. Del, they are the key to this, they are the ones that have been killing at Oakwood

Manor for years. They trained Ben to be a killer and didn't like it much when he died in front of you."

Del breathed out. "And that's it? All this killing because they didn't like that fact that Bos died." He half laughed sarcastically but then regretted it due to his broken ribs.

"What happened to them?" asked Harry.

Del looked sideways at him. "Are you saying you can't remember?"

Harry said the last thing he remembered was opening the door to try and knock Sue out.

"Okay well, you sent Belina for a six across the kitchen but she landed with rather more than a bit of a splinter in her eye. You tied Suzie up just before you collapsed. She is now on remand for all our murders and probably the ones at Oakwood Manor too. She will be going away for a very long time."

Harry sat up a little, or definitely tried to. "One tip for you, Inspector Martin."

"What's that, Sergeant Gorham?"

"Stop taking your fucking work home, it's not good for a copper or his family to do that."

*

Lady Suzie-Anne Wellingborough was eventually found guilty of the murders and assisted murders of seventy-six people. She was sentenced to life imprisonment without any chance of parole. Her mum, Lady Belina Wellingborough, also known as Bella, was cremated and her ashes scattered at the Oakwood Manor estate. It was presumed that it would be a quiet ceremony with only a few people in attendance. It was a shock to the staff at the crematorium to find a host of men coming and paying their respects. There seemed to be a disturbing number of mourners from around the country! It would have been the case in normal circumstances to have a huge congregation at a Lady's farewell. However, it was a bit of a shock with this one considering she had been publicly connected to a lot of horrific things in the media. It was amazing that there were as many as there were.

Printed in Great Britain
by Amazon